Beyond A Reasonable Doubt

Doubt Series Book 1

Sharon Johnson

Wicked Words Publishing

Published by

Wicked Words Publishing

PO BOX 712

Hamlin, PA 18427

Warning:

This book contains material that may be offensive to some people including graphic language, graphic violence, dubious consent, explicit sex, anal sex, male on male sex, oral sex, rimming, frottage, barebacking, rough sex, Mpreg, self-lubrication, and a few BDSM elements.

Author's Note

This work is part of a multi book serial that is not meant to be read as a stand-alone. Each book will include a new pairing, but they will all lead to the fulfilling of the prophecy. This series will be mainly an M/M universe, but will include episodes that feature different pairings. Future episodes may include M/M, M/F, M/M/M, M/M/F, F/F. I promise you by the end every question will be answered and every bridge will be crossed, but it may not lead you to where you were expecting.

DEDICATION

It is always difficult for me to decide how to dedicate my book. So many people help to guide and support me along the way, and it seems ungrateful to not mention them all. But this time the choice was clear, this book is dedicated to my co-workers, John and Jim. Thank you, guys, for all your kind, and not so kind, encouragements. You have inspired me to write every day, if for no other reason than to escape your constant nagging.

And a special thanks goes to Raissa Phoenix for all her late night pep talks and wealth of commas. Seriously I can't imagine doing this without you.

To the beta readers who read through all my horrid punctuation and still somehow like me.

Doubt thou the stars are fire, Doubt that the sun doth move. Doubt truth to be a liar, but never doubt I love.

William Shakespeare

The Importance of Time

Yesterday's the past, tomorrow's the future, but today is a gift. That's why it's called the present.

Bil Keane

Contents

Chapter 1 1

Chapter 2 18

Chapter 3 32

Chapter 4 45

Chapter 5 61

Chapter 6 80

Chapter 7 100

Chapter 8 129

Chapter 9 153

Chapter 10 176

Chapter 11 205

Chapter 12 222

Chapter 13 237

Chapter 14 256

Chapter 15 274

Chapter 16 290

Chapter 17 307

Chapter 18 320

Chapter 19 343

Chapter 20 351

Chapter 21 375

Epilogue 398

Chapter 1

Sean ~ July 2, Thursday, 5 a.m.

Beep, beep, beep.

Sean rolls over, pulling his pillow over his head as he goes, the shrill tone of his alarm screeching through his head like nails down a chalkboard. He can feel Sara reaching over to silence the clock even as he tries, in vain, to convince himself he can have five more minutes.

"Sean, it's almost five."

"Thanks, babe. Go back to sleep. I'm just going to grab a shower and head into the office," Sean mumbles as he rolls out of bed. Grabbing his clothes, Sean presses a kiss to Sara's forehead as she wiggles deeper into the covers. "I'll see you later. Maybe we can have dinner sometime this week."

"Mmhmm, yeah. Love you," Sara answers without opening her eyes.

"Thanks. You too. Just lock up before you leave." Sean hesitates before bending over to kiss her cheek and heading out for the most important case in his career.

Driving towards downtown Seattle from his home in Capitol Hill, the same way he has for the past five years, Sean takes in the scenery. The sky is overcast, shadowing the horizon as he passes the few cars he meets along the way, but there was no warning that today will be the last day of his normal life.

Pulling into his parking space at exactly 6:30 a.m., Sean grabs his suit coat and briefcase from the passenger seat and heads towards his twelfth floor office. Pushing past the double doors, a familiar smile and a cup of much needed coffee greet him.

"Good morning, my liege," Mary jokes in greeting, the way she always seems to do, even at this ungodly hour.

"Good morning, Mary. Oh my god, thank you," Sean replies as he inhales the aroma of his favorite blend. Sean walks toward his inner office, calling back, "Can you bring the case files from—"

Mary jumps in, "They're already on your desk, along with the court notes from last week."

Taking a long appreciative sip of coffee, Sean wonders out loud, "What would I do without you?"

He's about to hang his jacket when he hears her sassy reply.

"A whole lot less."

He snickers, throwing his briefcase on his desk, but Sean can't help but agree with that.

He grabs the first divorce case to ever cross his desk, and Sean can't help but remember why he has not taken that particular plunge. Although Sean specializes in family law, he has always handled the smaller cases that involve children— another subject he knows little about. His father's decision to make him prove himself by working up the corporate ladder means Sean often takes cases reminding him of why he's alone.

Marriage may look like a promising idea on the outside, but the thought of giving any one person that much power over his life makes him cringe. It isn't that he dislikes the idea of a family. He would love to have a family of his own, but he has seen firsthand that forever never seems to last. What starts as a blaze of lust, desire, and love can quickly turn into a pit of despair, contempt, and revenge.

Although if he's going to be perfectly honest, he has never connected with any one woman for longer than a few months at best. Sara is his most successful relationship to date, but she's not exactly marriage or family material even though she has recently hinted at wanting to make their relationship more official.

"Well, let's see what happened to your forever, Mrs. Malone."

After rereading the prenuptial agreement, Sean can't help but wonder what miracle his client expects him to perform. Without some explosive evidence, Mrs. Malone is trapped in the ten-year-old agreement. At least there aren't any children to be used as pawns.

Sean has never dealt with individuals with so much money at stake. Not for the first time, Sean wonders why he has been handed such an important client. Is this some elaborate test his father set up to see if he deserves this partnership? No matter; he will provide the best counsel he can no matter how hopeless the case may seem.

DeMatteo ~ 7:30 a.m.

Matthew "DeMatteo" Santiago makes his way towards downtown Seattle on his way to meet his client at the opposing counsel's office. His career as a divorce attorney is quite the joke amongst his pride—not that anyone would dare laugh at their Alpha. But since lions mate for life, even DeMatteo has to chuckle at his trade.

DeMatteo, however, is without a mate and childless, which is something that could be seen as a failure to some pride members. Being a gay Alpha, DeMatteo knows his true mate will be a man and his second in command, and as the Alpha Mate he will also birth their cubs into the pride. DeMatteo is not willing to consider breeding a female just to secure his pride cubs.

DeMatteo is always on alert to scent his true mate out when he goes to Alpha challenges or Pride Summits, which is why this meeting could not have happened at a worse time. What if his true mate is there this year and DeMatteo misses him?

At over fifty years old, DeMatteo has been waiting a long time. Most Alphas are ready to be mated by thirty-five, if not with their true life mate, then with a companion mate instead. Had his parents not been murdered by disgraced hunters, he would have been forced to leave his home pride lands to find or build a new pride, as all Alphas did. If he had, he might have found his true mate already.

Pulling onto the main roads, DeMatteo forces those thoughts from his mind. As the Alpha, he is the primary financial provider for his pride—not that they don't already have more money and influence than they'll ever need. He feels an instinctive need to provide for his pride, and this high profile client is extremely important to his firm.

As he waits in traffic, DeMatteo racks his brain to come up with why he's being dragged in for what's essentially an open and shut case. The only reason that makes sense is the new attorney of record for Mrs. Malone, Mr. Sean Herr, Esq.

DeMatteo had been shocked to learn that Mrs. Malone won't be represented by one of the senior partners, but by a virtually unknown, brand new junior partner. His client had surprised him with this revelation during their call on his drive this morning.

"What difference does it make? Honestly, you should be happy they sent their peon to settle a case they know they can't win," Mr. Malone had boasted.

The only thing DeMatteo hates more than losing is surprises, especially when information is intentionally kept from him. Suddenly, DeMatteo feels bad for Mrs. Malone.

Honestly, DeMatteo has nothing against the woman. If he had to be honest, he would say she's a better person than his client, but DeMatteo has a job to do. This is what he's good at, his passion and calling, but DeMatteo still hopes he can have it all wrapped up, by phone, in under an hour.

Now he is going to a meeting completely unprepared, and even worse, he has no idea who he's facing. All he knows is that he has never heard of Sean Herr, and DeMatteo can't help but wonder what other surprises this trip has in store for him. Deciding he's really not up for any more surprises, DeMatteo dials his phone.

"Timothy, I need you to pull up all the information you can find on a Sean G. Herr, Esq.," DeMatteo barks out as soon as the call is connected.

"Yes, Alpha. Is there a problem?" Timothy, DeMatteo's youngest sibling, asks.

"No, just turns out he is the attorney I am up against, and I know nothing about him. I had meant to speak to you before leaving the pride lands, but I ran into some issues this morning." DeMatteo sighs, pressing his finger and thumb to the bridge of his nose.

The morning had been filled with another fight with his lover Hugh. After years together, the other man resents that DeMatteo is putting so much effort into finding his true mate. DeMatteo has been satisfied with Hugh as a companion, but his lion yearns for its mate and no longer wants to settle. It is only a matter of time before he will have to end things with Hugh, even if he never finds his mate.

"I need it all emailed to me in the next hour and a half, sooner if possible. I'd like the chance to not walk into that office blind. I Googled him this morning and came up with nothing other than his schooling, not even his family. It's like he came out of fucking nowhere."

Timothy jokes, "Guess I'll have to go through our special sources. I know how much you hate surprises. I will send the information as an audio and written file. Consider it done, Alpha."

DeMatteo can hear his brother's smile as he disconnects the call. Shifters always have access to information. Over the centuries, they've learned that the only way to keep their secret is to become completely submerged in the human world. Doctors, lawyers, police officers, newscasters, and politicians, shifters make sure to reach positions of power that grant them access to, and control of, information.

Sean ~ 8:30 a.m.

"Good morning, Mr. Davis," Sean greets Frank Davis as he walks into his office, slightly taken aback by his early morning impromptu visit. Normally if Sean wants to see his father during business hours, he has to schedule it through the secretaries.

Not bothering to respond with social niceties, Frank grumbles, "I don't need to tell you how important this case is. Mrs. Malone and her family will make lucrative clients for the firm."

As if Sean doesn't know that. Mrs. Malone, soon to be Ms. Phillips, is from a family that is nearly as powerful as the man she's divorcing. The only thing Sean can't comprehend is why he has been given her case.

"I've gone over the prenuptial agreement. Barring any unforeseen circumstances, this case should be pretty open and shut. And I can't see how we can turn this into our favor—" He starts, but as usual Frank talks right over him.

"Mrs. Malone will be bringing new evidence that she believes will render that agreement null and void. It is your job to make that happen for her. Needless to say, Mr.

Malone's counsel is seeking to avoid any negotiation," Frank says.

Sean hears the implications: *make this happen or else.* "What is this evidence?" Sean asks, wondering if his father is using this case to punish him or push him out of the firm.

"She hasn't said. She said that she was bringing it in for today's conference." Frank starts to make his way back out of the office.

"What? So we don't even know what evidence she has? To get a ten-year-old prenuptial thrown out, she will have to prove malice or deceit beyond a reasonable doubt." Sean grimaces, trying to control his irritation at being put in a seemingly impossible position. "How the hell am I supposed to conduct this conference without a hint of what kind of case I have?" Sean growls at his father's dismissal.

His outburst stops his father deep in his tracks, and letting out a bark of laughter, Frank stares at him. After regaining his composure, Frank buttons his jacket as Sean watches him—as if he has sprouted a second head.

"That, son, is why I pay you the big bucks, so don't disappoint me," Frank whips back as he strolls out of the office.

Sean hits the button on his phone connecting him to his secretary. "Mary, have you heard anything from our client?"

"No, other than her call to confirm the meeting time. Do you need me to get in contact with her before the conference?"

"No. My father just informed me that she will be bringing something that she hopes will work in our favor. You know how much I hate surprises."

Sean hangs up the receiver when Mary walks in and flops in the chair directly across from his desk. Sean smiles at his oldest friend as she props her feet on his desk.

"Don't I know it? I thought I was going to lose my job over that surprise birthday party," Mary jokes.

Sean snorts. "Yeah. I remember having to get the carpets replaced after your date managed to bleed all over my carpet."

"Have a heart. He needed like thirty stitches in his hand," Mary tsks.

"Oh yeah, but he was the one who decided he could juggle knives. What grown-up even does that?"

"Okay, you're right. He was a complete mess, but that man was a beast in the sack," Mary says, making some ridiculous face Sean can only guess as her "O" face. "Do you need me to grab you another coffee?" she adds while smoothing her hair back into place.

"Yes, please. And start knocking before you walk in. I could have been naked in here," Sean scolds playfully, continuing on with their everyday banter. Mary had followed him into the firm, and while many of the more senior lawyers frowned on the casual relationship, Sean has always counted on Mary to keep him grounded.

"Come on, I've known you since we were ten. I doubt it's grown that much." Mary shrugs at Sean's indignation.

"Jesus, Mary, could you possibly be any more unprofessional?"

"Probably not, but that is why you love me," Mary sasses, throwing him a wink and blowing him a kiss on her way out the door.

Frank ~ 9 a.m.

Frank takes a deep breath as he leans against his desk. Today is the day that he has spent the last few years preparing for. But even knowing this day was coming hadn't really made it any easier to throw his only child into a war he hadn't even realized was being fought.

Last week had really thrown him for a loop when the entire coven showed up at his house to perform an unbinding ceremony. He knew then that the other person had been found, but he was shocked to learn that he would be instrumental in bringing the two together.

Mrs. Malone proved to be easy to convince of the change; she said she had new information that would make it easy enough for a child to win her case. Sean, however, was more than a little skeptical of his involvement in such a high profile case.

Instead of creating some fanciful story, Frank had decided to revert to his gruff demeanor. While it had the desired effect of ending Sean's never-ending questions, Frank had winced as he'd watched his son pull up yet another wall between them. But this was all for the best.

The sound of his phone ringing disrupted his musings. "Frank Davis speaking."

"Hey. So how did everything go?" Rebecca asks.

"About as well as anything goes with us," Frank answers, pacing in front of his desk. He can hear his wife rummaging through papers, no doubt the tome of rituals they would need for tonight's gathering.

She sighs. "That good huh?"

"Are you sure it's going to happen today?" Frank asks, for what seems like the millionth time, while pulling his fingers through his hair.

Time had been relatively kind to him up until now, keeping his hair more pepper than salt, but now it is the enemy. He needs everything to happen the way they have planned, and quickly.

Frank can imagine the warm smile on her face when Rebecca says, "Yes, Frank, I'm sure. We just have to make sure they meet, and the Goddess will see to the rest. The spell to unbind some of his powers will allow him to bond quickly. He will be able to sense their connection clearly. Stop worrying. Everything is going to work out."

"Okay, okay, you're right. I just hate hiding this from him," Frank confesses, stopping in front of the massive windows that overlook the courtyard.

"I know you do, but trust me, this is for the best. Not knowing is the only thing that has kept him alive. Once he has the protection of the pride, we'll tell him everything."

"I just hope he can forgive us when he learns about what really happened to you. It took a long time for him to get over the death of his mother, and our relationship suffered. I hope this isn't the thing that pushes him away forever," Frank confides. Some days it feels like his son is on the verge of walking away forever.

"Frank, sweetheart, this hasn't been easy for anyone, but I've seen it. Things will work themselves out. I'm going to need you to just trust me."

"Of course I trust you! This is just an old man's desperate bid to hold on to his son. But enough of my complaining. We still have a lot to do before tonight, and I still need to grab a few items," Frank replies earnestly. Of all the crazy things he's learned over the years, the most important thing he's learned is to trust his wife.

"Okay, good. I'm going to run down to the courthouse to make sure everything is in order. It will take a few days for all the transfers to clear, so anyone watching for them will hopefully be a few days behind us." After a few seconds, Rebecca adds, "Hey, Frank, we are almost home free. We just need to hold everyone off for a few more days. You know that I would never let anything happen to Sean, and neither will you. Okay?"

"Yeah, I know. Just a few more days," Frank says and ends the call. He heads down to his private executive exit. It is imperative that Sean remains unaware of his involvement until after. The less he knows, the less likely it is that he will trust the wrong person and expose himself.

He can only hope that soon he will get the answers to his prayers and Sean would be out of danger. So many sacrifices have been made to get them to this point, and he just has to keep going for a few more days.

As he heads to his vehicle, Frank notices he is no longer alone. He plasters on a smile before stopping to greet the person he is counting on to protect his son and save them all.

Chapter 2

DeMatteo ~ July 2, Thursday, 9:45 a.m.

Grabbing his briefcase, DeMatteo strolls toward the lower level of the parking garage. He's meeting his client's car to escort him to the conference room to face Mr. Malone's soon-to-be ex-wife. He had listened to a brief bio about the young Mr. Herr. Although he graduated at the top of his class, there is no evidence that the man had any experience in this level of warfare.

On the ride to the opposing counsel's office, DeMatteo feels his confidence about this case returning despite the surprise change in counsel. Thanks to the ironclad prenuptial agreement, he wonders if they will be done in time for him to take his private jet to Texas to the summit after all.

He had learned that Mr. Herr has mostly dealt with family law, and this is his first case dealing with the super wealthy. Mrs. Malone had cited irreconcilable differences as her reason for filing for divorce; even Mr. Malone had seemed shocked by her announcement. Maybe she had taken a lover? Maybe she had just changed her mind? DeMatteo had given up trying to understand human relationships decades ago; they just never seemed to work out.

Sensing someone approaching, DeMatteo looks up just as Frank Davis greets him. "Good morning, Mr. Santiago."

Turning to meet his law firm's biggest competitor face-to-face, DeMatteo offers his default intimidating scowl. DeMatteo is well aware that his mere presence makes most people he comes up against nervous, a fact that he shamelessly uses to his advantage.

Much to DeMatteo's surprise, Frank Davis's smile doesn't falter, and he quickly offers DeMatteo his hand. Shaking hands firmly, DeMatteo senses the man's inexplicable excitement.

"Good morning, Mr. Davis. I was just on my way to meet with Mr. Herr." DeMatteo's smile is tight-lipped, as he wonders why the man seems so pleased to see him.

"Yes, he is already in the conference room waiting for you. See you later." Frank is already walking away before DeMatteo can work out the odd exchange.

Shaking off the strange encounter, DeMatteo focuses on getting this over with as quickly as possible. His client is paying him a small fortune to make his latest failure as painless as possible, and DeMatteo is known for getting his clients what they want.

Sean ~ 9:20 a.m.

"Mr. Herr, Mrs. Malone has arrived and is waiting in the conference room with her associates," Mary announces.

"Associates...? I thought we were ironing out the details with her husband?" Sean replies as he gathers up his copies of the court transcripts and his jacket. "Never mind. I am heading there now."

Sean decides to take a few extra seconds to rinse his mouth and splash on some cologne before heading down the hall towards his client and her guests.

"Good morning, Mrs. Malone," Sean greets as he enters the conference room, wearing what he hopes comes off as a confident smile.

While Sean is at ease in the courtroom, swaying both juries and judges with his honest but charismatic approach, Mary has helpfully advised him of his sometimes arrogant demeanor with clients. And if there is ever a time Sean needs to woo a client, Grace Malone is the client to woo.

"Good morning, Mr. Herr." Grace Malone smiles as she stands to shake Sean's hand.

"This is Mr. Richard Price and Ms. Christine Winters." Grace's smile is nothing short of cunningly devilish as she motions towards her guests.

"Good morning. I understand that you have some new evidence regarding the divorce." Sean addresses Grace while shaking both parties' hands before grabbing the documents and disk that Richard hands to him.

"Now, I take it they have something to do with your case?" Sean hazards, motioning towards the two individuals as he scans the unmarked envelope.

"These two individuals, and the evidence you have in your hands, are going to win us this case."

Mrs. Malone quickly goes over the evidence she has gathered, and suddenly Sean feels giddy as she provides loads of audio and video documenting her husband's misdealings. It seems as though her husband has been gravely underestimating the abilities of his soon-to-be ex-wife.

DeMatteo ~ 10 a.m.

As soon as DeMatteo steps off the elevator on the twelfth floor, he inhales deeply, trying to clear the stench of cologne his client seems to bathe in. As he takes in a second breath, a new scent invades his brain, and his cock instantly stirs as his lion roars scratching to crawl to the surface. The only thing his body and lion can focus on is the indescribable scent of *mate*.

Reacting quickly and using his briefcase to cover his arousal, DeMatteo all but bolts from the elevator to follow the scent, eager to meet the shifter he has waited his entire life for. For all his searching and hoping for this exact moment, DeMatteo is ill-prepared for how fiercely his lion would react to being near their mate.

"Excuse me, sir. Can I help you?" a petite redhead asks as she steps directly into his path.

DeMatteo's lion roars in annoyance at the human, and he has to stop himself from physically shoving the tiny woman out of his way as his primitive side battles for control. His more rational side, realizing there are others watching, forces his lion out of the mating haze, allowing his human side to remain in control.

DeMatteo regains his composure enough to respond. "Yes, ma'am. My name is Matthew Santiago, and this is Mr. Kevin Malone. We have an appointment with Mr. Herr."

DeMatteo stalls to give what he hopes is his "butter won't melt in my mouth" smile as he struggles to contain his lion.

"Oh yes. Good morning gentlemen; my name is Mary. Mr. Herr is already waiting for you in the conference room, follow me please." DeMatteo tries to ignore her husky scent of arousal as Mary gives him what he assumes is supposed to be a flirty smile. With her hips swaying suggestively, she turns and leads them down the hallway.

DeMatteo is glad that the awkward situation of him charging through the building had been avoided. He hopes his mate does not get the wrong idea from the blatant musk of arousal wafting off the female.

The scent of his mate grows stronger as they go, causing DeMatteo's cock to bid desperately for freedom as his lion chuffs and rubs against his brain, begging him to go find their mate. But it is the other scents that give him pause, or rather the lack of the unmistakable scent of a shifter.

No, the only scent DeMatteo can discern is the scent of pure human, of multiple humans. Okay, so maybe his mate is not a shifter. Although every shifter knows this is a possibility, DeMatteo has never really entertained the thought; he has never met an Alpha with a human mate. It seems as though fate has a strange sense of humor. If his mate is indeed human, DeMatteo will have to be careful. It can be dangerous for any shifter to have sex with a human unless it is their true mate.

Scenting multiple females, DeMatteo prays the fates are not about to play the cruelest joke of all. DeMatteo's number one fear has always been that his true mate would be a woman. Not that he has anything against females; it's just he would have no idea what to do with one. The fates wouldn't be so cruel, would they?

Then there were the side effects of mating a human with any type of shifter, things that some humans might not be able to accept. Mating with an Alpha shifter would change a human even more drastically. It wouldn't give them a full shift into a lion like him, but they would become stronger, faster, live longer—as long as their mate lived—and have better senses.

They also would be able to partially shift, with claws and fangs capable of causing real damage during future matings or used for self-defense. If his mate is indeed male, he would also adapt internally to carry and nurse DeMatteo's cubs.

They would become, in fact, less human, and getting them to accept these changes as well as live a secret life is not something easily done. No one really knows how many more changes would occur with Alpha mates, since that knowledge had been long forgotten, and there were no known pairings.

But he doesn't have time to wonder why the fates have chosen to deal him this card. No, he will have to play the hand he has been dealt because his mate is sitting in this room waiting for him.

DeMatteo tries to calm his runaway pulse as they walk closer to the door. His mate is definitely in that room. Carefully schooling his features, DeMatteo braces himself to meet his other half, the one person created just for him.

Stopping outside the doors, DeMatteo breathes in deeply and quickly identifies Mrs. Malone, who he had scented on her husband. He also scents two unknown males and a second female whose scent is vaguely familiar.

Mary proceeds to knock on the closed door as if they weren't expected. "Come in," orders a smooth baritone, the sound sliding over DeMatteo's spine and further speeding up his thundering pulse.

God, I hope he is my mate. DeMatteo adjusts his painful erection behind his briefcase. Fuck, at this rate even the humans will be able to scent his arousal. Mary opens the door and turns suddenly to face him, pinning DeMatteo with a look that promises sex and more.

"Thank you," DeMatteo says shortly as he slides past her, trying to avoid any physical contact.

"Mr. Matthew Santiago and Mr. Kevin Malone are here," Mary announces unnecessarily, DeMatteo notices a peculiar look pass between her and his mate before she leaves, closing the door behind her. As DeMatteo makes his way further into the room, a tall, dark blond-haired man stands and makes the introductions.

"Good morning. I am Sean Herr, and this is Mrs. Grace Malone, Mr. Richard Price, and Ms. Kimberly Winters."

Shaking each person's hand in turn, DeMatteo is relieved that the female is not his mate. She is already obviously, to his nose, pregnant. The second male, while strikingly good-looking, is also not his mate. The only person left is the extraordinarily handsome lawyer, the lawyer he happens to be going up against in court. It seems the fates indeed do enjoy a good laugh.

Locking eyes with the male, DeMatteo has to physically hold his breath as his lion chuffs and rubs beneath his skin, desperate to get closer to their mate. Forcing his body to remain human, DeMatteo focuses on the other humans in the room as he greets his intended true mate.

"Mr. Herr," DeMatteo rumbles as he steps forward, extending his hand. His lion almost roars possessively at the contact, and he notices that his mate's eyes have dilated in response to that first contact. He wonders if Sean is somehow reacting to the mate bond, if he is in some way more than human.

Breathing in deeply, DeMatteo takes in his mate's scent. It is so potent he wants to roll around in it, but a subtle scent also reaches his brain. Slight, lingering, female arousal. His mate had been intimate recently with a female. His mate was straight?

Wrestling with the panic of having a mate that may not want him, who may have already bonded with a woman, and the possessive rage from scenting someone else on his mate, DeMatteo has to step back to avoid causing a scene and shifting right then and there, exposing himself to humans.

Standing around six feet tall, Sean is slightly shorter than DeMatteo's six-foot-four height. DeMatteo can tell that under that finely-tailored suit is a muscular body with strong shoulders. Sean's dark blond hair and emerald green eyes make a striking contrast to his tanned skin. His features speak of a Mediterranean ancestry. Simply put: the man is beautiful.

DeMatteo wants to drag him closer to mark—and mate—him right fucking now, and the fact that he is human is the only thing keeping DeMatteo in his human skin. But one thing is certain: DeMatteo has met his mate. Now he just has to find a way to keep him. But first, they have to deal with this case before DeMatteo can speak to his mate alone.

Stepping back, DeMatteo runs directly into his client—fuck, he forgot the man was even there—who is rooted to the floor with his mouth agape.

What the fuck is going on? There is a sudden building tension in the air, and he can scent his client's growing anger. Looking at the smug expression on Mrs. Malone and his mate's faces does little to ease his mounting fears. DeMatteo realizes that this case is not as open and closed as he had once thought, and he has the suspicion that it is him that the fates are laughing at.

Realization slaps DeMatteo in the face a fraction of a second after he stands near his client. DeMatteo now understands why he recognizes the scents from both women and why the wife seemed so confident. Obviously Mrs. Malone's scent would be on her husband, but Ms. Winters's scent is also on the man.

Fuck. Ms. Winters is Kevin's lover, a lover Mr. Malone had failed to warn DeMatteo even existed. This transgression will change some of the parameters of the divorce settlement, giving the wife a larger amount of the assets due to adultery, but that won't remove the prenup. There will need to be some seriously damaging information, beyond a simple affair, to void the entire contract.

DeMatteo's mind is raging with being lied to, and his lion is growling in frustration while he is grappling with both his absolute anger at his client, who had knowingly withheld pertinent information, and lust for his mate. DeMatteo has never felt the need to throttle one man within an inch of his life and fuck another man through the headboard at the same time, but needless to say, it is disorienting.

It is going to take all of his Alpha control and strength to get through the next few hours. Focusing on the case will be a daunting task with his mate sitting teasingly right across from him. His lion wanted to throw the man on the floor and mount him, humans be damned, and the pheromones his mate is leaking are doing little to calm him down.

DeMatteo watches his mate while they all sit at the conference table. The man is perfect; if DeMatteo was forced to describe his ideal mate, he'd be hard pressed to imagine someone better than the opposing counsel.

Chapter 3

Sean ~ July 2, Thursday, 10:15 a.m.

What the fuck is that? Sean resists the urge to jerk back when an unfamiliar but overwhelming feeling of lust slams into him as their hands meet for the first time.

"Mr. S-Santiago," Sean stutters as he stares into the deepest brown eyes he has ever seen.

He is beautiful, but as soon as the thought enters his mind, the moment is over. Matthew pulls his hand away with a swift step back, leaving Sean feeling suddenly adrift. It is like every part of him wants to stay close to the other man, which makes no sense.

Shaking the haze of lust out of his mind, Sean manages to get his brain to remember how to use words. "Everyone, if you would please have a seat."

That lawyer, Mr. Matthew Santiago, somehow completely unsettles him; never has Sean felt such an instant attraction to a person. He also has never, not once in his life, wanted to pounce on a man in public, but he did now. The confidence he had felt just moments ago has fled, and now he struggles to regain control of the meeting.

Sean's internal freak-out is drowned out when the defendant completely loses his shit, and he realizes he should have had security on standby. Sean watches the man practically foam at the mouth as he shouts at his estranged wife.

"What the hell are you doing here?" Kevin stalks over to his wife. "What the fuck do you think you are doing?" He continues staring at his wife and lover. Sean steps in front of his client, ready to physically restrain the irate man, by the time Santiago intervenes and grabs his client's arm.

"Let's all sit down and discuss what is going on here," Santiago growls, and Sean knows he has to feel like he has just stepped into a well-laid trap.

Guilt begins to twist his gut as Sean, for some reason, feels the need to comfort the man guiding his client away from a smirking Mrs. Malone. Although Sean is just doing his job, a part of him feels the need to step in and calm the obviously angry attorney.

"As we all know, we are here to discuss the dissolution of this marriage. My client is willing to sign divorce papers today if your client signs over half the marital assets," Sean says coolly, regaining control of his wayward mind and traitorous dick.

"Excuse me?" Santiago exclaims, jumping to his feet "There is an existing prenup—"

"As of record, your assets are estimated at sixty-eight million; we know there is more but will be satisfied with thirty-four million, no alimony, and with Mr. Malone retaining all physical property," Sean cuts in, not allowing the outburst to derail his demands.

"I have no idea what game your client is playing at, but the prenup stands. She will get only what she agreed to," Santiago growls out while Mr. Malone starts a string of cursing that would have impressed a seasoned sailor.

"Mr. Santiago, as I am sure your client is aware, the prenuptial agreement is null and void if abhorrent moral misconduct can be irrevocably proved," Sean says as he queues up the flat screen on the wall.

There it is, in high definition: Mr. Malone and Ms. Winters are engaged in activities that would make a porn star blush. There is also audio in which Mr. Malone states how he only married his wife to gain her shares in the company. Sean mercifully stops the video after a few painful minutes.

"Ms. Winters is also pregnant with your child, Mr. Malone," Sean adds as if the video needs anything else to back up their claims.

Sean watches, silently amused, as Santiago sits utterly dumbstruck. His client yells, "Clean this shit up!" Without offering a word of explanation or apology, he storms from the room and slams the door behind him.

Sean glances at Santiago, beaming with pride after a hard won victory. It may be considered bad form to be so smug at effectively ending someone's marriage, but to be able to wipe the floor with that slimeball is a reason to celebrate.

"Mr. Herr, it seems as if my client will be willing to come to a settlement regarding this matter. I will contact you before close of business tomorrow to go over the details." Shaking everyone's hand again, Santiago hands Sean his business card with his personal contact information before racing out the door to catch his sniveling, lying, rat-bastard of a client.

Walking back to his office, Sean can't help but smirk. What a slam dunk! This day is turning out to be epic. Reaching Mary's desk, Sean tells her that the enemy will be calling to schedule a meeting.

"Oh really, he is too handsome to be the enemy," she purrs. They have always had more of a friendship than a boss-employee relationship.

"Mary, just patch him through to my office when he calls," Sean growls out, inexplicably annoyed, before stalking into his office and slamming the door.

Trying to clear his head of the unpleasant thoughts surrounding his recent behavior, Sean focuses on drafting a divorce agreement and confidentiality clause. Now that he has Mr. Malone on the ropes, Sean has no intention of backing off. The only thing not going according to plan is the erection Sean has had since he set eyes on Mr. Santiago—Matthew—walking into the conference room.

Everything about the man calls to him on a level so primal that Sean is terrified to rationalize the depths of his own need. Hearing his secretary gush over Matthew had evoked a wave of jealousy that had raged through his body so fast he was unable to reign in his harsh words. Pushing those thoughts out of his mind, Sean focuses on the familiar. He begins wrapping up the biggest monetary settlement of his career.

"Well, I take it everything went well. What did you think of Mr. Santiago?" Sean jumps when he hears his father's voice.

"Yes, things went well. Did you know about the evidence? He seemed like a confident lawyer that got side-swiped by his client's lies. Is that why you gave me the case?" Sean accuses as he watches his father cross the office.

"No, I told you that this morning. She never said what evidence she had, only that it was conclusive. I gave you the case because it was important you met Mr. Santiago. I am sure you will see him again. So I guess I owe you congratulations. I've never seen Mr. Malone's tail tucked so tightly between his legs." Frank chuckles as he takes a seat in the chair in front of Sean's desk.

Mr. Frank Davis is a lot of things, but he is not one for flattery or handing out undeserved praise, so Sean is shocked when he sees the pride in his father's eyes. The shock must have been showing on his face when his father adds, "I am very proud of you, son. Never doubt that."

As he stands to leave, Sean finds his words stick in his throat as he watches his father exit the room. Before he could completely vanish, Sean calls out, "Thanks, Dad."

Frank turns back, looking at him with a fondness Sean has not seen in years. Frank simply nods and smiles in acknowledgement before heading through the door.

Unless he gets struck by lightning, Sean is sure that nothing could surprise him more than the fact that he has somehow finally pleased his dad. His father's newfound interest and vocal praise is completely out of the norm, so much so that Sean can almost ignore how strange the exchange had really been.

Richard ~ 8 a.m.

"Richard, I know how you feel about relying only on my visions, but the Alpha Guardian is about to be born," Tien states.

"I thought you saw the birth of the Alpha Guardian years ago, but we have yet to see any sign of them. If the prophecy is true, the Alpha Guardian will be mated to an Alpha in my family line, and the only Alpha available to mate in our family is DeMatteo," Richard offers, pacing his office.

As the Alpha Apex of North America, he and with his mate, Guardian shifter Tien, govern over all the prides and hold seats on the Shifter Council: a coalition of shifters that work with humans to safeguard treaties that regulate both sides.

"Yes, and he has yet to find his true mate. So it is possible that he will be the Alpha the Goddess has chosen to bring shifters back," Tien counters.

"Tien, DeMatteo is gay!" Richard exclaims, running his hands through his hair before continuing to pace around his desk. "There are no known records of gay Alpha Pairs, let alone one with an Alpha human. Tien, listen to me. There are reasons why many shifters no longer believe the prophecies are real. When we mated, many believed that we were what was foretold. You are the first known half-human Alpha mate, and the first Guardian shifter ever."

Tien jumps in angrily, "Yes, but I told you at our mating that the Goddess told me that I was to train and nurture the Alpha Guardian. So tell me, do you not believe me? Or do you believe that the Goddess has lied to me?"

"It's not that simple, Tien, it's not just what I believe as your mate. You want me to address the Council on something that we have no way of proving until we meet this Alpha Guardian."

"Since when do I need proof to tell others what the Goddess has instructed me to do? I simply need access to all of the scrolls and to be able to conference with the magic users in the prides," Tien sneers sarcastically.

"You don't, but you know the Council will want more than just your vision. They will want to know who you have seen," Richard barks, eyes flashing Alpha red in annoyance.

"And since when have you taken issue with your favorite nephew being gay?" Tien questions incredulously, flashing her own Alpha mate eyes in warning.

"Never. I am just saying what others are too afraid to say to your face."

"Afraid? Of this face?" Tien asks innocently, batting her eyelashes.

Richard rolls his eyes at his sassy mate. While she is the best mate that any shifter could have ever asked for, her shifted form has been known to send more than one Alpha running with their tails firmly tucked between their legs.

Richard strokes her face. "No, not this face, baby, but your other face can be quite intimidating to those who aren't intimately involved with your more animalistic ways."

Tien snorts and bats his hand away. "Clever distraction, but I'm more interested in those things people are too afraid to say to my face."

"Well, the biggest disagreement is that it will be a human Alpha," Richard begins, but as usual, Tien cuts in.

"But I was mostly human."

"Yes, but your family was also mixed with shifters for generations before your kind went extinct. Many argue, correctly I might add, that you were never really completely human to begin with! You were at least a quarter shifter.

While you were unmated, you lived your life as a human, but you were almost a hundred years old, Tien."

"But—"

Butting in, Richard adds, "Yes, I know what you are about to say, but I am telling you that this is what they are saying. Many shifters resent the thought of some human coming to save us when we were here generations before any primate climbed out of the trees."

"That is ridiculous; we know that we all come from the same Goddess. Our species have evolved together since the beginning."

"Tien, you know that it is not only humans that have lost their faith in the old gods. I just want you to be prepared to have many of the others against the very idea, and not just shifters. Even the humans are likely to reject this."

Richard takes his mate's hand, silently begging her through their mate bond to understand the battle she is about to start. The hostilities between the different shifter species have turned shifter against shifter as each group battles for control. Their only common thread is the distrust and hatred of some humans hell-bent on wiping out their entire species.

"That is even before you tell them that they are a gay Alpha Pair. I have no issues with DeMatteo being gay, but you know that there is talk that this is the reason why he has yet to find his true mate."

"That is crazy talk, Richard. You yourself were almost five hundred before we met."

"I know, but you know the bigots will grab anything that even seems to support their cause. There has never been a case of a gay Alpha and Alpha Mate. Every other gay Alpha has taken a female companion mate, and they have all been killed when they lost their pride to other mated Alphas."

"The Goddess has told me there will be many that try to stand in the way of the Alpha Guardian. That is why I was sent before, to ensure their enemies do not succeed, and that is why I was given such a powerful mate to fight beside me."

"You have a wicked tongue, mate. But yes, I will always stand with you, Tien. If what you see is indeed DeMatteo, then we will have to make sure our allies stand firm. There are still many shifters who oppose the thought of a gay Alpha and many more of them who distrust humans completely. I will contact the members of the Council and advise them that you seek their audience. Do you need to speak with the Human Council as well?"

"Yes, all sides need to know that the time has come. I will be leaving soon to hold a ceremony with our mages to seek the Goddess's protection."

"Alright, I'll head down to the Council this morning. Be careful, Tien. We have a lot of work to do."

Tien nods then quickly presses her lips to her Alpha's. They will need each other's strength for the upcoming battle, for their enemies will be many.

Chapter 4

DeMatteo ~ 1 p.m.

"Just do whatever it takes to make them go away. Give her the thirty-four million. I already called the bank to have the funds made available. I want it over. Now!" Mr. Malone bellows at DeMatteo before hanging up.

If someone asked DeMatteo to come up with a list of things that pissed him off, being disrespected by those of a lower rank and being hung up on would be at the very top. His client had done both.

After today, he's adding being forced to publicly roll belly up for his mate to the list. The worst part about it is that he realizes it may not be a onetime thing.

Leaving his office, DeMatteo climbs into his 2014 Bentley Continental GTC and heads back home to his pride lands.

Loon Lake in Stevens County, Washington, has been his family's home for over five hundred years; his father and uncle had established the pride before his uncle ascended to become the Alpha Apex.

Eight hundred acres of land make up DeMatteo's territory, and there are three hundred and fifty members of the pride. They are negotiating buying more land to continue to grow; unlike their full-animal cousins, there is more than one male in the pride so they need ample space to avoid the inevitable clashes surges of testosterone tend to bring.

Being gay means DeMatteo does not have to fight with other males within the pride for access to breeding females. Since most of the females in the pride are his sisters or cousins, and inbreeding is incompatible with producing cubs, it wouldn't be a problem even if he was straight.

Occasionally, a rogue male wanders into his territory looking to take over, and the price for that is death. The Santiago pride is large and healthy, and because he has earned the devotion of the entire pride, every member is willing to fight to keep order.

Even before DeMatteo pulls up to his home, his lion is roaring for him to go back and claim their mate. DeMatteo knows he will need to speak to his uncle, and he will need a plan. Having a human mate makes everything that much more complicated. Add to the fact that his mate was most likely straight, or at least he had been until their handshake, and the problem had grown tenfold.

DeMatteo knows that the mating pull will override the gay part; his mate would be drawn to him and that need will intensify every time they were near each other. The biggest problem will be getting over the mental stigma. Humans attach so much of their self-worth to their sexuality.

So if his mate has issues with homosexuals, his mind could cause him to rebel against the mating. If they mated and he could not accept it, then the human spirit could go insane with mind splintering from an incomplete mating bond.

There is also the little problem of exposing shifters to a human. This Is always a dangerous prospect; if the human rejects the bond, they could expose shifters to the world and start a war between the species in doing so.

Humans tend to want to destroy things they do not understand. At one time, humans and shifters lived side by side. Then some humans turned away from the old gods and created new ones in their image. Not long after that, the wars started.

Fighting to prove their new gods were supreme, the humans had nearly wiped themselves out. After most of the world's written records were destroyed, the world entered the Dark Ages.

The Council of shifters had decided it was too dangerous to expose their dual nature, and that had been when the veil had gone up. Over time, the humans who knew of shifters died and the story of their existence, and the old gods, became a myth.

Few humans remember the old ways of the Gods and Goddess, so each time a shifter takes a human mate, it's a huge risk; DeMatteo will need to speak to his uncle for advice on how to approach claiming his human mate.

Climbing out of his car, DeMatteo is not surprised to see his sisters in their lioness forms, sunning themselves on the front porch. A few members of the pride have jobs and apartments in the human world, but most choose to stay on the pride lands.

When he makes his way to the front door, each sister presents her belly as he reaches down to stroke them in passing. As he opens the front door, DeMatteo can feel the ripple of magic when his sister shifts from lioness to human.

Being full siblings of the former Alpha and Alpha Mate gives DeMatteo and his siblings an advantage. They are more powerful and much larger in both their human and animal forms, and as their cats, they are around seven feet tall and weigh over eight hundred pounds.

True-mated Alpha's children are almost always born Betas; having an Alpha child is not guaranteed and Omegas are extremely rare.

Being an Alpha, DeMatteo is the largest, easily surpassing his father's size. DeMatteo tips the scales at over eleven hundred pounds; shifted, he is even larger than his Alpha Apex uncle. This is why he has been so successful in defending his pride even against true-mated Alphas.

Because he has raised his siblings, they are closer than most. They often seem to be able to read each other's minds. Samantha, who also serves as his lead enforcer, has always been particularly in tune with him so it is no surprise when Samantha embraces him as soon as he arrives. Never one to start with pleasantries, she instead greets him with a barrage of questions.

"What's with the constipated grimace? I'm guessing the meeting went crazy wrong if you're still in town. Don't tell me some fresh-face junior lawyer sent the great Alpha DeMatteo home with his tail tucked between his legs."

DeMatteo lets out a sigh. It is pointless to try lying; any shifter could easily scent his wariness and his lion's general dissatisfaction. "I am not grimacing. I'll have you know this is my standard 'Samantha is talking me to death' face. The meeting went to shit sideways, but also proved to be the greatest moment in my life. I met my true mate today."

DeMatteo rattles off the facts, hoping against hope that this will be enough information and that his sister will be too excited to press for more details. He really doesn't want to explain that his mate is human and straight, especially not before he has a drink and a chance to speak with their uncle.

"Oh. My. God! DeMatteo! That is amazing! Well, come on, spill it. Tell me all about him. What's his name? What pride does he belong to? What does he look like?" Samantha rambles excitedly, barely dragging in a breath between questions.

Although Alphas have the ability to hide their scents and emotions from the pride, DeMatteo has never felt the need to hide what he is feeling from his siblings. It is an ability evolved from the Alpha's need to protect his position in the pride, and his siblings will never be a threat.

"DeMatteo, where is your mate? Why is he not here with you?" Samantha questions seriously; as he had thought, it hadn't taken his sister long to realize that he had come home alone.

When shifters find their true mate, they generally begin the courting process immediately. This is especially true for Alphas, who tend to be highly possessive and territorial during the first stages of mating, rarely letting the other shifter out of arm's reach.

So DeMatteo returning alone is highly abnormal, even though their younger brother had waited months before claiming his mate.

Well, isn't that a great question?

He had waited twenty-five years for this moment, but having a human mate had never been part of his plan. "I wouldn't say that anything is wrong, but I need to consult Uncle Richard and Aunt Tien about how to bond with my mate."

"Uncle Richard? I think you are a little too old for the birds and bees talk, DeMatteo," Samantha jokes.

"Well, I need to know how to bond with a human. So I'd say this is a pretty special case, since my mate is both a human male and straight."

DeMatteo wants to laugh at how quickly Samantha attempts to school her look of utter shock into neutrality and sets out to support her brother, but he just can't seem to find any humor in his current situation.

Samantha's smile is real when she says, "I am sure that your mate will be happy to be with you. You know that the gods don't give us true mates who are unable to bond with us. That human is the other half of your soul and you're the other part of his. I am so happy for you; now we need to plan a celebration!"

"You are right, I just need to talk to Uncle Richard about how to properly bond, and mate, with a human." After giving her another quick hug, DeMatteo goes off to deal with the barriers to properly claiming his mate.

DeMatteo knows one of the first things he has to do is to call it off with Hugh. They have been lovers for almost fifteen years, providing each other with companionship while waiting and hoping to find their true mates.

Deciding that a quick break will be for the best, DeMatteo heads straight down to the barn to have what he knows will be a painful conversation.

"Hey, Hugh, are you out here?" DeMatteo calls as he rounds the corner. Although he can feel the other shifter's presence through the pride bond, DeMatteo has never wanted to be the type of Alpha that abuses his authority on and over the pride.

"Hey, DeMatteo, how did the big showdown with Mr. and Mrs. Malone go?" Hugh chuckles as he pops out from behind one of the stalls.

"Things got pretty interesting, but the case is over. I just need to finish up the paperwork," DeMatteo says as he watches Hugh gather up his horse grooming kit and blankets before approaching.

The last thing DeMatteo wants is to hurt his longtime friend, but his lion is growling at the presence of the man and his open affection. But he knows—if he is honest, he has known for a while—that this is going to hurt. Samantha had warned him over the years that Hugh was growing too attached and would have trouble stepping aside for his mate, but DeMatteo had enjoyed their easy companionship.

DeMatteo recoils when Hugh reaches for him for their usual kiss, unable to control his immediate reaction to someone other than his mate trying to touch him. His lion had always been indifferent to their relationship, but now that he's scented their mate, his lion will kill anyone who tries to interfere in order to protect that bond.

"Okay, what the hell is wrong with you?" Hugh asks, and DeMatteo is hit with his scent that reeks with hurt and sadness.

"That is why I came to find you. We need to talk," DeMatteo says, rubbing his hand across his stubble. He understands Hugh's confusion. As the Alpha, he needs to deal with this, even though his cat wants nothing to do with the other man.

This is a pride member, DeMatteo reminds his lion, *and we have to keep the pride strong.*

"I really don't know how to tell you this, other than to just say it: I met my true mate today," DeMatteo rushes out, "so we have to end this." He gestures between the two of them. Both Hugh and DeMatteo know that if his lion feels that Hugh poses a threat to his mating, it will attack. The look of hurt is so stark across Hugh's face that even DeMatteo's lion manages to back down enough to sense his despair.

DeMatteo tries to be discreet as he scents the air to gauge his former lover's mood, hoping to soothe his lion's uneasiness. Fear, anger, and sadness roll off Hugh as he stares at DeMatteo, and the Alpha feels helpless as to how to offer comfort in a way that won't cause further distress.

"You know we discussed this before we started dating. If either of us found our true mate, the other would back away. Of course I don't want you to leave the pride; this is your home. I just need you to give me space until I complete the bond. My lion is feeling aggressive, and I would never want to hurt you."

"Oh, okay. I will move all my stuff out of your room as soon as possible," Hugh mumbles as he avoids DeMatteo's gaze.

"Thank you, Hugh. I don't want to sound like an ass, but I hope that we can remain friends." DeMatteo lets out a breath, relieved that things are going smoothly. He doesn't want to hurt the man any more than he has to.

"Yes, Alpha," Hugh says around a growl of displeasure as he stomps out of the barn.

DeMatteo sighs, pinching the bridge of his nose. "Or maybe not," he says, already feeling the headache he's sure he'll be nursing. Which is a feat in itself seeing as his healing is so quick he's never really had one before.

But then Hugh's always been special.

DeMatteo ignores his lion's desire to just grab the shifter and force him to submit for such a blatant act of disrespect. Although they had made that agreement, DeMatteo had understood that Hugh would not take the news kindly after fifteen years.

DeMatteo walks up to his private office to contact his uncle, still needing advice on how to bring a human into the know. Richard had assisted Carla when she had taken a human companion mate a few years earlier.

"Hello, DeMatteo, it's been a while. To what do I owe this phone call?" Richard greets warmly.

After the death of his parents, Richard had instantly stepped in to help DeMatteo claim the role of Alpha. DeMatteo had been at a clear disadvantage, being young and unmated, and having such a large and desirable pride. Richard had worked hard to prepare him for the challenges he would face, but more than that, Richard and his mate had become surrogate parents for DeMatteo and his siblings.

"Hello, Uncle. It has been too long, but I am afraid that this is not just a social call. I need your help, as both my uncle and my Alpha Apex."

"Okay, that is vague and troubling."

"Today I met my true mate. My male, *human* true mate."

"Oh, I see. A human Alpha Mate? I agree. You do need my help, but you will also need to speak to your Aunt Tien."

The line goes silent, but DeMatteo can feel his lion calming. The bond they share is enough that even his Alpha lion feels at ease knowing the older Alpha will help them.

Tien is the first to speak again.

"DeMatteo, you have found your mate? And he's human?" Tien asks unnecessarily.

"Yes, which is why I called. I have never heard of a human Alpha Mate; I was hoping that you or my uncle would have information on how this is possible."

"Of course. First, I must say that this is very powerful magic. It is true that there has never been a full human Alpha Mate, although the prophecies spoke of the day when one would be born. So this is a great honor," Tien says.

Richard adds in, "We believe that mating will occur just as it would with a Beta shifter and human mate. It is unclear if you will form an Alpha knot since you'll need to remain human to mate. Unfortunately, there are no clear answers since you will be writing history."

The conversation goes on for hours before DeMatteo ends the call to contact his mate. His uncle had advised him to contact his mate immediately and invite him to the pride lands to "finish the legal paperwork" as soon as possible. This will give him time to assess his mate's mental state and also give the magic of the mating bond time to deepen their connection.

It was unclear if, being human, Sean will be affected by the mating bond before DeMatteo bites him. When Betas find human true mates, they are always unaware of the connection. So Betas are forced to court their mates like a human would, which is much slower than with shifters. But DeMatteo knows that he will court his mate for a lifetime if that is what it takes.

His lion especially likes the idea of spending time with its mate; DeMatteo can feel it chuffing and rubbing just beneath the surface. DeMatteo's uncle had explained during their call that mating with a human is only truly dangerous when they are not true mates. So he can at least be confident that even when his lion is mostly in charge, it will instinctively protect their weaker mate, even from itself.

After having his fears put to rest, DeMatteo had been able to speak with his aunt, a Guardian shifter, about the prophecy that foretold of this type of mating. She is able to communicate directly with the Goddess and is the physical manifestation of the old ones. Although DeMatteo had been raised to believe in the Goddess, this is the first time he has ever heard of these stories.

Tien had confided to DeMatteo that she had received a vision years ago that predicted that his mate would be human. She'd told him that the Goddess herself would bless their union. DeMatteo found himself both overjoyed that the fates seemed to have destined him a mate and frustrated that his aunt and uncle had hidden this from him. All the time he wasted with Hugh could have been avoided if he knew his mate was waiting for him.

By the time he had hung up, DeMatteo had been instructed on how to care for a newly formed human Alpha Mate. He made a mental note to question both Tien and Richard about why these prophecies had been hidden, but right now he had more pressing matters to attend to.

It is time to contact my mate and put my plan into action.

DeMatteo heads to his office to place the call to his intended mate. *My mate.* DeMatteo chuckles to himself, thinking of the sexy man. It is impossible for him to point out the human's single best feature. With his blond hair, green eyes, and at least six feet of lean sculpted muscle, Sean is more than handsome enough to grace the covers of magazines. Add in his intelligence, quick wit, and sharp tongue, and DeMatteo had never stood a chance.

Although DeMatteo has often attracted smaller men, he has always known his mate would be strong. Yes, Sean checked all the boxes in his ideal mate list, and after speaking to his aunt and uncle, DeMatteo has no fear that his mate will reject him. Picking up his cell phone, DeMatteo places a call to the man that he will spend the rest of his long life with.

Chapter 5

Sean ~ 9 p.m.

When Sean finally arrives back home that evening, he is bored beyond distraction, wondering why Matthew hadn't called yet. As he hops in the shower, Sean reviews the meeting—in detail—and tries to make sense of his feelings.

The man in question had phoned the office right after their meeting to tell Sean's secretary that Mr. Malone would be agreeing to the terms. He had then asked for Sean's personal number so they could detail the contract and set an appointment for finalizing the paperwork.

Now Sean had to wait over the long weekend. With Saturday being the fourth of July, everything will be closed until Monday. *Now I won't get to see him for three days,* Sean muses over his dinner for one.

The fact that he is so bothered by this both pisses him off and confuses him. *Why the fuck am I so worried about a man calling me? I barely know him, but I feel like I need to be with him.* Nothing about his reaction to the other man makes any sense; it's almost as if something is drawing him in.

Sex is easy. Even though Sean has never been with a man or even had a desire to try, he understands sex in and of itself. If it was just sexual attraction, that would be easy to sort through, but this is different. The thing that frightens Sean the most, and he can barely admit this to himself, is that he doesn't just want sex.

When Sean ponders his reactions to Matthew, he knows he wants something long term. He wants to own every part of the man, and that is something he should not be thinking about a man he just met. When Sara had hinted at the possibility of marriage, Sean had completely panicked, but after a single meeting with Matthew Santiago, Sean is ready for that and more.

Those thoughts make Sean remember his mother and all of her stories of true love and happily ever afters. Sean's mother had been a hopeless romantic; Sean had loved to hear about when his parents first met. They had what he thought was the love of a lifetime; she had told him that he would meet his perfect match, too. She had said there was a perfect person who was made to be with him, that he would be drawn to this person who would love him in a way that no one else could.

That is what Sean feels: drawn, and it's as if everything in his life has been leading him to this place. It feels like every story his mother had ever told him about magic and love but with an intensity that defies all logic. But Sean is no child, and he knows the feeling of being magically drawn to a soulmate is just a story his mother had told him.

Needing to get out of his own head, Sean heads out for an evening jog. Just like always, thoughts of his mother make his heart throb painfully. No child is ever ready to lose a parent, but to have her ripped away so suddenly had left Sean reeling. After two miles, Sean hopes the aches in his legs and another hot shower will distract him from his earlier thoughts.

The run back has given him even less insight. He strips on his way to the bathroom, not caring about the mess. He hurriedly washes away the day, stubbornly ignoring his half hard dick. Getting out of the shower, Sean is proud of the fact that he did not jerk off thinking about that frustrating man. The fact that his dick is so hard it hurts confuses Sean to no end; he is by no means a virgin, but he's never really craved sex before.

Yes, like every other red blooded male he enjoys getting off, and in most cases his hand would do. In those rare moments he needed a connection with a warm body he could normally be satisfied with once or twice a month, sometimes less. Not that he doesn't enjoy sex; he does, but sex is just not something that demands his attention.

Until now. Now it seems as if his dick has a mind of its own.

Drying himself roughly, Sean is left with two thoughts: he is extremely attracted to the sexy-as-sin lawyer, and he just knows he has to follow his gut. He just needs to figure out how and when to make his move.

But the biggest question is the one that is the hardest to answer: is Matthew interested in him? Sean doesn't even know if the man is gay, it's not as if he could tell by looking at the guy. Sean had had several gay friends in college, so he knows most stereotypes were untrue.

While he has never been sexually or emotionally attracted to a man before, Sean has never been one to completely dismiss an opportunity or go against his gut feelings. But one thing he has no interest in is hitting on someone who could probably snap his neck with their bare hands if they wanted to.

Seeing he missed a call, Sean listens to the message, disappointed to hear Sara's voice asking if he wants to get together again tonight. Sean had promised to call her this morning, but after meeting Matthew and winning a career building case, he had been flying so high that Sara had never crossed his mind.

Sean finds himself hesitating to call her back, wondering how to tell his girlfriend that he does not want to see her again. How would he explain? Dialing her number, Sean decides to just stick with the half-truth: "I met someone else and I want to see how it goes." No need to tell her that the other person is a man.

"Hello, handsome," Sara purrs over the line as soon as the call connects.

Normally Sean would feel content at hearing her voice, but now the sound causes his stomach to roll and he feels strangely irritated by the pitch. Swallowing his irrational annoyance, Sean attempts to sound conversational.

"Hey, Sara. Sorry I missed your call. I was in the shower," Sean explains, hoping to stall long enough to get his head together.

"Perfect, since I am just about to pull into your driveway."

Shit. Telling her on the phone would have been hard enough. Now he will have to break up with her and convince her that he does not want to have sex while his hard, angry dick stares up at him. Throwing on clothes, Sean has a firm conversation with his dick, willing it to behave.

Sean is amazed at the stubbornness of his erection at just the thought of Matthew, when just last night when he had sex with Sara, he had barely been able to maintain his erection long enough to ejaculate. Now he can't get the damn thing to go away.

Well, that settles it. I guess my dick knows who it wants.

Opening the front door, Sean almost winces at the speed in which his dick deflates. Sara slides into his arms and immediately presses their bodies together as she licks across the seam of his lips. It is difficult to not just shove her away. Instead, Sean gently pries the clinging woman from him while steering her into the house. He does not want an audience for what is sure to be a scene.

"Come on in, Sara," Sean says, shaking his head at the strange twist of fate his life seems to be taking.

Steering her towards the couch instead of his bedroom, Sean finds himself saying what has to be the most cliché and dreaded phrase in any relationship.

"We need to talk."

By the time he gets the irate woman out of his house, Sean is completely done with the day. He almost ignores the phone, thinking it's likely Sara calling to tell him, again, what a piece of shit he was. She had left in tears once he had told her that he had met someone and wanted to pursue it. But at the last second he decides she deserves the chance to tell him off, only to be surprised by the husky voice that sends his pulse racing.

"Can you meet me at my home office tomorrow morning to finalize the settlement? Mr. Malone will be on hand to sign the agreement," Matthew's voice seems to purr through the line.

"My client will be unavailable tomorrow," Sean mutters, hoping to disguise any trace of longing his voice may give away.

"That's fine. Wouldn't want World War Three breaking out in my backyard with those two. It might ruin the party I'm having," Matthew jokes. His laugh alone is enough to get Sean's dick from half hard to raging instantly. "You are more than welcome to stay for it."

After getting his address and about ten minutes of small talk, saying he has no plans and would stay for the party, Sean knows he had to get closer to that man. Talking to him is easy, like they have known each other for years.

Crawling into bed, Sean wraps his fist around his cock, which had filled back out while talking to Matthew. Closing his eyes, Sean begins pulling his hand up his shaft. All he can see is a six foot four Hispanic male with brown hair flowing past his shoulders, brown eyes that burn into his soul as he stares into them. Sean imagines those large hands stroking his cock and that strong-looking mouth taking him down to the root.

Quickening his pace, he imagines how it would feel to have rough hands sliding down his ass as one finger gently circles his hole. Gently rolling his sack with his free hand, Sean lets a finger ghost over that puckered flesh, while picking up the pace with the other.

Suddenly the image of Matthew sliding his cock home inside of him has Sean's orgasm racing down his spine. With that in mind, Sean comes hard, hissing through his teeth, "Matthew!"

Fuck. I am losing my mind. Now I'm jerking off thinking about that man fucking me? I never thought of myself as the woman in a relationship.

But then again, there really wouldn't be any woman in this relationship.

He can almost hear Mary's snarky voice in his head. *Careful, Sean. Your misogyny is showing.*

He needs to re-think everything he knows about relationships. That thought should scare him, but as much as Sean wants to fuck that gorgeous man, he also wants to get fucked. But that raises another question: *would Matthew let him fuck him?*

Now with all the possibilities in his head, Sean knows that sleep will not come. Hopping out of the bed, Sean decides that if he is going to actively pursue a man, he should probably do some research.

It only takes a few minutes to find all types of information: how to prep his lover, how to give a blowjob— *hmm, that might be a skill that comes in handy*—and the joys of frottage. After a few hours of learning ways to fuck in positions that he isn't sure he could get into, Sean decides to watch a few movies. For research...

After educating himself in a very pleasurable way, Sean is able to finally climb back into bed. After thinking about it to death, Sean knows he wants the man in question, beyond a reasonable doubt. Now he just has to figure out how to get him.

God, I hope he gives me some kind of clue.

Sean ~ July 3, Friday, 5 a.m.

"There had better be a great, goddamn reason you are calling me at the ass crack of dawn on my day off," Mary groans.

"Is that the way you greet your boss and best friend?" Sean chuckles. Mary's manners can be lacking in the best of times, so early morning wake-ups were especially unpleasant.

"News flash, asshole, you are not my boss on Saturdays, and it's only your soon-to-be-reevaluated position as best friend that got me to answer in the first place," Mary fires back.

Sean can almost see her epic bitchface at the thought of him being her boss. Friends since childhood, Mary had always been the one who'd led their group. If it hadn't been for their friendship, Sean never would have survived his mother's death. No, if anyone was ever the boss, it was Mary.

"So feisty. Look, I'm sorry to wake you, but I'm at the office looking for the Malone files. I need to run them down to the opposing counsel today for signatures."

"Yeah? Well, butter my butt and call me a biscuit. Mr. Malone must be desperate to settle before she changes her mind if he is seeing you on a weekend. I can meet you at the office and fax them to Mr. Santiago if you want."

"Wow, one second you are threatening to revoke my best friend status, the next you're offering to drag yourself out of your coffin to come help me. Must be that time of the month," Sean jokes as he goes through the contained chaos that is Mary's desk.

"Very cute, fucktard. Now you can try to work that fax machine on your own. Mr. I-can't-figure-out-how-to-use-my-own-phone. And stop going through my desk. The files are in the safe, with Mrs. Malone's signatures," Mary replies.

"Thank you, my cranky goddess, but I will not need your services today. I will be hand-delivering the files to Mr. Santiago's home for his client's signature and notary. This way it will be filed in court before either party can draw blood."

"Wow, now I know I want to come with you. That Santiago is one fine piece of—"

Sean cuts in, "Thanks, Mary. I got them. See you next week," and ends the call before she can finish whatever raunchy comment she is about to make.

Sean pushes aside his annoyance of his friend's obvious attraction to the other lawyer, it is insane to be jealous over someone he'd just met. Yes, he had decided he wanted to pursue his interest in the other man, but there was no guarantee Matthew would want him back.

Deciding to skip that train of thought, before he can talk himself out of making a move, Sean concentrates on making sure he has everything in order. Business first. He couldn't wait to see his father's face at the start of business next week, when the man finds out that everything has already been taken care of.

DeMatteo ~ 5 a.m.

"So how exactly do you expect to woo your mate in the middle of a party?" Samantha asks as they go over the food preparations.

"What you mean is: how do I plan to woo my mate with my nosy siblings interfering?" DeMatteo laughs at her guilty look.

"That too."

"Simple, my siblings—under the threat of death—will stay away from him. Tonight is very important and as my Head Enforcer, I'm relying on you to keep everyone in check. He is human, so there is a chance that it will take a while to bond," DeMatteo cautions.

"What about Hugh? How do you want me to control his access to the future Alpha Mate?"

"I know there is no love lost between you two, but he is still a member of the pride. That being said, I expect you to watch him. I don't think he'll interfere, but with my mate, I'm not willing to take any chances."

The thought of treating one of his shifters like an enemy doesn't quite sit well, but until they are fully bonded,

DeMatteo's lion will be an over-protective, possessive ass. No one is safe if his lion perceives a threat, so it is best to proceed carefully.

"Hopefully he will make himself scarce. I'd like to be able to enjoy the party without having to babysit your ex. So how are you planning on telling him about shifters? Oh god, do you remember Carla with Nick? I thought she was going to pass out when she brought him here for the talk." Samantha laughs at the memory of Carla pacing the halls as Timothy and DeMatteo had spoken to her human companion.

DeMatteo rolls his eyes. "No, I don't think anyone can make it as dramatic as she did. I plan to just ease him into it after a few dates," he says.

Nick ~ 7 a.m.

"So, what? You're going to pull all my resources and reallocate them to Nick?" the female hunter snarls over the speaker.

"You said it yourself. Your mark has been pulled out of play, and anyway, there has never been any proof that he is anything other than human. Nick, however, has been grooming this mark for years," Chris replies calmly.

"Grooming? All he has been doing is fucking some animal! Please, tell me how this is so useful to the hunters."

Nick is here for a face-to-face meeting with the most important hunter in the community, and now he has this washed-up hunter reducing his work to fucking. There is no way he's going to let his sacrifice be belittled by this uppity bitch.

Nick jumps out of his chair, screaming at the phone, "Hey! Don't act like I'm just fucking, or like it is something I am enjoying! I'll have you know—"

"Enough!"

Nick snaps his mouth shut, and Chris jerks his hand in the direction of his abandoned chair, the unspoken warning clear. He takes his seat, grinding his teeth so hard it's surprising he doesn't lose a molar.

It's not that he's afraid of Chris; the man may be demanding, but he has never so much as raised a hand against him since taking him in. He's just unwilling to risk his chance of finally destroying the pride and smart enough to realize these two nut jobs are his only way in.

Chris ~

"Enough!" Chris bellows, shooting Nick a stern look as both young hunters go silent.

Chris points to the chair and Nick flops back down like a petulant child. Chris takes a minute to let each of his underlings get control of their tongues. He will not allow for any infighting. They need to present a united front if they want to win the war.

"This is not up for debate. If you don't like my orders, then feel free to walk away. Nick, you are cleared to make a play. Call me directly with whatever gear you need."

"Yes, sir. Thank you, sir."

"And you, miss, will be available to assist him in any way I see fit. If I hear that you have been anything but helpful and supportive, I promise you will live just long enough to regret not walking away when I gave you the chance. Do you understand me?"

"Yes, sir. I understand you perfectly," she said.

After the call ends, he waits in silence. Nick needs to learn his place. Chris watches as Nick tries to rein in his temper before the young hunter speaks, "Sir, I want to apologize for my outburst."

Chris learned long ago not to confuse a person needing to work with him to further their own goals and being loyal to him and the cause. There is no doubt what Nick's intentions are, but for now he has come closer than anyone else.

"This is the last time, Nick. I can't afford to have you two at each other's throats. Do you think you'll be able to keep it together long enough to complete your mission?"

"Yes, sir," Nick answers gruffly.

Chris watches the young hunter as he slinks out the door, he doesn't have the time to babysit him, and now that the female hunter has lost her target he needs to get another hunter in play to follow him. There is something about that family that Chris doesn't like and until he figures out how they are involved he'll need to have someone keeping tails on them.

Chapter 6

DeMatteo ~ July 3, Friday, 10 a.m.

DeMatteo figures that it would be best to have Sean meet him on the ranch in the morning. This way, they can conclude their business, and DeMatteo will have the opportunity to be alone with his mate. Humans tend to be predictable with their mating rituals, which is yet another reason this would be easier if Sean was a shifter.

Most attorneys would scoff at the mere suggestion of a meeting over a holiday weekend, but DeMatteo knows that Mrs. Malone must be desperate to get all the paperwork over and done with before her husband can try to find some way to weasel out. He also hopes that the subtle signs of awareness he had noticed in Sean's eyes are a signal of mutual attraction.

After his talk with Samantha, he is sure that she will keep Sean and Hugh carefully apart. The situation between him and Hugh is shaky at best. No doubt any interaction would make both his mate and Hugh uncomfortable. Hugh had removed all his belongings from the Alpha's den without as much as a word—not that DeMatteo had attempted to coax the man into speaking. Maybe some space would allow Hugh to come to terms with the breakup.

No such assurances can be made about the rest of them. DeMatteo knows his lion will be desperate to keep their mate close, but it's also important that eventually the entire pride is introduced to their Alpha Mate, especially his siblings.

DeMatteo had spent most of the night before convincing his other sisters that he would not need their assistance in courting. Thank god Timothy had had the great plan to convince the sisters to help by cooking and staying invisible. DeMatteo does not need his siblings or his pride members making Sean uncomfortable by their excited crowding.

DeMatteo can't begin to imagine how Sean will react when he learns that humans are not the sole masters of the planet—not to mention the added bonus of going from an only child to being the Alpha Mate of a large pride and having a few dozen siblings. Suddenly, DeMatteo realizes that easing his mate into their bond by inviting him to a full pride gathering might just prove to be a huge mistake.

DeMatteo had initially been shocked to learn that Sean is the only child of Frank Davis, the founding partner of the law firm where his mate is employed as a junior partner. Sean had used his mother's maiden name in law school, having legally changed it at eighteen. This will make his mating even more complicated. Frank is a powerful man; hiding his true nature may prove to be more of a problem than DeMatteo had initially anticipated.

DeMatteo is pleased that his mate is the type of man who wants to achieve things on his own merit without riding on the coattails of a famous last name. The more he learns about his mate, the more DeMatteo realizes that the fates have chosen the perfect person to help him lead the pride.

DeMatteo ~ 2:30 p.m.

"Sean, I'm so glad you agreed to meet me here to finish this unfortunate series of events," DeMatteo says.

"Not a problem. My client is also eager to get this part of her life behind her," Sean says. "As long as it's no trouble, I'd love to stay for the party after."

DeMatteo watches closely as Sean tries and fails to discreetly hide how his body reacts to their proximity. DeMatteo has the unfair advantage of scenting Sean's arousal.

There is no sense in lusting after the man until after business is concluded. If nothing else happens today, DeMatteo is grateful to have the chance to get to know his human while sharing a good meal.

"As I told you last night, I've already drawn up a few documents outlining what my client expects, and if it's acceptable, we can draw official documents and have the papers submitted to the court by Tuesday morning," DeMatteo says. "I am glad you will be staying for the party; if you decide to drink, there are guest rooms available for anyone who needs to stay."

DeMatteo has to choke off a growl as his mate watches a group of women pass. The smell of lust his mate is exuding makes DeMatteo's lion want to maul everyone within reach. Needing the distraction, he pulls the man back into the subject of business.

"We can use the library to go over the documents before my client arrives," DeMatteo offers, his voice more aggressive than he wants it to sound.

"Of course, yes, let's get this settled," Sean answers cautiously.

DeMatteo wants to punch himself for losing control. The musky scent of arousal that had been curling around his mate has been replaced with the unpleasant burnt scent of wariness.

After spending two hours hashing out the details, the documents are finally ready for his client's signature. DeMatteo has been trying to find a way to get back to the easy conversation they had enjoyed before, but his mate seems determined to keep the conversations short and on topic.

"Well, that should just about cover it. Mr. Malone has just arrived. After he signs and it's notarized, I will give you a copy for your client's signature. After that, we can head down for lunch."

"That's great, and of course I will be staying for lunch. After spending the last few hours soaking in the amazing smells, you couldn't kick me out if you wanted to," Sean says, standing up to stretch.

DeMatteo is ridiculously pleased that his jealous behavior hasn't ruined their lunch plans. "Well since kicking you out would be the last thing I did, I guess it's settled," DeMatteo counters with a wink, although most of his attention is diverted to the patch of skin his mate is revealing.

Sean ~ 4 p.m.

After Mr. Malone leaves, Matthew and Sean head back down poolside where the party's well underway. Sean is introduced to the variable list of who's who in Seattle's rich and powerful scene.

Sean tries not to feel inferior as Matthew introduces his family; being an only child, he can't help but wonder what it must be like to have so many siblings. Besides the large numbers, Sean is taken aback by the fact that apparently the entire family are winners of the genetic lottery.

They spend hours talking about their families and careers, and Sean realizes about halfway through their meal that they shared many common goals and beliefs.

"Why don't you join me in my office for a drink?" Matthew gestures down the hall.

"Sure, that would be great. You have to show me the rest of the house."

As Matthew takes him through the three levels, Sean decides that the word house does little to describe the impressive structure. The architecture is an interesting mix between old world and modern, with grand entrances and high ceilings. Matthew obviously comes from an old, rich family.

"And that was the two-cent tour," Matthew announces as they make their way out of the library.

"Wow, this place is amazing. How long has your family lived here?" They climb the spiral staircase in the west wing.

"This property has been in my family for generations. I've tried to keep the original look and feel of the place, although I have made several additions and modifications recently," Matthew says as they return to his office.

Sean smiles as Matthew pours them each a finger of whiskey; he isn't normally much of a drinker, but if there was ever a situation that required liquid courage, this has to be it.

DeMatteo ~ 10:30 p.m.

"Thank you for having me over for your party. It was wonderful. I better get started on the long drive back to the city," Sean says standing up.

Wait, what? DeMatteo pauses, caught off guard by Sean's sudden statement.

You cannot let our mate leave! DeMatteo's lion roars in his head.

Up until now DeMatteo had thought that things were going well. After the tour of the pride house, DeMatteo had escorted his mate back to his office. DeMatteo is almost positive that his mate had been flirting with him, and that he isn't just an overly friendly drunk. Although his uncle had cautioned him to proceed slowly with the human, he had not hesitated in returning Sean's casual touching.

Sean makes it all the way to his office door before he reacts. A wave of panic hits him as he realizes his mate is leaving. Without thinking, DeMatteo grabs his arm, turning him around, his lion all but in control.

"What the hell!" Sean yells, his features morphing from surprise to anger.

"I'm sorry," is all DeMatteo manages before his lion races to the surface. His brain barely registers Sean's scent spiking with fear as his fangs drop. DeMatteo's eyes flash. He drives his fangs deep into Sean's shoulder, initiating their mate bond.

The sweet taste of Sean's blood rolls across his tongue, and DeMatteo instinctively clamps down harder, his lion roaring out its victory in his ears. He can dimly make out his mate's pained whimpers, but he can't stop now, even as the man inside him recoils at taking this much without consent.

Sean ~ 10:30 p.m.

Five hours. I have been flirting with this man for five hours and not once has he made any move towards me. Sean curses in his head. Sean is a lot of things, but he is not desperate. He also isn't willing to sit around and pine after a man who obviously does not want him.

He is suddenly very happy that he had limited his alcohol consumption; now he is free to drive home and drink away the bitter taste of rejection by himself. Deciding it is time to cut his losses, Sean waits until Matthew finishes his drink before making his exit.

"Thank you for having me over for your party. It was wonderful. I better get started on the long drive back to the city," Sean says as he stands and heads to the office door.

Sean glances at his watch. It's ten thirty; if he leaves now he might be able to get Mary to come to his house and help him drown his miseries.

He is almost out of the office when Matthew grabs his arm, forcing him to turn or suffer a broken appendage. Sean is just about to knee the bigger man in the balls when he realizes that the asshole must have drugged him.

Looking at Matthew's face, Sean swears the man's eyes flash red as he whispers something indiscernible. Whatever confusion he feels is forgotten as Matthew suddenly bites him.

Fire and pain race down his shoulder as this man—no, this beast—sinks its way-too-sharp canines into his flesh. Sean grabs on to his arms to push him away just as the pain melts away and a wave of euphoria and pleasure washes over him.

Sean's cock becomes instantly, painfully erect as pleasure unlike anything he has ever felt races through him. Sean's knees nearly give out as Matthew bites down harder and growls. That sound short circuits something in Sean's brain, and suddenly he is no longer desperate to get away; no, now he feels as if he can't get close enough.

Sean's rational mind completely disconnects from what is happening as something new fills him. Without his permission, Sean's body reacts. He can hear himself whimpering as he rocks his ridiculously hard dick against Matthew's thigh.

Just as Sean begins to feel light-headed, Matthew pulls away and starts licking his shoulder, making a noise that Sean can only equate to a cat purring in contentment. His tongue feels too rough, too long, but before Sean can work out why, the sound intensifies. Shaking in shock, Sean is strangely comforted by the purring. He raises a seriously shaking hand up to touch his tender shoulder.

"What the fuck w-was that?" Sean stutters, while trying to remember how to breathe.

Snapping out of his trance, Matthew looks at Sean in shock. "I'm so sorry... I didn't mean for it to happen like this. When you went to leave, I panicked... I couldn't control my lion. Oh fuck, are you okay?"

Sean reels, adrenaline coursing through his veins as he tries to make sense of Matthew's words.

"Am I okay? Of course I'm not fucking okay. You bit me! And what do you mean, you *didn't mean for it to happen like this*? So how did you mean for this to happen? Is there some other way you were planning to bite me? What do you mean *your lion*? Don't tell me you're insane and think you're a lion. Jesus, fuck, you're insane, aren't you? What the fuck is going on, Matthew?" Sean asks, his hand pressed against the ache.

There is blood on his hand as he pulls it away, and suddenly the room begins closing in on him. He goes to step back, and his legs are unsteady. This is not happening. This is all some crazy dream, and he is going to wake up any minute alone and in his bed. He just needs to wake up right the fuck now. He squeezes his eyes tight, and opens them again only to see Matthew's bloodied face staring back at him.

Sean hasn't had a panic attack since he was a teenager, but now he can barely breathe. His vision starts to blur in on the edges as his heart rate soars. He knows he's about to pass out, but there isn't a damn thing he can do to slow it down. He had come here tonight hoping that something would happen with Matthew, but never in his craziest nightmares had he ever considered he'd be maimed and bleeding all over an expensive rug.

DeMatteo ~ July 3, Friday, 10:40 p.m.

DeMatteo mentally slaps himself as he reaches for Sean as the human begins swaying. If he could, DeMatteo would claw his own throat out instead of having to watch the blood ooze from the mating bite. He berates himself as he tries to keep Sean on his feet.

How many ways am I going to fuck this up? DeMatteo is at a loss; he has never lost control like this.

"How the fuck are you doing that?"

"Doing what?" DeMatteo asks warily, eyeing his mate and looking for whatever is causing Sean's scent of panic to grow stronger.

"I... I heard you, talking in my head," Sean whispers. His eyes are glassy, and DeMatteo knows that the bite is starting to take.

Is it possible? Could a partial mating allow them to have a mental link?

Can you hear me, mate? DeMatteo whispers through what he hopes is their mind link.

"I… I can hear you?" Sean says as if it was a question.

DeMatteo hesitates. He is unsure how to explain to the man that they now share a mental link that will allow them to communicate without words and feel each other's emotions. He realizes that Sean must be picking up on some of his projections when he starts to struggle to get away.

"What the fuck are you? What the fuck is going on!" Sean demands as DeMatteo takes his hands away.

He has already fucked up so much that he isn't willing to do anything to frighten the man further. Almost immediately, DeMatteo regrets letting go of him as Sean's eyes roll to the back of his head.

Well, fuck.

Just barely catching his mate before he can hit the ground, DeMatteo cradles Sean against his chest. Drawing in a deep breath and taking in his mate's scent, DeMatteo can feel his lion purring, satisfied that it is finally able to make its claim.

"Fuck!" DeMatteo grunts as he gently places his mate on the couch in his office, unsure if he should try to wake him. DeMatteo gently strokes Sean's hair, waiting for him to wake up. After what seems like an eternity, Sean's eyelashes begin to flutter as he crawls his way back to consciousness.

Sean ~ 11 p.m.

That was a crazy damn dream. Sean thinks as he slowly regains consciousness, normally he just wakes up but this time it feels like he's wading through syrup.

I thought just having sex dreams about a man I barely knew was strange, but now I'm dreaming that he bit me, Sean muses without bothering to open his eyes.

I would be happy if you allowed me to make all your dreams come true, mate, Matthew's voice whispers back to him in his mind.

Sean jerks his eyes open only to gaze upon a very real, very concerned-looking Matthew Santiago staring down at him. "Are you okay?"

Oh my god, did I say that out loud? Sean scoots away from Matthew. "Yeah, um yeah, I'm fine. Did I pass out? Did we finish signing the documents?"

"Yes. We finished that hours ago. You are in my office; we were having drinks. Do you remember anything that happened?"

He doesn't like the way Matthew is looking at him, as if Sean is missing something. Sean's confusion starts to clear and Sean begins to remember when and, more importantly why, he passed out.

"We need to talk," Matthew quickly interrupts.

"I'm not sure of what happened, but I'm pretty sure I don't want to talk to you," Sean snaps, reaching his hand up to feel what now appear to be healed scars on his shoulder.

Snapping his eyes back to Matthew, Sean notices that his chin and neck are matted with blood, his blood. *Oh my god, he is breathtaking*, Sean gazes into his mate's eyes. Mate, that is what Matthew called him in his mind; it's the same word he thought in his dreams.

What is going on? I must be having another dream.

Sean squeezes his eyes shut, trying to calm his runaway heart. When he opens his eyes, he is only mildly surprised to see Matthew staring at him.

This is not a dream; this is a fucking nightmare.

"I just need to go home." Sean is desperate to get away from this man, but pain stabs at his heart even as the words leave his mouth.

The fuck is wrong with me? This man just fucking bit me. I need to get far, far away from him. Even as he thinks these words, his heart stutters at the thought of leaving.

Matthew is my mate? Why does he seem like the most important thing in my life? More importantly, why the hell did he bite me? How is Matthew my anything, we just met yesterday? But isn't this what I wanted even when I thought I was completely straight? Sean's thoughts are confused and jumbled; nothing makes any sense.

"Well, you might be straight, or you might have thought you were straight, but you are definitely my mate," Matthew interrupts Sean's apparently not-so-private monologue. Although Matthew's face is blank, Sean can feel it: the fear, pain, and aggravation rolling off the man.

For some strange reason, every fiber of Sean's being wants to comfort him. Gritting his teeth, Sean barely manages not to reach out to Matthew.

"Okay, you want to talk. So talk. You can start by telling me how the hell you are reading my mind." Sean tries not to fidget as Matthew carefully watches him, but his entire body feels feverish and foreign. He can still feel an odd throb in his wounds, but there is no real pain. In fact, he is feeling warm and tingly, like there are tiny fingers running all over his body.

Something strange is happening to Sean's body, and he can't tell if it's reacting to shock or if that bite is doing something to him. The only thing he is certain of is that the only person who can tell him what the fuck is going on is the same person who is approaching him like he's a frightened animal.

Chapter 7

DeMatteo ~ July 3, Friday, 11:15 p.m.

Through their barely-formed connection, DeMatteo can feel his mate's fear. But along with that fear and confusion, there is unmistakable awareness and attraction— awareness of their shared connection, along with a healthy dose of longing and need.

These emotions alone are enough to give DeMatteo hope; these are emotions he can work with. This can still work out despite their rocky start. Sean seems to be responding to the mate bond better than DeMatteo could have hoped, but he knows he still needs to explain everything.

Carefully taking a seat next to Sean, DeMatteo takes in a deep breath and prepares to explain the existence of the paranormal and magic to his very human, very nervous mate.

"There is no easy way to tell you this, and what I am about to tell you will be hard to believe, but I need you to promise to let me explain."

DeMatteo waits until Sean nods his head in reluctant agreement before continuing.

"I am *not* completely human; I am what some like to call a shifter. I have a dual spirit: one is human, and one is that of a lion."

Sean lets out a hysterical giggle, before clapping his hands over his mouth.

"We have lived beside humans since the dawn of time, keeping our existence secret."

"So why tell me, if this is a secret? Why expose yourself? If you're part of some secret society of *shifters*?"

"Because you are my mate, my true mate. Humans search their whole lives to find love. Just like shifters search their entire lives for their one, true mate. I will never hide anything from you, or hurt you in any way."

DeMatteo can sense Sean's tension as he stiffens; it would've been easy to guess that his mate is remembering being bitten even without the vivid mental image his mate is sharing with him.

"That was a claiming bite. I will never hurt you, but my lion was desperate to start our bond. That should never have happened without your permission, but I lost control. That is no excuse, simply the reason, and I hope you can one day forgive me. Every shifter has one true mate; we are able to find them by their scent, and the physical attraction is instant, whether if it's with another shifter or not."

"I don't believe you… This is impossible… You're crazy…"

DeMatteo cuts off Sean's rambling, pushing into his mate's thoughts. *Please don't be afraid of me, mate. I am not crazy, and this is very real.* Verbally, he adds, "I am sorry for the way our bond started. I will spend the rest of my life earning your forgiveness."

Any chance he has of Sean accepting their relationship will live or die by his mate's reaction to his Alpha form. "There is more, but it might be easier if I show you. You need to see me in my other form. I want you to see all of me." DeMatteo stands, quickly stripping off his clothes and shifting before Sean can argue.

Sean ~ 11:20 p.m.

One moment Sean is staring at what he believes to be a crazy man, but in the next, that man quickly transforms into the largest lion Sean has ever seen. Stumbling to get away, Sean leaps from the couch and promptly falls on his ass.

The animal must stand at least eight feet and weigh over a thousand pounds. It peers down at him, and Sean doesn't know if he should so much as take a breath or if that would provoke the animal to attack.

It is still me; I would never hurt you. Matthew pushes into Sean's mind through their link when Sean starts to panic. His panic quickly bleeds into curiosity as Sean rocks up on his knees. He tentatively reaches out his hand and carefully brushes against Matthew's mane.

"Oh my god!" Sean whispers as Matthew gently pushes his giant head into Sean's hand and lets out a gentle purr. Before his brain can connect the dots and register his shock, Sean is staring into the eyes of a very nervous, and very naked, Matthew Santiago.

"Oh my god, I must be going crazy. You just turned into a lion. Am I going crazy, Matthew?" Sean knows he is rambling, but he is trying to come to terms with what he has just seen.

Matthew is not human, or at least, not completely human. Sean is sure of that because Matthew just turned into a lion—a gigantic fucking lion—and that is not shit humans do. As if turning into an animal isn't enough, Sean has to contend with some freaky mind meld with the thing, which is how he knows the beast is nervous and not hungry as it watches him. On any other day, Sean is capable of rational thought, but right now everything he ever knew about anything has been turned on its head.

If anyone else had come to him with this story, Sean would be calling a psychiatric hospital. But there is no way for him to deny what he has seen with his own eyes and felt with his own hands.

The most amazing part—and yeah, at this point that is really saying something—is that he can not only hear but feel Matthew's presence in his mind, begging Sean to accept him. And every inch of Sean's being is screaming out, *"Yes!"*

DeMatteo ~ 11:30 p.m.

Quickly grabbing the sweatpants he always keeps in his office, DeMatteo dresses and hurries back to his mate.

"No, you're not going crazy. I know this is a lot to take in, but you're strong enough to deal with it," DeMatteo answers, taking a seat on the floor beside Sean.

"How... how do you know that I'm strong enough? That I won't go running to the police the moment I get out of here?"

"Because I can hear your thoughts and feel your feelings, and I know you want to be with me."

DeMatteo feels Sean relax as he moves closer, like his presence alone is enough to calm the skittish human. DeMatteo wants to prance at his mate's scent of acceptance; his lion is eager to finish the mating, but DeMatteo is content with being allowed this close.

"I can feel your every emotion," DeMatteo continues as he gently touches Sean's hand. "Also, I know because the gods would never give me a mate who could not accept me."

He slides their palms together, relieved when Sean does not pull away. They have a long way to go, but he knows if he can get them through the next few hours then he stands a real chance at winning his mate's trust. He just needs a little patience and no small amount of luck.

But the fates have so far been in his favor, and he has no choice but to believe in them now. For years he had lectured that Alpha same sex true mates didn't exist, but he had never given up hope. Privately, he had chosen to believe the legends that predicted this union, and now he must choose to believe that the gods would not allow his mate to wander into his life just to be taken away.

Sean ~ July 4, Saturday, 12 a.m.

Sean watches as Matthew slides their palms together, his fingers opening and entwining of their own volition. He knows he should be frightened; he should be kicking and screaming and running for the door. But as he sits here and stares at their hands, Sean only feels contented and safe.

Sean sits mutely as his more practical side wars with his heart. It is true that he feels drawn to Matthew in a way he has never felt, and he wants things he has never even considered with anyone else. Sex would be one thing. If it was only that, he could write this feeling off as just lust. But no, Sean has the desire to spend his life with the man. He wants to know everything about him. He wants to grow old beside him, to build a life and a family with him.

A family? What hopes would a gay couple have of raising a family? Adoption would be difficult and costly. What would his family and friends say? Just thinking about his father's opinion makes his blood run cold.

"Have you done this before? Been with a man?" Sean asks, even though he is pretty sure of the answer.

Matthew nods. "Yes, I have always been gay."

Sean can't stop the sudden bolt of jealousy and anger that blazes through him.

"But it was never like this. You are my mate. Now that I have found you, I will never want to be with anyone else. I can't. The bond will not allow me to touch another in a sexual manner."

"Will it be the same for me?"

"Yes. I am sure that when your girlfriend touched you after we met, you found it repulsive," Matthew answers, and Sean doesn't need to feel his emotions to know his mate is just as jealous as he is. He can't help the image of Sara's face and flashes of exactly what they had been doing the night before Sean had met the shifter.

"Girlfriend? What are you talking about, girlfriend?" Sean asks.

"When we met, I could tell you'd had a recent sexual encounter. And just now, you were recalling your last interaction with her. I can still scent her on you." Matthew answers bluntly. Sean is surprised to hear the rumble of what must be his lion bleeding into his voice as his eyes flash red.

The sound should have frightened Sean, a reminder that Matthew is not just a man. Instead the sound went straight to his cock, causing his balls to throb and tighten.

"Sara isn't my girlfriend; we are just friends," Sean explains.

"Do you fuck all your friends?" Matthew growls.

Sean can sense the tension and rising rage swirling inside the man, and he relents, feeling the need to soothe the beast of jealousy riding Matthew.

"No, I just mean we broke up. And no, I couldn't stand the thought of being with her after we met." His quick and honest confession seems to instantly calm the man beside him.

Matthew takes a deep breath, massaging the bridge of his nose. "I apologize; I have no right to be jealous of your past. This is not the time to discuss our past lovers. I want to work on our future together," he says. Sean's pulse races as he realizes that yes, even with all he now knows, he wants a future with Matthew.

"May I kiss you?" Matthew asks.

Sean is surprised to see what can only be vulnerability in Matthew's eyes. Sean closes his eyes as he slightly nods.

The kiss is gentle, a mere brushing of skin. It isn't at all what he was expecting—hoping—it would be.

"Let's get you cleaned up and then you can ask me the million questions in your head."

"Okay." Sean is about to stand when he realizes he has come in his pants. *WTF?* He thinks before his mind replays him clutching Matthew tight as his fangs sank in and as he comes faster than a middle schooler who finally made it to third base.

"Um, I'm going to need a change of clothes," Sean mutters, horrified and unsure if the entire situation could possibly be more embarrassing. "Matthew..."

"Please, call me DeMatteo. That is my name in Spanish, what everyone close to me uses."

"Matt… DeMatteo, I'm not sure I can stay here all night."

They come to an immediate halt, with DeMatteo turning swiftly and putting them face to face. Looking into DeMatteo's warm eyes, Sean quickly forgets why he wanted to leave, and instead he hears himself saying, "But, I guess it's too late to drive home now." The silence stretches as they continue down the hall, and Sean can't help the ongoing debate in his mind.

Why did I agree to stay here? Because you wanted him the moment you saw him. He is an animal, an actual lion. He could kill you, Sean's fear warns him. *He would never hurt me,* Sean reminds himself.

"This is the master bathroom; I hope you find everything that you need," DeMatteo says. Although Sean can feel his concerns, he is unable to decipher all the different emotions or thoughts he can feel swirling inside DeMatteo's mind.

"Okay. I'm going to go shower."

DeMatteo ~ 12 a.m.

DeMatteo isn't sure if that was a statement or an invitation, but he knows that his mate is still nervous and needs time to think about everything he has learned today.

"I'll get you some clothes and wait outside," DeMatteo says as he leaves the room and heads to his brother's old room. When Timothy had been mated, he had built his own home on the pride lands, although he still sometimes stayed at the pride house when he worked late.

Is that disappointment Sean is feeling?

DeMatteo steps into the closet. It seems his mate wants him to join him in the shower. He can't help but smile as he feels his mate's internal struggle to come to terms with his feelings. Yes, he has made the right choice giving his mate this time alone.

Sean is about Timothy's size, so these should work, DeMatteo guesses as he pulls out a pair of jeans and shirt that still bear the tags. Leaving the clothing on the bed, DeMatteo tries to contact Timothy to prepare for his upcoming mating. DeMatteo will not leave anything to chance, so he will have his brother stay during the entire change.

Sean ~ 12:35 a.m.

After taking a long shower in a massive stone and glass enclosure with fourteen side jets and an overhead rain shower, Sean steps into what can only be described as the most luxurious bathroom he has ever seen. Looking around, Sean figures this is as good of a place as any to learn about his mate. He has always believed that he can learn a lot about a person from such a personal space.

Sean is impressed with the luxurious amenities and the use of beautiful designer pieces. There is a corner Jacuzzi tub large enough for two that is surrounded by some sort of stone.

There are what look to be speakers built in, but he can't see how to turn them on. Not wanting to snoop but needing to pee, Sean opens a door looking for the toilet. It is in its own smaller room with a sink. Sean has to smile at his mate's over-the-top style; DeMatteo obviously spares no expense when it comes to amenities.

Another door reveals towels and other toiletries. Rubbing himself dry with a fluffy, white towel, Sean has to wonder how his life had taken such a drastic turn. In less than a day he has gone from a single heterosexual man to the mate of a male lion shifter.

When he comes to the realization that maybe he is not one hundred percent straight, he also realizes that he has some reservations about the stereotypes associated with being gay, or at least bisexual. They are mostly concerned about how his family would react.

Not so much his stepmother; she has—so far—supported his choices. She is almost as young as he is, but his father is a different breed altogether. But Sean has never lied to his parents about the important things. And he will not start now, not with something so life-altering, so he will have to find a way to tell them.

Last night, after coming to terms with the fact that he was indeed coming out as bisexual late in life, Sean had decided to pursue DeMatteo. Boy, had that turned out to be more than he had bargained for.

Knowing that talking to himself is not going to get him any closer to understanding the turn his life had taken, Sean wraps the towel around his waist. Opening the door, he takes a deep breath and steps into the unknown.

Sean squeaks when he walks into the bedroom, staring at a very large man seated at the foot of the bed. "Who are you?" While this man is not as large as DeMatteo, he is similarly shaped and would be handsome if his face wasn't currently twisted in a scowl.

"I could ask you that, but I am sure I know the answer," the man drawls as he gets to his feet and starts walking towards Sean.

Sean wonders if this man is another lion shifter.

"You would be my replacement? You don't seem like much," the man sneers.

Sean's question is answered when the man's eyes glow eerily yellow and he bares his teeth. Sean startles when a low, menacing, rumbling growl slips out of the shifter's throat, causing Sean's spine to tingle at the threat.

Oh my god. I am going to be killed by a crazy man. Is this DeMatteo's lover? Where is DeMatteo? As fear and jealousy fight for control of his thoughts, he has to stomp down the sudden urge to strike out at the other man. *Don't do anything stupid; this guy could gut me.*

Sean watches claws slip out of the man's fingertips. Acting purely out of self-preservation, Sean slowly retreats, planning to lock himself in the bathroom. But as suddenly as it had begun, the man stops moving, schooling his features and turning around as if he had not just been threatening Sean.

DeMatteo ~ 12:40 a.m.

"What the fuck are you doing in here, Hugh?" DeMatteo roars, not waiting for a reply as he rushes over to Sean. "Is everything okay? You were screaming for me." Sean's heart sounds like it's trying to beat out of his chest as DeMatteo searches his eyes and scans his body for any signs of distress or injury.

"I didn't call you."

"Alpha, I was just coming over to remove the last of my things from our room…" Hugh starts.

DeMatteo feels Sean bristle at the implications. *Our room? So this is his lover.* Sean's entire body vibrates with anger as he seethes beside him, his thoughts battering DeMatteo's mind.

"Former lover, I ended it the day we met," DeMatteo offers. "It meant nothing." He doesn't miss the way Hugh flinches at his words.

He may not have expected Hugh to become Sean's best friend, but he'd never dreamed the man would insult and threaten his mate. DeMatteo had been shocked as his mate projected the scene that was unfolding in their bedroom through their mind link.

At first, he had been surprised at his mate's ability to project what was happening through their bond so clearly. But once Sean's projection had showed Hugh baring his teeth and growling in obvious warning, DeMatteo had barely contained his shift when his lion had recognized the threat to their mate.

Hugh ~

"Our room?" DeMatteo growls.

Hugh is shocked by DeMatteo's aggression. He instantly drops to his knees, throat bared as DeMatteo's Alpha power fans across him. Hearing the mate-stealer gasp, Hugh peeks up to see the human pressed against DeMatteo's side.

"This is the Alpha and Alpha Mate's den. You will show my mate the respect he deserves or I will rip out your intestines and feed them to you," DeMatteo warns, his eyes flashing red.

"Yes, Alpha. I apologize, Alpha Mate," Hugh mutters as he remains prostrate from the magnitude of his Alpha's rage.

"Leave us, Hugh," DeMatteo snaps.

Jumping to his feet, Hugh keeps his gaze lowered as he hurries from the room. He doesn't stop moving until he is outside his office. Hugh can feel his lion shivering at their mate's rejection. His life is truly over. DeMatteo has chosen that sniveling human to be his mate, and Hugh knows he will have to leave the pride.

Hugh can feel someone coming up behind him, and his claws are already out as he turns to take on whoever the human has sent. Nick's eyes are wide as he steps back. Hugh's lion is so distressed he hadn't even sensed his closest friend before attacking.

"Hey, slow down. What's wrong?" Nick says, his hands up in the universal sign of surrender.

Hugh immediately sheathes his claws; Nick has been his only confidant over the last few years.

"Fuck, I'm sorry, Nick. I thought you were someone else."

"I can see that. Who were you ready to attack?" Nick asks as they close themselves in the soundproof office.

"I can't believe he brought that bastard to our bed before I even had a chance to grab all of my things. I mean, first he dumps me without even a conversation. Then the very next day he is parading his *mate* around the pride, and I'm supposed to just roll over and take it after he has humiliated me in front of everyone?" Hugh begins.

His mind reels as he paces in front of his desk. Once again, he is being thrown away after an Alpha has no more use for him. *I don't know why I thought this would be any*

*different. He is just like every other Alpha out there. 'Sorry,
Hugh, you were good enough to warm my bed, but now I have
a mate.'*

"Wait. When did you two break up? And he has
already brought someone to your bed? DeMatteo? I don't
understand," Nick cuts in, stopping his mental tirade.

"Yes, DeMatteo! I'm surprised Carla didn't tell you.
Lord knows all of them have had it out for me since the
beginning. Yesterday DeMatteo met his *true mate*, and today
he brought him here."

"God, I'm sorry, Hugh. I've been away on business
and haven't seen Carla since yesterday morning. Are you sure
he said this man was his true mate? Who is this guy?"

"I don't know. Samantha and all her thugs have circled
around the two. I was told to stay away, so I only heard bits
and pieces. His name is Sean Herr; he's supposedly some
lawyer from Seattle."

"Wow! That is so strange and sudden, but you know
how protective Samantha can get. But still, I can't see why
they are suddenly treating you like a leper."

"I know. Everything is happening so fast that I can't
wrap my head around it. Just yesterday we were madly in

love, and boom, this guy walks in and suddenly DeMatteo
can't stand the sight of me. I just need to calm down. Maybe
once everything settles, he will see me."

"Don't be so hard on yourself. You aren't the bad guy
here. You two were together for years. It makes sense that you
need time to grieve," Nick soothes.

Nick ~ 12:50 a.m.

Nick needs to sit down to conceal how much the name Sean Herr means to him. It is almost impossible to believe that the two marks are connected. He had just heard the name Sean Herr from his associates. He has to find a way to confirm that this Sean Herr is one and the same; if so, this changes everything.

Nick needs to get more information. If DeMatteo mates, he will be nearly impossible to kill. Suddenly it looks like Nick has wasted all the years he has spent getting close to the Alpha through his sister. Unless he can find some way to turn this around.

Hugh says, "Yeah, you're right. I just need to get control of my lion. Can you believe I almost attacked DeMatteo's precious mate?"

"Really?"

"Yeah; if DeMatteo hadn't come into the room, I don't know what would have happened to his little human," Hugh admits and Nick notices that the shifter's claws slip out when he mentions the mate, but that's not what catches his attention.

"DeMatteo's true mate is a human?"

Hugh's eyes flash and he growls. "Yeah. But he expects me to accept someone so fucking weak as my Alpha? Never," he vows.

Nick watches as the shifter begins to pace, his eyes flashing as he becomes more agitated. "So you didn't feel the need to submit?" Nick questions.

At that Hugh's face shifts, eyes and fangs, and Nick takes a step back from the unbalanced lion. Hugh breathes heavily through his nose, his eyes clenched tight as he forces his face back into its more human shape.

Suddenly Nick is starting to see that the damaged shifter could be used as a possible weapon. If his mind is so broken that his lion is willing to attack his own Alpha Mate, there is a real chance they can use him to do all the dirty work.

Nick just needs to keep the shifter angry but passive. Maybe with the right motivation and tools, Hugh can be the pawn they need to clear out the pride. Hugh is not very strong or smart, but that could be the best way to let him stay under the pride's radar.

"No, I wanted to claw his eyes out, and all he did was tremble in the corner and wait for someone to save him. What kind of Alpha Mate does that?"

"I don't know? Hugh, I want to do something for you, but you are going to have to trust me and not say anything to anyone in the pride about this. You do trust me, right? Because what I am about to suggest could get us both killed."

This part is pivotal. Nick doesn't want to seem overeager to challenge the Alpha Mate, but if he can find some way to convince Hugh that Sean is dangerous, he will be less likely to ask too many questions.

"Of course I trust you, Nick. I did just tell you I was going to attack the Alpha Mate; that statement alone would cost me my life. What are you offering to do?"

Nick smiles at the shifter. It's almost a shame to hit such an easy mark. When Nick had first started to befriend the damaged animal, he had mostly done it for entertainment purposes. It amused him to fill him with ideas of how each sibling was plotting to destroy his relationship with the Alpha. But now it seems as if his project is going to pay out in spades.

"Yeah, okay. Something about this story doesn't sit right with me. I want you to let me contact some friends I have, someone that has no contact with the prides, and see what we can find out about this guy. Sean Herr is his name, right?"

"Yeah, Sean Herr, an attorney out of Seattle. Why? Do you think he is dangerous?"

"I don't know, but do me a favor and be careful around him until we can find out who this guy is. It may be nothing, but when you look at everything together, something seems fishy. But first I have to get his picture so we are sure that anything we find is about this guy."

Nick spends a few minutes comforting the shifter before heading back to his office. He locks his door before calling his associates. This is just what he needs to show that uppity bitch why Chris put him in charge.

"Hello?" Chris answers, his voice thick with sleep.

"Hey, it's Nick. You won't believe this, but I think your old mark just showed up as a mate in the pride. And not just any old mate. Oh no, they claim that a human is the Alpha's true mate."

That seemed to wake the older hunter. "Is that so? I will need a photo of this human for confirmation, then we have to move fast to stop them from completing the bond. We don't want her making any cubs. What is the Alpha's name?" Chris asks.

Nick laughs. "I doubt we have to worry much about cubs. The Alpha's mate is male," he replies, copying the photos of the Alpha with an unknown smaller male.

Chris grunts. "A male? I thought you said they are true mates? There are no gay true mates."

"I know, but I'm just telling you what the shifters are saying."

Nick can hear the other man typing in the background as he says, "This is highly unlikely, but go ahead and gather that information. If what they are saying is true..."

"I'm way ahead of you, sir. I will be sending you his pictures tomorrow. He attended a pride gathering, so I am sure there will be some at every angle. As far as planning, I might already have someone in place to do the heavy lifting," Nick sneers.

"Nick, if this is everything you say it is, you will be going down in the history books."

"Be expecting the photos in the next few hours; if it is who I think it is, we need to schedule another face to face. I think you will like my plan of using one of their own to spring the trap," Nick gloats, he will finally be able to prove that he is more than capable of taking down these abominations.

Chris's voice breaks him out of his mental celebration. "Alright, send the photos to this number. Oh and Nick…"

"Yes?" Nick queries distractedly.

"Happy hunting," Chris says before disconnecting the call.

Nick wants to shout, but has to settle for a fist bump with the air. He has to contain his celebrating for now. All the years he'd spent training are finally paying off in a big way. He's so busy going through the pictures from the party Carla had so helpfully posted online, looking for good photos that he almost falls on the floor when someone pounds on his door.

"Who is it?" Nick answers, his voice steady despite his rising panic.

The person on the other side tries the knob. "Hey, baby, why is the door locked?" Carla asks, when it doesn't open.

"Oh, I didn't realize it was. Hold on," Nick answers as he closes down his laptop, locking it and his phone back in his safe.

Clicking buttons to wake up the monitor on his desktop computer, he pulls his hands through his hair a few times and heads over to the door.

Carla pulls him into her arms to lick into his mouth the instant the door open. Even after years of this, it is only his discipline keeping him from vomiting as he returns the kiss passionately. He has worked hard to reconcile bedding this abomination with his ultimate motives.

"There you are; I was wondering if you were back yet. What are you doing locked away in here? I have some incredible news to tell you."

"Wow, I missed you too. I was just catching up with some paperwork. So what do you need to tell me?" Nick says as he leads his *mate* into his office.

Chapter 8

July 4, Saturday, 2 a.m.

Gathering his mate in his arms, DeMatteo breathes in his scent in part to comfort the man in his arms, and also to reassure his lion that their mate is safe.

"I am sorry, Sean; I didn't think Hugh would react like that."

"So that was your lover?" Sean asks.

"Yes, he was. But I called it off the day we met," DeMatteo confesses. He knows that it is important that his mate knows the whole truth. "I am a little over sixty years old, and I took him as a companion a little over fifteen years ago," he continues, getting the entire story out there so no more surprises can spring up.

"Fifteen years!" Sean exclaims. "And you what? You just dumped him the day we met? Oh my god, no wonder that man hates me. How can you just leave someone after all that time for a complete stranger?"

"He knew from the beginning that my mate would trump all when I finally met him. The same way he would have left if he had met his. I know this all seems sudden and new to you, but my lion has claimed you, and he is, as humans would call it, *in love* with you. So there is no way I could have stayed with Hugh, even if you rejected me."

"Claimed me? In love with me? DeMatteo, you just met me. You can't be in love with me!" Sean says, shaking his head.

DeMatteo can sense his mate's panic, his thoughts coming rapid-fire through their bond. *This is just ridiculous. I can admit that I want him; on some levels, I feel I need him. But I don't think I love him, not yet. This is crazy.*

DeMatteo tries not to get upset with his mate's feelings, but the words still sting. *Our mate is human; he needs time to accept us,* his lion reminds him.

"Relax, Sean. I know you don't love me yet, but let's finish the bonding; everything will work itself out."

"Wait, you're over sixty years old? What do you mean, we need to finish the bonding? How? I have so many questions that I don't even know where to begin," Sean rushes out. DeMatteo purrs as his mate presses their bodies together, resting his head on his shoulder.

DeMatteo wonders if Sean even notices how much he is leaning into DeMatteo. He has to dig his claws into his palms as his mate's erection presses firmly into his hip. It seems that even though his mate is still mentally processing everything, his body is all aboard to complete their mating.

"Well, let's start by finishing the bond. That is the easiest part to explain, and the most crucial. We have sex, tie together, and I bite you again. After that, I will answer any questions you have."

"Tie together?" Sean asks, his body growing tense again.

DeMatteo chances rubbing his mate's arm, hoping the gesture and his scent would help the human. "Yes, I have a knot. When we mate, it will swell, releasing my barbs and locking us together," DeMatteo explains.

DeMatteo can feel Sean's heart rate pick up. "Barbs?" he gasps, and if the subject wasn't so sensitive, DeMatteo would laugh at the way Sean's eyes nearly bulge out of his head.

Instead DeMatteo aims to remain comforting. "Yes, but don't worry. It will not hurt you. You were born to be my mate; my body is incapable of giving you anything but pleasure. Once we get past the initial discomfort of penetration, your body will naturally adjust," he explains. The longer they maintain physical contact, the more his mate's body reacts to the pheromones he's producing.

Sean's eyes are so dilated he looks stoned as he looks up. "So we will be stuck together? How long?" he asks, nervous but willing. The mating pheromones will soon have them all but swept up in an almost mindless rut.

"I don't know; I've never knotted anyone. We are only able to completely tie with our true mates. The barbs will release the mating chemicals."

Pressing his nose deep in the bend of his skittish mate's neck, DeMatteo inhales deeply, enjoying the scent of claim and mate. No shifter can ever get enough of their mate's scent, and DeMatteo is no different. His lion wants to stalk the man, hold him down, and rut until he spills his seed, and then bathe in his scent. It is intoxicating.

Sean's doubts seem to clear as DeMatteo wraps his arms around him. DeMatteo pulls his head away enough to capture his mate's lips. DeMatteo moans when Sean's lips open immediately in submission, and he quickly dips his tongue inside. Electric currents slide up his spine as the mate bond flares to life.

DeMatteo cannot resist rocking his cock against Sean as his lion begins to chuff, causing his mate's body to shiver and his pulse to skyrocket. Trying to resist the urge to just mount the man on the floor, DeMatteo rubs his hands down his mate's waist, reaching around to palm the swell of Sean's ass.

Leaning down to rub his face into the column of Sean's neck, he lets his rough tongue run over his mark.

Sean ~

Gasping, Sean clasps onto the strong arms caging him, his cock growing painfully hard at the scrape of stubble traveling up his neck. When DeMatteo licks back into his mouth, Sean opens immediately, whimpering as their cocks rub through the fabric separating them.

The most intoxicating taste bursts in his mouth, sweet with a strong chocolate flavor. Sean wants to be consumed by the mouth tasting his. Running his hands up impossibly strong arms, Sean groans at the sensation, not the least bit put off by the feeling of hard muscle.

As Sean's thighs hit the bed—*when did we start moving?*—DeMatteo gently presses him into the mattress. He submits willingly, eagerly, his normal aggression and dominance taking a back seat to his need to please his mate.

Sean moans embarrassingly loud when DeMatteo unexpectedly grinds his denim-covered cock down hard against him. The sudden bite of pain intensifies the pleasure, short-circuiting his brain.

Sean obediently lifts his hips when DeMatteo undoes the towel that is covering him, desperate to feel his mate skin to skin. Sean's hands find the hem of DeMatteo's T-shirt and tug, begging DeMatteo to remove the offending article.

"Want to see you," Sean moans as he runs his palms up DeMatteo's eight pack. Holy shit, no human could have muscles like these.

DeMatteo is up and off him in seconds, stripping his clothes until he is just as naked. Sean feels disorientated without his weight pressing him into the mattress. Looking for a way to distract himself, Sean grabs his cock and starts stroking.

DeMatteo's low growl grabs his attention, and Sean has to squeeze the tip of his dick hard to keep from coming on the spot with the way DeMatteo's eyes flash and his face shifts slightly. The thought that both the man and the lion are looking at him with such lust makes his dick twitch, forcing a spurt of pre-cum from the tip.

"You're huge... How is it going to fit?" Sean asks, faltering a bit on his movements as he takes in the sight of DeMatteo's impressive length and girth.

"It'll fit. We just need to prep you," DeMatteo says as he reaches into a drawer and pulls out a tube of lube.

"Don't worry, mate. You were created just for me. We are meant to fit together in every way. One day we won't even need this," DeMatteo teases before reclaiming his lips in a mind-numbing kiss. Sean would question that last part if he could remember how to speak, but now all he can think about is continuing this.

Sean's body melts as DeMatteo moves down his chin, nipping along the way. Sean's eyes roll back in his head when DeMatteo pauses to nibble on his mating mark.

Those marks seem to be connected directly to his dick; Sean writhes and drags his blunt nails across DeMatteo's shoulder. Continuing his assault, DeMatteo licks Sean's nipple, purring as the flesh pebbles under his ministrations.

"Oh god. DeMatteo! Feels so good," Sean praises as he lifts his hips, desperate to feel some friction on his cock.

"Easy, mate. I'll give you what you need," DeMatteo admonishes as he pushes Sean's hips firmly down.

Much to Sean's despair, DeMatteo seems content. Following his leisurely path, he stops to dip his tongue into Sean's navel.

"Fuck, DeMatteo, please, please," Sean moans, desperate. Any thoughts of pride have been abandoned as

DeMatteo noses his way lower. Sean grips the sheets beside him, his legs tremble as he tries to resist grabbing DeMatteo by his hair and shoving his cock in his mouth.

DeMatteo~

Taking a good look at his mate's cock, DeMatteo's ass clenches. Not as large as him, but his mate's cock still stands at least a proud eight inches. DeMatteo has never bottomed, but as he takes his mate's cock deep in his mouth, he knows he will happily give this man his ass. He has to in order to fully bond, and to combine their life forces, they will need to be fully mated.

Easing up on the suction, DeMatteo slides his lips up the shaft until just the tip remains, giving it teasing licks as he slicks three of his fingers. Releasing his prize, DeMatteo slowly circles his mate's hole with one finger, letting him adjust to the cold and the feel of being touched there.

Sean moans softly as DeMatteo pulls off. He continues to jack Sean slowly as he presses on the opening, teasing the muscle until it begins to open. He keeps applying pressure to those resistant muscles as he noses Sean's balls, enjoying the fresh wave of lust that rolls off his mate.

Once Sean starts pushing back against his fingers, DeMatteo decides to reward him by licking his cock from root to tip. He presses harder until just the tip of one finger is able to breach those tight, virgin muscles.

"Shit." Sean gasps, clenching down hard on his finger.

DeMatteo pauses, unwilling to hurt his mate any more than is absolutely necessary. Sensing their mate's pain, DeMatteo's lion begins rumbling, which makes Sean's body go lax.

Taking Sean's cock back into his mouth, DeMatteo continues to deepthroat while pumping his finger, speeding up his rhythm until the pleasure outweighs the pain. He can tell that Sean is ready to continue when he starts to pick up on that rhythm.

"That's it, mate. Push out your muscles as I push in," DeMatteo encourages, before going back to the task of stretching him to take his cock.

Slowly, he can feel Sean's muscles relaxing around his fingers as he does as he is commanded. DeMatteo barely resists his lion's urge to roar at their mate's submission.

One by one, DeMatteo inserts his fingers until all three are scissoring, pushing, and pulling while his mate pushes back, seeming so desperate to chase after those infrequent brushes to his prostate. DeMatteo can no longer ignore the throb between his legs as he pulls his fingers free, and lets Sean's cock fall out of his mouth.

"Please, DeMatteo! What are you doing? Why did you stop?"

"It will be easier if you don't come before I am inside you."

DeMatteo offers comfort to his mate, kissing his inner thigh. Even with the prep, DeMatteo knows that there is no way to completely eliminate the pain of this first mating. Not until he's inside where his pre-cum can do its job of readying his mate to breed. He compensates by putting an obscene amount of lube on his cock, to avoid any drag, as he encourages Sean to roll onto his stomach.

"It will be easier for you this way; I don't want to hurt you."

He opens him up further by pulling Sean's left leg up towards his chest. DeMatteo's larger frame completely covers him as he lies partially on top of Sean's back, similar to a wrestler's pose.

Gripping the base of his cock firmly, DeMatteo rubs his crown against Sean's hole, coaxing those slightly loosened muscles to relax further. Pushing with his hips, slightly harder on each press, they both let out startled gasps when his engorged head is finally able to slip inside.

"Fuck!"

"Relax, Sean. Just breathe and push out against me."
DeMatteo groans as he desperately fights the urge to bury
himself into his mate.

Waiting a few beats, DeMatteo feels his mate slowly
relax. He thrusts forward, sliding in another inch as Sean
pushes out.

"Fuck, yes just like that," DeMatteo praises. "You're
doing perfect. Just let me in, mate." He accompanies each
word with a small thrust until his groin is flush with Sean's
ass.

Stilling, DeMatteo smooths his hands up and down
Sean's sides. "Tell me when I can move," DeMatteo grits out.

His lion is riding him hard, demanding that he fuck,
mark, and breed their mate. The man in him knows he must
take care to avoid injuring the precious man lying under them,
while the lion is desperate to seal their bond.

Sean ~

Sean makes a few exploratory thrusts, causing DeMatteo's cock to stroke something deep inside him that makes his toes curl with pleasure. Sean arches his back as much as he can, and he shoves his ass back hard, trying to get that feeling again.

"Mmm… ahhh... Do that again," DeMatteo orders.

More than willing to feel that amazing pleasure again, Sean wriggles his hips, looking for that perfect spot. "Please move."

Sean can feel every inch dragging against his inner walls as DeMatteo pulls his hips back; it feels like liquid fire spreading through him as DeMatteo pushes his way back inside. His body spasms and clenches as that spot is hit again.

"Oh god!" Sean wails as DeMatteo picks up a slow, deep rhythm, each thrust rubbing against that magical spot. Desperate for more contact, Sean begins rocking harder, forcing DeMatteo to pick up his pace.

"Careful, mate. I don't want to hurt you," DeMatteo warns as his grip tightens on Sean's hip.

"Fuck me, please fuck me. I am so close!" Sean yells. It is difficult in this position, but he is finally able to reach between himself and the bed to wrap his hand around his cock.

DeMatteo ~

As he moves in and out, DeMatteo tilts his hips so his cock brushes Sean's prostate on every stroke; ever so slowly, he increases the speed and force of his thrusts as his orgasm begins to build.

Once he is sure he will not rip the delicate tissues, DeMatteo pushes a faster pace, and Sean bucks back eagerly, matching his tempo.

"Yes, that's it, Sean." DeMatteo's thrusts become nearly brutal as he winds his free hand in his mate's hair. "Submit to me. Mate with me," DeMatteo growls. His lion is all but in control, his voice more beast than man as his claws extend.

DeMatteo can sense his mate's impending orgasm through their bond, and his canines extend and sharpen. Licking over his mark in warning, DeMatteo rolls fully onto his mate as he slams his cock in to the root.

"*Mine!*" DeMatteo roars just before he strikes, biting deep.

Pinning his mate to the bed with his cock and teeth, his mark is so deep that no one will doubt their mating.

Sean's body locks down tight as the force of his orgasm snatches his voice reducing his scream to a gasp. Tasting his mate's blood, DeMatteo distantly hears his mate climax as DeMatteo's knot forms and the mating barbs latch onto his mate's prostate.

Take care, his lion says in his mind. His teeth clamp harder as the first spurts of semen flood his mate's guts. As he empties himself in Sean, he releases his teeth to lick the wound closed.

"Oh my god!" Sean wails.

DeMatteo can feel everything clearly through the mate bond; the sensations are so detailed it is as if he experiences them himself. The burning that courses through Sean's body, DeMatteo's shifter DNA bonding them on a molecular level, changing him. Sean grits his teeth as spasms wrack his body, and only DeMatteo's weight keeps him from flailing off the bed.

Easy, mate. Relax. I've got you, DeMatteo whispers in his mind. Sean can only whimper in response as his entire body rebels against him.

"Oh god, I'm dying," Sean sobs weakly.

"No, you are not dying. You are changing," DeMatteo soothes him. He clasps his mate tighter to his body, his knot and barbs still tying the pair together.

Changing? Changing into what? are Sean's last thoughts as he slips into darkness, where DeMatteo knows he will welcome the escape from the pain.

They remain locked together for three hours in which Sean's body orgasms four times, each one wracking his body and pulling DeMatteo into his own release. DeMatteo continues to rub his mate as Sean's body breaks out in a sweat and his temperature skyrockets.

This is normal; he is just going through the change, DeMatteo keeps reminding himself. His lion basks in the feel and scent of their fully-claimed mate, and he cannot help but rub his scent over every part he can reach.

When he is finally able to pull away, DeMatteo goes straight to the bathroom to get warm rags and towels to clean his mate's body. By the time Sean is clean enough to put his underwear on, Sean's breathing has become so shallow that the rise and fall of his chest is almost unnoticeable.

DeMatteo hurries to phone Timothy to come check his mate. DeMatteo knows his mate is still alive; he can feel his life force slightly through the bond, and he is not going feral.

It's a real fear. DeMatteo knows that when a mated shifter dies, his mate also dies shortly after. Once the spirits have been bonded, they refuse to live without each other. Alphas, however, do not just die with their mates. Because of their strength, they can live a few months, or maybe a year or two, but they go completely insane.

Feral is one of the most feared terms to shifters. Once an Alpha turns feral he will attack anyone at any time until their spirit can no longer fight and joins its mate. The kindest thing that can be done is to put the Alpha down.

"Timothy, I need you to come to my room, now," DeMatteo barks as soon as the phone connects.

"Yes, Alpha," is all he hears before he hangs up and returns to his mate's side.

A tentative knock sounds before the door opens. He can scent his brother's fear before the shifter even approaches.

"Enough! Get over here and check on my mate. Something is wrong. His temperature is still climbing and his heart is barely beating."

Timothy ~

Regaining his composure, Timothy quickly goes to work checking Sean's vitals. "Everything seems fine, DeMatteo. He is still going through the change," Timothy states calmly. trying to get DeMatteo to focus on him. "I do not know why his heartbeat and temp are so off, but we knew that there could be some abnormalities due to him being human. The rest of the change should be similar to a human Beta mate. He could be in and out of consciousness for the next few days or even weeks."

"And that is normal? What will I tell his job? His father will worry if he is missing, and I have no idea if anyone knows where he is."

Touching his brother's arm, Timothy exudes his Omega calming influence, hoping to settle his Alpha.

"Yes and no. This is somewhat normal for a human with any shifter, but since you are an Alpha, his adaptation will be more extreme, so he might be out of it longer. And when he wakes up…" Timothy hesitates, "DeMatteo, you do realize that there needs to be a *full* mating to complete the bond."

"Yes, Timothy, I realize that, and you can stop pushing calmness on me. Tien explained Beta and Alpha mating rituals. I am not angry at you; I am only worried about my mate."

"Yeah, well, it's my job to look after the mental and physical needs of the pride, and that includes our Alpha," Timothy states. "Seriously, just try to feed him every time he wakes. Lots of protein and water. I will send up a powdered vitamin and hormone supplement. Until he can produce enough of our hormones on his own, he will need the boost. Congratulations, big bro, and remember, now that you are mated he can become pregnant," Timothy says as he heads out of the den.

DeMatteo ~

DeMatteo quickly composes a message to one of his contacts to have Sean's personal email account inform his family, friends, and co-workers that he has a personal issue to deal with and will return in a few days.

He knows it is unethical, by human standards, to hack into his mate's personal accounts, but they cannot afford to have any humans searching for Sean. Shifter connections will make this go smoothly, allowing them to explain why Sean will be unavailable for the next week or two.

Hearing his mate stir, DeMatteo quickly gathers the almost liquefied food Timothy had sent, along with the vitamins to feed his new mate. After Sean's third feeding, DeMatteo starts to feel his own effects of their mating.

His lion will not allow DeMatteo to stray too far from their vulnerable mate or get much sleep, so he needs to depend on his pride to care for everything else as he cares for Sean. Calling down to have his sisters bring him a plate of meat, a pitcher of water, and his vitamins, DeMatteo settles into what will be his only duty for the next few days.

Samantha ~

"So how is he doing?" Samantha asks as she delivers the items DeMatteo will need over the next few days.

She is surprised by how pale and lifeless the human appears. He lies unconscious, covered mostly by a light sheet, in the middle of the Alpha's den. If it wasn't for her superior sense of smell and hearing, she might have thought the man was dead.

"Yes, Timothy said that his vitals are fine and that it's normal for him to stay out of it while his body adjusts to the changes."

Samantha tries to step closer to her new Alpha, but DeMatteo's deep warning growl stops her mid step.

"Don't go near him."

She can tell without seeing that DeMatteo's fangs are beginning to drop, his voice is pitched low into his lion rumble. Samantha cautiously takes another step back and bares her throat, showing her brother that she is no threat.

"I'm sorry, Samantha. Just don't," DeMatteo apologizes around his fangs.

Samantha is quick to cut off any guilt her brother might be thinking. "No, DeMatteo, I am the one that's sorry. I know better. It's just that it's so amazing that we now have our Alpha Mate. My lion just wants to go to him, but I won't! I'll just tell the others to stay away," Samantha offers as she backs out of the Alpha Pair's den.

Chapter 9

Sean ~ July 16, Thursday, 8 a.m.

Sean hears voices and the sounds of animals, and they pull him back to reality. *Did I leave the television on again?* Slowly opening his eyes, the first thing Sean realizes is that he is not home, but he is alone. As he starts to sit up, sounds and smells slam into his mind, making him gasp and wince at the intensity.

Easy. Don't hurt yourself, mate. DeMatteo's words caress his mind.

Before he can rationalize his situation, DeMatteo is beside him. "Good morning. Are you hungry?"

"I'm starving," Sean replies before he realizes it's true.

DeMatteo quickly bites into his wrist and shoves the bloody offering to his lips. Sean reaches up to push his arm away, but once the first drop hits his tongue, he instead finds himself clasping the offering and gulping the sweet-tasting liquid.

Oh my god, what am I doing? Sean's mind races as he feels uncomfortable pressure in his gums.

Pulling back, he gasps, hands reaching up to touch as his canine teeth elongate and sharpen. Spurred on by both a hunger Sean has never felt and the wonderful smell emanating from DeMatteo, Sean reaches up, fisting DeMatteo's hair to pull the man closer.

DeMatteo gasps as Sean roughly pulls his head to the side and strikes, his fangs burying deep in the juncture of his neck.

"Easy, mate," DeMatteo warns, stroking his hands gently down his mate's sides. The first self-feeding can be very dangerous for a shifter if his mate drank too much.

Blood is not something lion shifters consume outside of mating, and it is only done with humans to assist with the change. Human mates suffer horrible injuries when the shifter is forced to stop them from draining them dry. DeMatteo would never injure his mate, not even to save himself. "That's enough," he encourages.

Releasing his prize, Sean laps at his mating mark, healing the wound. Lying back with his mate, DeMatteo gently caresses his sides as they both drift back to sleep.

Waking up, Sean notices two things, the hard cock that is wedged between his ass and the gentle purring in his ear. *Did the man always purr like that? And why is that so sexy?*

Turning slowly, as to not wake the giant cat beside him, Sean gazes at the face of the man that has changed his life completely. While he cannot remember everything that has happened, what he does remember is amazing.

The sex was amazing. Yeah, it had hurt like a bitch at first, but then, god, nothing had ever felt so good. And as long as he was admitting the truth, he had to say that the bite was the catalyst to the most toe curling orgasm of his life.

DeMatteo rolls onto his back and Sean stills. Realizing that the man is still asleep, Sean continues his visual exploration; pulling back the sheets slowly, his mouth waters as he gazes on what has to be at least ten inches of uncut cock.

Suddenly the thought of tasting his lion is at the forefront in his mind. Scooting down until his prize is eye-level, Sean wonders if he can give his mate half the pleasure he has received.

Gently grasping DeMatteo's dick, the first thing he notices is how soft the flesh feels; so much like his own, but undeniably different, like velvet over steel. Although this is the first dick other than his own that he has ever touched, Sean is eager for a taste.

Stroking up to the tip, Sean curiously licks across the engorged head. A burst of salty, bittersweet fluid explodes in his mouth. The taste is nothing like Sean expects; it is so much better, and he wants more.

A quick glance up assures Sean that his mate is still asleep. He needs to taste more, and Sean probes the slit before sucking the tip into his mouth. Not satisfied with the small amount he is coaxing out, he dips his head lower and sucks as he would a straw. It isn't long before Sean is rewarded with another burst of pre-cum. A low moan causes Sean to look up and lock eyes with his very awake mate.

"Don't stop, Sean," DeMatteo groans as he gently palms Sean's short locks. Encouraged by the sound, Sean takes more into his mouth. It's too much, and the broad tip pushes on the back of his throat, triggering his gag reflex.

"Don't rush. Breathe through your nose, and when I touch the back of your throat, try to swallow around me," DeMatteo says as Sean wipes at his tears.

Sean has no intention of disobeying that command. Taking him back into his mouth, Sean concentrates on his breathing, using his hand to measure how deep he can go to keep from gagging again. He experiments with suction, twirling his tongue around the tip, taking DeMatteo deeper each time. This time, when he feels DeMatteo touch the back of his throat he forces himself to swallow around the intrusion.

"God. Yes… fuck, Sean, just like that." DeMatteo's fingers slide through Sean's hair. "Too short," he grumbles, thrusting gently.

He wants to make it last, but sucking his mate's cock has him so hard it feels as if he'll be able to come without even touching his cock. Sean drops his head as far as he dares and reaches down to tug frantically on his neglected dick.

Sean's orgasm creeps closer as DeMatteo grabs him by his ears. His hand falters as he nearly chokes when the Alpha starts with quick, shallow thrusts that broadcast his imminent release. Sean moans low in his throat, coming on DeMatteo's leg.

Spurred on by the quick jerks of DeMatteo's cock, Sean realizes his mate is close, but he is still not quite prepared for the warmth flooding his mouth. He swallows quickly, not wanting to lose a drop of DeMatteo's essence.

Some escapes from his mouth and dribbles down his chin anyway, and Sean attentively nurses at his lover's softening cock, cleaning up every drop. Sean is amazed by the strong but sweet taste of DeMatteo's seed. He had had no idea what cum tasted like, but that was not what he expected.

"Good morning," Sean greets the sated and surprised shifter staring down at him.

"Good morning, mate. Not that I'm complaining, but what brought that on?" DeMatteo asks as he tries to get his breathing under control.

"Nothing. I wanted to taste you, so I did."

"Well then, come up here and let me say good morning properly."

Crawling onto his mate, Sean takes his mouth in a searing kiss. Their tongues meet and twine as the passion roars up between them. Pulling back when the need for air can no longer be ignored, Sean stills when his tongue runs across his sharpened eye teeth.

"What happened to my teeth?" Sean inquires, while touching the point with a finger.

"That is part of the change, mate. Let's get dressed and have breakfast. Then we can speak to the pride doctor and he can explain it all to you."

Dressing quickly in his sleep pants and a T-shirt— *when did these get here?* —Sean walks back into the room to find his mate similarly dressed. Heading down to the formal kitchen, Sean is amazed with the amount of food and people present.

"Good Morning, Alpha," says a large male as he dips his head. DeMatteo goes over to the platters of food, grabbing a mountain of eggs, bacon, sausage, steaks, and a variety of baked goods.

After taking a few quick bites, DeMatteo grunts, "It's good. Eat." With that said, everyone else starts making their plates. Sean is slightly confused by the gestures.

Then something clicks in his mind, something he had read or saw on television. "Are you their king?" Sean whispers, waiting to get his plate.

DeMatteo grabs his arm and leads him to a smaller table that seats ten.

"I am the Alpha of the pride, not a king. Just like my father before me," DeMatteo answers after they are seated.

"Here. Eat from my plate," DeMatteo orders, handing him a fork.

"I can get my own," Sean replies. Sean's eyebrows shoot up as he hears the low, angry growl from his mate.

"Just let him feed you, Alpha Mate," says a familiar-looking female. "His lion needs to provide for you," she continues once Sean takes a piece of bacon, chuckling. "My name is Samantha. I am DeMatteo's sister, the oldest after him." She points at DeMatteo.

"Older by two minutes," says another female, joining their table. The table quickly fills up with seven more females and one other male.

"Let me introduce my siblings: Samantha, Julia, and Cassandra, they are the oldest. On this side there is Carla, Jenny, Rebecca, and our baby brother Timothy and his mate Kim."

The family resemblance is unmistakable. While DeMatteo is by far the biggest, the others are not far behind.

"Timothy is also the pride's doctor and Omega. We will need to speak to you after breakfast." DeMatteo addresses the last part to Timothy, who bows his head in response.

Breakfast goes by quickly. After eating the equivalent of his body weight, Sean feels the need to take a nap.

"Sean, are you ready?" DeMatteo asks, pulling him out of his food-induced coma and steering him towards his office.

"Good morning, Alpha Mate. It will be my honor to be your primary physician. I am also a board-certified surgeon," Timothy states as they enter DeMatteo's office.

"I am sure you have a ton of questions; I will start by explaining all the changes your body went through." Timothy begins once they are seated at the small conference table. "First, let me assure you that you are still mostly human, in that you will never completely turn into a lion. But the changes that come with mating with a shifter make it necessary that you no longer see any human doctors."

"Why? If I'm human, what difference does it make?"

"I said you will not turn into a lion, but I am afraid that is where you being human ends. There have been physical and genetic changes, things that can be discovered if you partially shift unexpectedly. If they do extensive testing, they will notice abnormalities. Your rate of healing will be unexplainable, as will your lack of aging over the years,"

Timothy explains as he shows slides of different genetic characteristics.

Sean can only understand half of what he is looking at. There are pictures of humans and lions together, photos showing people with fur and claws and glowing eyes but mostly human.

"There are arguments that at one point in our history, we shifters were closer to our animals' forms, but we evolved alongside humans. The evidence suggests that we were successfully mating together from the beginning. As time went on, humans and shifters fought wars over religion and race, much like today, but those wars resulted in huge losses on both sides."

Timothy explains as the images of old text and drawings depicting various scenes of fighting come on the screen. Sean is strangely fascinated with the graphic details of a history he never knew existed.

"The survivors, both human and shifter, sought to bring peace between our species. These treaties separated our clans to the point where no one other than the ancestors of those humans who created the treaties knew of our existence."

The next slide comes up, and Sean is drawn to the weird symbols and figures, the scene of a body with two oddly formed shapes melting into one.

"That brings us to the biggest, and hardest to explain, change you have undergone. You now have a dual spirit, one of a human and..." Timothy inhales deeply. "One of a lioness." Timothy waits as if willing Sean to understand.

DeMatteo ~

"A *lioness*? Are you saying I am part female now?" Sean asks, hands flailing wildly.

DeMatteo immediately places his hand on his mate's knee, attempting to soothe the irritated human.

"No, Alpha Mate, you are still a male, but the fates have bonded you with a lioness spirit," Timothy scrambles to explain, but it is too late. The growl that comes from the Alpha Mate is one hundred percent pissed off lioness.

Sean moves from his chair so quickly even DeMatteo fails to react in time. Face and hands shifted, Sean's eyes glow a fiery orange and claws long enough to disembowel extend from his fingers. He wraps his claws around Timothy's throat and bares his fangs in warning. Timothy immediately offers more of his throat and whines in submission as waves of dominance roll off the furious man.

"Easy, mate," DeMatteo says, his voice a rumbling purr as he slowly approaches his upset mate.

When he doesn't respond, DeMatteo is forced to let his own dominance roll out. After a second, Sean whimpers in distress before looking over to him.

"Let him go, Sean. You don't want to hurt him, do you?" DeMatteo encourages, still letting his dominance roll across the room.

Sean looks to the man he is holding and jumps back, suddenly horrified at what he is doing.

"Oh my god. I am so sorry, Timothy. I don't know why I did that," Sean says, shifting back.

DeMatteo wraps his mate up in his arms to comfort the confused human coming back from his first shift.

"It's okay, Alpha Mate," Timothy chokes out. Even though he knew Sean would be strong, the power DeMatteo could feel radiating off him was stronger than DeMatteo would have ever thought possible.

Timothy ~

"Timothy, we are done for the day. I am taking my mate to bed," DeMatteo states, herding Sean towards the door.

"Was that his first shift?" Timothy asks, his voice scratchy from being choked.

"Yes," DeMatteo answers gruffly.

"Well, I have to examine him first," Timothy says, walking toward the Alpha Pair. He completely ignores his Alpha's irritated growl, back in doctor mode.

"Okay, but do your Omega thing and make it quick," DeMatteo tells his brother, who is already checking the human.

Releasing large amounts of calming waves, Timothy quickly checks Sean's eyes, mouth, hands, and vitals. They have no idea what to expect with a human Alpha Mate, so Timothy proceeds with extreme caution.

"Thank you, Alpha, Alpha Mate, everything looks good," he says to the pair. Timothy will need to consult with others in his field, and maybe even Tien, but apart from Sean trying to kill him, he is comfortable with how the change has settled.

DeMatteo ~

Before DeMatteo can make it out of the room, Timothy calls out, "You need to complete the bond now, to stabilize his shifts."

Leading his mate to their bedroom, DeMatteo knows what he has to do. Hell, he wants to do it; he just isn't sure if his mate is up for it.

"What's wrong, DeMatteo? Are you angry at me?" Sean asks when he can no longer feel his mate in his mind.

"Nothing is wrong, my love, and no, I am not angry with you. We need to complete the bond; your lioness is blocking our connection," DeMatteo answers as he closes them off in their den.

"My lioness is blocking you… why would it do that? We are mated. And I thought we completed the bond last night?" Sean asks, his long frame stretched out on the bed.

"Twelve nights ago," DeMatteo replies warily. Sean looks up at his mate, trying to figure out what he is saying.

"We started the bond twelve nights ago. You've been in and out of a coma since then," DeMatteo offers, hoping not to push his mate into another involuntary shift.

"Twelve days! I've been here for twelve days and you're just getting around to telling me that?" Sean balks, jumping out of the bed. "I have to call my father. He has probably gone to the police!"

"Relax, Sean. I had an email sent from your personal account stating you went off to New York with the love of your life to get married."

"Are you insane? No one will believe that!"

"Oh, they'll believe it, since your dad had your itinerary checked as well as the hotel you are staying at. I even managed to get your photos fed into surveillance tapes. Shifters have a lot of influence."

Sean ~

Sean paces, going through what DeMatteo has told him. He can't really be angry. It's obvious that DeMatteo has done everything he could think of to keep their secret. Even though people rifling through his home and email rub him the wrong way, he knows DeMatteo had little choice. He will still have to find a way to explain this to his parents, but that will have to wait.

"Okay, mate, what do we have to do to finish this bond?" Sean asks.

He can feel something moving just beneath the surface of his skin, and although he would prefer to talk this through, the lioness inside him is restless.

"You have to claim me," DeMatteo states flatly, but Sean can see the fear and hear the uncertainty in his voice, even without the mate bond to guide him.

"Claim you? You mean I have to fuck you? Have you ever been with someone like that?" Sean asks, unsure why this was important and only knowing that it is.

"No, I was saving that part of myself for you. I would never allow anyone but my mate to claim me."

"The night before I came up here, I did research on gay sex," Sean confesses. "I knew before you bit me that I wanted you. And while it was hot I'm still not sure how to make this good for you," Sean confesses, his eyes shifting to that of his lioness.

He can feel a wildness inside that's untamed, unashamed, and eager to claim their mate. Sean pulls off what is left of his clothes after his partial shift. The confidence and grace he feels with the movements are foreign, and whatever confusion or fear his human mind still holds is stamped back by the overwhelming need of his lioness.

"I don't need you to do anything. I know you will not be able to be gentle, not after your first shift, so I have been wearing this butt plug all day," DeMatteo says as he strips out of his clothing. Sean can feel a tingle in his fingertips as he catalogs every inch of skin being displayed.

As soon as he is naked, DeMatteo climbs in the bed with predatory movements. Sean's cock is already straining as he imagines DeMatteo walking around all day with his ass stuffed full. When DeMatteo starts that deep rumbling purr, Sean feels it like a punch to the gut.

Sean is still surprised how the sound of his mate purring makes his cock ache; it is such an unusual sound, yet it has an undeniable effect. "Let me," Sean says as he reaches forward to rub DeMatteo's back. DeMatteo climbs into the center of the bed on his hands and knees, offering his mate his most vulnerable position.

DeMatteo doesn't hesitate before dropping his chest low, braced on his elbows. Sean can feel his fangs drop as he crawls behind his mate. There is something about the way DeMatteo is shamelessly presenting himself that makes Sean just want to mount him, fast and hard.

He focuses on DeMatteo as he pushes back against the lioness. Regardless of what his mate said, Sean is determined to take his time. Sean slowly pulls the plug out, marveling at how DeMatteo whines and wriggles. Eager to see what other sounds he can pull out of the man, Sean pushes the plug back inside. DeMatteo groans, pushing his hips back onto the toy, while arching his back.

"Sean, I need you inside me. Now," DeMatteo growls when the plug is finally removed, spreading his legs further until he is exposed obscenely.

Sean's pulse races as his mate presents him with the sexiest view he has ever seen. Sean tries to calm his breathing as he grabs the needed supplies from the nightstand. Kneeling behind his mate, Sean feels his lioness pacing in his mind, impatient with the foreplay and eager to claim her mate.

Quickly spreading lube on his aching cock, Sean eagerly pushes the tip into DeMatteo's stretched hole. Once he is in past the flare, Sean stills, not so out of his mind that he forgets that no one has ever touched his mate this way. He is overwhelmed with the enormity of what he is about to do, and he knows without a doubt that this is the point of no return.

DeMatteo ~

DeMatteo holds his body rigidly, presenting his most vulnerable areas to his mate. His lion has completely rolled onto his back, eager to complete the bond and merge their souls for all of eternity. He can feel the mental link as it opens, Sean's emotions washing into his mind.

"Are you okay?" Sean hisses through clenched teeth, and DeMatteo can sense his mate desperately trying to hold off his sudden impending orgasm.

DeMatteo doesn't answer with words; with a grunt he pushes back, seating Sean's cock to the root. "Fuck!" DeMatteo wails as fire spreads from his ass through his entire body.

Sean clutches at his waist. "Don't fucking move. Just don't move or I'll come." Sean pants, his hand squeezing between their bodies as he pinches off the base of his cock.

DeMatteo feels the lioness brush against his mind as Sean reaches out through their bond to get a read on how he is feeling. As soon as their souls make contact, he feels the lioness race to the surface, where DeMatteo's lion is already waiting. They meet and merge, entwining into one being; in his mind he can see a bright light growing until it completely surrounds the two mating lions.

Time freezes until the light recedes and each lion leaps back into the human it had left behind. When Sean opens his eyes, DeMatteo knows they'll glow bright Alpha-Mate-orange. Once DeMatteo feels his need for release subside to a dull ache, he pulls away from Sean slowly before shoving back hard, spurring his human into action.

"You feel incredible, better than I ever imagined it could be," Sean groans before sliding his cock out at an agonizingly slow pace and shoving back in. After four or five slow thrusts, Sean begins to speed up with each pump, until he finally sets his hips to a brutal, punishing pace.

DeMatteo knew that Sean would not be able to control his lion, but he never thought that he would love having his ass taken. Gritting his teeth, DeMatteo holds on for dear life. Between the growls of pleasure and the pinch of pain from Sean's claws digging into his hips, DeMatteo feels indescribable pleasure as his orgasm pulls closer to the surface.

Sean seems to connect with his prostate on every other thrust; DeMatteo can't think or speak, and the only thing he can manage is a combination of babbled out curses, moans, and Sean's name. His orgasm builds at a fevered pace; there is no way he can hold back much longer.

DeMatteo nearly misses the warning lick to the juncture of his neck. Suddenly, Sean grips his hair in an unforgiving hold and sinks his canines deep. DeMatteo roars as his orgasm slams into him like a Mac truck, cum pumping out without anyone so much as touching his cock.

Sean growls and clamps his teeth down harder as he floods DeMatteo's insides with his release. Once the spasms end, Sean gently withdraws his teeth before licking the wound closed and collapsing on his mate.

Chapter 10

DeMatteo ~ July 18, Saturday, 8 a.m.

DeMatteo rolls onto his side to look at his now-sleeping mate; stretching out, he winces at the pain in his ass. Normally his lion would have healed any damage almost before he could recognize it, but it wanted to keep this reminder of their claiming.

He had heard that when humans mated with shifters, their new lions were insatiable for the first few months, but that does not begin to describe the last two night's activities. Sean had taken him three times, with DeMatteo taking him four times in return.

Whether they went to sleep or merely passed out from exhaustion was debatable; they hadn't left the room the entire time. His sisters kept a steady stream of meat coming to their room to fuel their marathon mating. DeMatteo hopes that with the bond fully formed, Sean's lioness will settle. As Sean cuddles in closer, DeMatteo feels his lion pushing towards the contact.

"That seems like a good sign," DeMatteo mutters, mostly to himself, as he feels Sean's lioness purring through their mate bond. Feeling the overwhelming need to provide for his mate, DeMatteo slips from the bed and quietly leaves the room. Knowing he will feel the instant his mate awakes, DeMatteo heads outside to catch a fresh meal.

Stepping off the front porch, DeMatteo starts his shift. Being the Alpha, DeMatteo can complete his shift in a matter of seconds. Humans that had witnessed shifting said it looked and sounded horribly painful, hearing the bones break as the body was reshaped. DeMatteo thought of it more as a full body stretch, like waking up from a long sleep.

Relaxing his body, DeMatteo lets his lion rise to the surface; his entire body tingles as he crouches towards the ground. His lion takes shape before his hands touch the dirt, stretching out the kinks from remaining human too long, and DeMatteo shakes out his dark mane.

Unlike their animal counterparts, shifter lions are huge. A few decades ago some humans accidentally found some of their remains, mistakenly classifying them as prehistoric cats. Humans gave them the name American lion or Panthera Atrox.

The shifter community had decided this was a lucky break. Due to their long life span, the bones were over twelve thousand years old, even though the shifter had only been dead fifty. Shifter lions also did not need to hunt in a pride, though like the animals they were close social creatures.

Standing at a little over eight feet tall and weighing over eleven hundred pounds DeMatteo is larger than most shifters.

Trotting off a few miles deeper into the pride lands, DeMatteo's mouth waters when a delicious scent wafts through the air. *Hmm, how nice, an elk*, a more than sufficient meal to bring home to his mate. Scenting the air, DeMatteo picks up the trail of the hapless animal that has wandered into his sights.

DeMatteo circles the elk, staying out of sight and downwind until he gets into his striking range. Although DeMatteo can cover large distances at top speed, long hunts would wear him down for the long haul home.

Once he reaches a comfortable distance, DeMatteo stills as the animal looks around uneasily, sensing danger. *Oh, no you don't, little girl, I've already caught you.* DeMatteo bursts into top speed towards his prey.

The elk turns and tries to cut back into the heavier trees, but DeMatteo is already springing on her back and clamping his powerful jaws around the back of her neck. It is over before the animal hits the ground, her neck snapped instantly. DeMatteo stops long enough to thank the gods for allowing him a successful hunt before gutting the elk and dragging his prize home.

Sean ~ Saturday, 9 a.m.

Sean stretches as he wakes; a slight twinge in his ass reminds him of why he is so tired. DeMatteo had been wonderful; Sean had apologized profusely after he realized how brutally he had claimed his mate.

DeMatteo had quieted his words with a sweltering kiss that left him dazed, aroused, and desperate to start again. Sean had lost count of how many times he came, but each orgasm was more devastating than the one before.

Rolling over to cuddle with the man, Sean is surprised to not only find his space vacated but the sheets cold. Grabbing his sleep pants from where they lay crumpled on the floor, Sean quickly gets dressed to find his wayward mate. His instincts are screaming that he needs to stay close to DeMatteo, which brings up a host of other questions that need to be answered.

They had never finished speaking to the doctor about his changes but Sean is eager to do so. Strange things are happening to his body, and he is determined to find exactly what is going on. Since waking his thoughts have been filtering with strange instincts, it's almost as if his body's been co-opted by someone else.

Reaching for the door, Sean feels a presence inside his mind for the first time. It isn't like what he felt with the mind thing with DeMatteo; it's like the presence of another person lurking in the corner.

Mate. The presence purrs in his mind, the voice eerie in the sense that, while it is not the sound he normally hears, he instantly recognizes it as his lioness. While he slept, Sean had been confounded by dreams of a lion that spoke to him.

I am the Alpha Mate, the voice had said. *Don't fear me. We have always been together.* Sean had wanted to write it off as just a dream, but now that voice was still speaking.

"Fuck, I really need to talk to Timothy," Sean says to himself as he steps out onto the porch. Sitting on the rocking chair Sean wonders, not for the first time, if he is losing his mind. Hell, he doesn't even know why he is outside; he just has a feeling his mate is out here. As he gazes into the tree line he thinks that he has imagined the whole thing.

Suddenly, a giant cat comes into view, its mane long and darker than its coat, and in its mouth it drags something. An elk. Standing to get a better view, Sean realizes that it is his mate walking toward the steps. DeMatteo drops his prize as soon as he reaches the porch and shifts back into a human.

"Good morning, mate," DeMatteo says as he climbs the steps to join Sean on the porch. "I didn't expect you to wake so soon. I went hunting."

"I can see that. I can also see that it went well," Sean replies as he points to the elk. He tries not to laugh at the way DeMatteo puffs up like the giant cat, preening at Sean acknowledging his catch.

Sean takes a step back when DeMatteo steps forward and reaches towards him. He can tell that DeMatteo is thrown when Sean stops him with a hand to his chest.

"You got a lot of…" Sean waves in his mate's general direction to the blood covering DeMatteo's face, frowning at the gore that covers the rest of DeMatteo's body.

DeMatteo ~

"Ah, yes... so sorry, mate, I forgot," DeMatteo grumbles, looking down at his bloodied torso.

He has to remind himself that humans are often put off by the sight of blood, even though they themselves eat large amounts of meat. They prefer their meat to come in a sanitized container, free from the realities of death.

"Is that for me, mate?" Sean asks. His head dips, displaying his mating marks, as he looks up at DeMatteo through his lashes.

"Yes, of course I hunted for you," DeMatteo answers, his voice pitched lower in response to his mate's presentation.

"Well, come shower with me, and let me thank you properly," Sean suggests as he heads back into the pride house.

DeMatteo quickly tosses the elk in the giant freezer room that sits next to the pride house—he will deal with that later—before pursuing his flirtatious mate back upstairs.

After a steamy shower and mutual blowjobs, DeMatteo plans to butcher the elk he caught and prepare his mate's breakfast while Sean meets with Timothy. Now that the bonding is complete, Sean's lioness will be more stable, so he should be safe alone.

He watched as Sean runs the razor across his neck, their mating mark a dark contrast on his pale skin. "While you're with Timothy, I plan to go over our travel details in my office. I can stop down when I'm done," DeMatteo says.

DeMatteo can see Sean roll his eyes in the mirror. "I'm sure it'll be fine, DeMatteo. I don't need you to babysit me. I feel fine," Sean groans. DeMatteo drops it; he can feel through the bond that Sean wants to do this on his own.

Sean ~ 11:30 a.m.

After a quick breakfast, Sean walks into the room adjacent to DeMatteo's office where he is scheduled to meet with Timothy. This office is almost as large as DeMatteo's but lacks any office equipment or personal touches.

While the space is immaculate and smartly furnished, it is easy to see no one has used it in many years. Walking back to the door, Sean is fascinated by the intricate scrawl craved into the mahogany door, "Άλφα σύντροφος."

"It means Alpha Mate in Greek," Timothy offers with a weak smile that doesn't reach his eyes as he enters the office. "This was our mother's office and now it will be yours."

Unsure of what to say, Sean blurts out, "DeMatteo has a similar tattoo." Sean winces, trying, and failing, to find a more comfortable topic.

"Yes, it is also on his door; it means Alpha. Most shifters have a mark of their rank."

"I am not sure I'm ready for a tattoo."

"We'll cover that after we finish with the physical and I answer all the questions I'm sure you have," Timothy says.

Sean can only hope this meeting goes better than their last as they each take a seat. "I know it must be hard to accept all the information that you have been given in such a short amount of time. I hope to answer any questions you may have. We were born shifters, part human and part lion. There are other shifters that are connected to the wolf and the bear. There were many others, but they were exterminated during the wars. There are tales told of humans who possessed dual Alpha spirits, but they were discarded as myths," Timothy explains.

Sean blinks. It's hard to imagine that entire races were wiped out in the wars. While evidence of mankind's ability to make war with and destroy each other is still displayed all over the world, shifters seem so strong in comparison. It's hard to believe that humans found a way to kill them.

Timothy ~

"Much like us shifters, some humans like you are born with dual spirits and are mated to shifters, but they are never Alpha. That spirit was believed to be too strong for a human to control. This is why your mating is so special. It is believed that your family is connected to the ancient tribes and fused with magic. I searched the archives to find another example of a human Alpha Mate, and you are the first."

Timothy pauses to let Sean absorb just how special he is; no one has ever heard of a human Alpha Mate.

"The closest there has been before you is the Alpha Apex Mate, Tien. She is what we considered mostly human. Her ancestors bred with shifters, but it is believed that after the wars, her family was forced to blend with other humans. After generations of not mating with shifters, the genetic markers were buried, until Tien. With you, we believe the Alpha Mate spirit has always lived in you but was dormant. It only awakened when you met your true mate."

Timothy can't hide his excitement about the knowledge that his uncle is the only shifter in recorded history who has a partially human Alpha Mate. Tien is a Guardian shifter, and she possesses great magic. But there is no way of knowing if Sean is like her and is able to fully transform into his animal.

But unwilling to frighten his Alpha Mate with the unknown and risk getting his throat torn out, Timothy and DeMatteo had decided to wait to speak with their aunt before revealing this information.

"Now we get back to the changes you have gone through. As I told you yesterday, your body is no longer human. The first change you must have noticed is your ability to communicate with DeMatteo telepathically. All mates share this connection with each other, but as the Alpha Mate, you will also have a connection with every member of the pride. You will be able to sense their well-being and any strong feelings. As Alpha Mate, you are second only to the Alpha and can use your dominance over others to co-lead the pride. As you've seen, you now have fangs and claws, and your vision and sense of smell has sharpened to that of your lioness. These traits are for protection, and you will be able to control them at will. Shifters have very long lives, as in thousands of years, and your life has been extended to match that of your mate."

"Wait, are you telling me that I will live for thousands of years?" Sean stammers out.

"Yes, our father was over two thousand years old before he met his mate, our mother. Many of the older members of the pride are our half-siblings. Technology and travel has made it easier to find a mate. Our mother was from Greece and did not come to America until around the sixteen hundreds. It is common to live over ten thousand years if the pride is strong and the Alpha is fully mated. His longevity is shared within the pride."

"But what about my family? My friends? How am I supposed to explain to them why I am not getting older?"

Timothy had expected the human to have a lot of questions; luckily they have more information than he would be able to read in a lifetime. "You can find more of our history in the library. DeMatteo will take you there after you have settled in," he suggests and makes a note to ask Carla to get together a good set of books for Sean to start with.

"Library? That still doesn't explain how everyone in my life will fail to notice that somehow time just seems to stand still for me."

"The short answer is magic. We have evolved to be able to seem to age to those without the ability to see the magic. Of course, there are magic users who will know what we are, but they are also bound by the treaties."

"Magic? But what about my parents? Would DeMatteo be able to change my father?"

"No. I'm sorry, but it doesn't work that way. The only humans who can be changed are the fated mates. We can take on human companions and they receive some benefits, but soul bonding is something that can only happen with mates. All this information is kept in the libraries. My suggestion is that you write down any questions you have. I will be available to answer them all, and what I don't know, we can find. Carla serves as a historian, if you will. I am sure she would love nothing better than to help you explore our history."

Timothy takes a moment to send Carla a text explaining that Sean will need a full tour of the libraries and access to all books regarding Alpha Mates. Her reply is instantaneous and affirmative; Timothy forwards a copy to both Alphas.

"So now you are set with Carla, but there are a few more things we need to discuss about your transition. It is important that you understand everything that is happening. Normally we would have had these talks before the mating began, but due to the uncommon situation we are a bit pressed for time."

"You mean that DeMatteo threw a wrench into your plans with his surprise mating? Trust me, you couldn't be more surprised by any of this than I am."

"Of course, Alpha Mate, I didn't... I wasn't trying to imply that. I wasn't..."

Sean ~

"Timothy, fuck, I'm sorry! I'm not normally this much of an asshole, but this is a lot to fucking process!" Sean exclaims as he runs his fingers through his hair, giving it a sharp tug. "Okay. I'm okay. Please continue. You were explaining the role of the Alpha Mate," Sean says as he takes his seat.

He hadn't meant to lose it with the man; besides it's not as if any of this is Timothy's fault. Actually, Sean has found that he liked the man who looks younger but is likely older than he is. Something about him just seems to click with Sean; being around him made Sean feel more relaxed.

Timothy shoots him a look of disbelief, making Sean laugh and raise his hands in the universal, I give up, manner. "I swear I'm calm, go on."

Timothy eyes him warily for a few seconds before continuing, "As Alpha Mate, you will be expected to provide the Alpha and pride with a litter of cubs within the first few years. This, along with the true mate bonding scars, cements your status as Alpha Mate in the pride and fulfills your obligations to the pride as well as the Alpha."

Sean laughs incredulously, "In case you haven't noticed, I am a man; how can I be expected to produce cubs?"

Timothy ~

Timothy opens his mouth then closes it. Had DeMatteo not warned his mate about pregnancy? Sending out a massive wave of calming influence before speaking, Timothy explains. "Alpha Mate, I apologize, I thought you knew. The most stunning change your body has made is that you have adapted to be able to carry and nurse the Alpha's cubs."

He hesitates, but there is no way he can put this off.

"Please remove your clothing, Alpha Mate, because I will need to examine you internally and take a urine sample," Timothy orders gently.

He is going to strangle his brother; he had warned him to use protection once they had completed the bond. Timothy hadn't been certain that Sean could become pregnant, seeing as they were always told male Alphas could not carry—but then, those were the same people who said there couldn't be gay true mates.

"This may seem a little invasive, but due to the changes your body went through, I am going to need to give you a rectal exam," Timothy explains.

Sean's movements seem to falter. Timothy can't begin to imagine what must be going through the human's mind, but if it is anything like what he's thinking, DeMatteo is a dead man.

DeMatteo ~ Saturday, 1 p.m.

DeMatteo has just finished making lunch when he feels a burst of panic through his mate bond. Racing from the kitchen, he nearly runs over Hugh as he makes his way to his mate's office. Whoever is frightening his mate will pay with their life.

Bursting through the door, DeMatteo is shocked to find his mate naked, lying across the desk with Timothy between his legs. DeMatteo's lion roars as he covers the space in a blur of motion, snatching his brother away from his mate by his throat.

"What the fuck is going on?" DeMatteo snarls, barely suppressing his urge to gut the man he now sees as a threat to his mating.

Jumping up, Sean wedges himself between his snapping Alpha and the terrified Omega. "He was examining me! Let him go right now!" Sean barks. DeMatteo releases his brother only to grab his mate, growling at the scent of another male all over him.

Seemingly unfazed by his mate's jealous rage, Sean unleashes his own anger. "Did you forget to tell me something, DeMatteo?" Sean growls. "Or was it your plan to keep this bit of information secret?"

Confused by Sean's outburst, DeMatteo struggles to understand the questions. What did he not tell his mate?

"When were you planning on telling me I could get fucking pregnant?" Sean bellows, eyes flashing.

DeMatteo's eyes bulge as he realizes that he has, in fact, forgotten to tell his mate something vitally important. *Well, fuck my life.* "Sean, I'm sorry. Things have been so crazy. I forgot." This cannot be happening; he has never managed to mess up anything as badly as he is screwing up his mating.

"You forgot? You have got to be shitting me. How the hell could you forget something as crazy as this? I cannot get pregnant, DeMatteo. What the hell would I tell people? We just got together. This is too soon. Where the hell does the baby come out from?" Sean rattles out question after question, and DeMatteo knows that the human is on his way to a panic attack.

The scent of panic and anger grows with every word out of the man's mouth. There is a real possibility that Sean will go nuclear if he stays on this path. Even DeMatteo's lion cowers in the face of his wrath.

"Please, mate. I'm sorry. I was going to tell you." DeMatteo cautiously steps closer to his mate.

"It is your responsibility to tell me these things, DeMatteo. I have a career I have to get back to. I have been here for almost two weeks! And still there are important things you have *forgotten* to tell me!"

This is not happening. DeMatteo tries to calm his mate through their bond but is met with nothing but a wall of fury. He has been so wrapped up in finally being able to claim his mate that he completely forgot that his mate did not know everything that could happen once the bond was fully formed.

"Sean, if you give me the chance to explain..."

"Explain what? How you have turned me into a girl, and your freaky shifter sperm was going to get me pregnant?"

"Yes! I mean, no! Dammit, Sean, I mean I would have explained everything that would happen when the bond was complete. I should have—"

"There are a lot of things you should have done, DeMatteo. You should have given me a choice to be mated to you. You should have told me I would magically turn into a lion hybrid. And you definitely should have told me I could get fucking pregnant," Sean seethes.

DeMatteo recoils, stunned, looking at his mate. Sean is angry, betrayed, hurt, and DeMatteo is the one to blame. He is the one who put that look on his mate's face, and there isn't one thing he can say in his own defense.

"Do you regret it?" DeMatteo asks, after a long silence.

"Regret what?"

"Regret going through with the bonding. Yes, I bit you without your consent, but you could have walked away. You can still walk away."

Sean pulls back, his face full of pain and asks, "What? You want me to leave, now that we are fully bonded?"

"We are bonded, but that doesn't mean you have to stay with me. I don't want you to stay and resent me. A tainted bond can be worse than a broken bond. I want you to stay; don't misunderstand that, but I have been selfish from the start and I wouldn't blame you if you left," DeMatteo confesses and his lion whines at the thought. But DeMatteo will never do anything to force his mate's hand.

Timothy ~

Timothy edges away from the Alpha Pair to check the results of the special pregnancy test he administered. He tries not to listen as Sean continues to ream his brother out, but DeMatteo sounds broken in a way that the Omega in him can't ignore.

"I don't want to walk away, but you have to be honest with me. I've been playing a game of catch up, only finding out the truth after things have already happened. If this relationship is going to work, I am going to need full disclosure from you," Sean replies.

Twice in less than a week, Timothy has almost had his throat ripped out. When he was studying shifter medicine, he had been warned that treating Alphas and their mates could be dangerous for the pair, but their warnings failed to indicate how extreme the danger was to others around them.

"Of course. I was never trying to hide anything from you. I would never. I want you to stay, I have waited my entire life to meet you. I would never do anything intentionally to hurt you or hide anything from you," DeMatteo says.

Carefully emitting more soothing waves, Timothy prays that the test results come back quickly and that they are negative although the internal examination seemed to show changes that might indicate pregnancy.

Two tense minutes later, both of his prayers go unanswered.

"Okay, we can work through this," Sean answers and reaches out to grasp his mate's hand.

Hugh ~ July 17, Friday, 12 a.m.

"And they're sure that Sean is the head witch of that coven?" Hugh asks as they wait in the car for the person that Nick said could provide proof that Sean is a witch.

Hugh had almost started to believe that maybe he had finally lost it and gone totally insane. For years Hugh had wondered; how could it be that DeMatteo couldn't recognize that Hugh was his true mate? He was completely isolated from most other members in the pride, but he had often heard them speak of his obsession with the Alpha.

He had all but given up on making any connections until Nick had joined the pride. Being human, he was able to resist the influence of the Alpha siblings that had systematically poisoned the others against him. They had soon become friends after finding shared interest in movies and other pop culture.

At first Hugh had been hesitant of befriending a human, but as DeMatteo had started to pull away, Nick had been his constant companion. Nick's presence lessened Hugh's pain at his mate's ambivalence towards their bond. Once DeMatteo had brought that human home, Hugh had confided in Nick that he believed DeMatteo was his mate and this imposter was trying to steal him.

Nick had promised to check the human out with some of his other human contacts, ones that had no association with the pride, and within a few days Nick had come back with the answers.

"I told you, Hugh; this person has had contact with Sean before. This is not the first time this coven has stolen a mate and killed them. They are nuts. They believe in some crazy prophecy that speaks of a human mated with a shifter. If you changed your mind, now is the time to say it, because they just pulled in," Nick stresses as they watch a tan SUV pull into the parking lot.

"No, I'm sure. I'm just worried about going against such a powerful witch."

"Well, that depends on how serious you are about saving your mate," Nick offers as he steps out of the vehicle to greet their guest.

Hugh and his lion bristle at the challenge. Getting out of the car to stand beside Nick, Hugh growls out, "Oh, I'm deadly serious."

"Well that's good to hear, since you will be the one to help me kill the witch," their guest quips as they shake hands.

Nick ~

Nick smiles as Hugh sits down with the other hunter; it's almost too easy. When he had first infiltrated the pride, he had thought it would be difficult to get to the Alpha. He was constantly surrounded by the rest of his filthy pride, and making a move would be a death sentence.

But then he had met Hugh. It had been clear from the beginning that this one was mentally unstable, so his family decided to bide their time. The opportunity presented itself when DeMatteo got more active in searching for his mate. Hugh became more and more unstable as the other man pulled back, making it easier to get closer to the weak link and give him gentle nudges.

"Now we just need you to stay close and bide your time until we have what we need to kill the witch," Nick offers.

"But they have already started the mating process. Once he finds out DeMatteo isn't the one in the prophecy, he'll kill him," Hugh protests.

"No, it will take a few years before the witch can be sure, and we just need a few weeks to be ready," says the hunter.

"You're sure?"

"Like I told you, this isn't the first time this coven has done this, but with your help they will never be able to do it again."

Nick and the hunter shake hands before returning to their vehicles. Never once had Nick guessed that it would take a psychotic shifter to help them reach their goals. Wiping out the entire pride of abominations will finally make amends for the destruction of Nick's clan twenty-five years ago. Now all he has to do is wait.

He cannot wait to see the look in his companion mate Carla's eyes as he slits her throat.

Sean ~ July 18, Saturday, 1:55 p.m.

Sean can feel something in him aching for his mate, and he knows that he will never—he could never—leave this man. There is something wild and alive that courses through him whenever they touch.

Yes, he is upset to find that so many changes have happened, to not only his life, but his body, without his consent. But that doesn't mean he would change mating with DeMatteo. It just would have been easier to absorb if he had learned all this before he was thrown into it.

Adapt and overcome, that is the advice his mother had given whenever he'd faced challenges. He can't help but wonder what his mother would think of the challenge he is up against now. That thought brings him back to his father.

The knowledge that he has to hide so much of his new life from his father makes his guts twist. They have just begun to mend their relationship after it had been interrupted by his mother's death. Though he loves her now, his younger stepmother had served to further the divide between them. But maybe the possibility of being able to give him grandchildren would serve as a common thread they could bond over. Not that he would be rushing to have children.

Chapter 11

Sean ~ July 18, Saturday, 2 p.m.

Clearing his throat, Timothy announces, "Congratulations."

Jerking his eyes back to Timothy, Sean takes about two seconds to process what he has just heard.

"Congratulations? Are you fucking kidding me?" Sean drops DeMatteo's hand to whip around towards the Omega.

"Sean, I'm gonna need you to take a few deep breaths and try to relax," Timothy tries.

Relax?

If Sean was pissed before, they haven't come up with a term to describe what he's feeling right now. How the fuck can he be pregnant? He is a human male; his parts don't work like that—or at least, they shouldn't.

"Relax? Are you fucking shitting me? Tell me you're fucking shitting me. Cause if you're not then there is no fucking way I'm gonna relax!"

DeMatteo tries to grab his hand, but he is not having any of it.

"And you! You don't get to touch me! Matter of fact, you need to stay ten paces away at all times!" Sean screams. He knows he doesn't mean it, but he cannot believe what is happening.

And DeMatteo?

DeMatteo is just looking at him with some stupid wounded look like he's the one that's just been told he's magically knocked-up.

DeMatteo ~

"Calm down, mate. I already said I am sorry. Can you tell me exactly what's wrong now?" DeMatteo asks, realizing that unless he keeps a cool head, he will never figure out the problem.

He understands that he should have told his mate about the possibility of pregnancy, but surely, with all that has happened in the last few days, Sean will forgive his forgetfulness. What is still left unexplained, and to him the most important part, is why Sean was being examined naked. That is the only question DeMatteo really needs answered.

"What's wrong? What, are you fucking deaf? Well, I'll tell you what's wrong, DeMatteo. Apparently I'm *fucking pregnant*!" Sean says, and the look his mate fixes on him would make a weaker shifter tremble.

Wait, did he say he's pregnant?

"Pregnant? Timothy, are you sure? How can you tell so soon?" DeMatteo addresses his brother.

"Yes, Alpha, although I won't be able to tell you how many cubs he's carrying for three months. But you should hear the heartbeats before then. The internal sample test I drew can confirm pregnancy after twenty-four hours."

Thank the fates! This is fantastic news!

DeMatteo locks eyes with his mate. "Timothy, please leave us," DeMatteo orders gently.

With his eyes lowered, Timothy swiftly leaves the room, leaving DeMatteo alone with one seriously angry, newly pregnant male. *Well, this does not look good.*

DeMatteo wants to jump for joy, but something in Sean's eyes warns him that his mate will explode if he doesn't handle this just right. DeMatteo has always wanted a family, but he never wanted to spring it on his mate without his consent. They had been so caught up in the mating heat that DeMatteo had honestly forgotten to use protection after that first time, but now his mate is looking at him with suspicion.

"Sean, please believe I did not do this on purpose." His mate watches him warily as he eases closer. "I was so swept up with the mating heat, I forgot." DeMatteo silently begs his mate to believe him.

"Okay, well, is there a way to get rid of it?" Sean asks flatly.

DeMatteo's heart falls to his feet. "Get rid of what?" DeMatteo hedges, praying he is misunderstanding his mate.

"The pregnancy. Is there a way to get rid of it?"

DeMatteo can't think as a roll of nausea strikes; his lion roars in his head, he either has to kill his children or risk losing his mate. "Yes, there is a way, if that is what you want to do, mate," DeMatteo answers honestly; he will never lie to his mate and risk losing the love of his life.

It would kill DeMatteo if this is the option his mate chooses, but he has forced him into an unplanned pregnancy, albeit unintentionally. Unable to hide the fear in his eyes, DeMatteo braces himself for the real possibility he might lose his first litter.

Sean ~

Sean isn't prepared for DeMatteo to answer him so quickly. At first he had been furious, thinking his mate had knocked him up intentionally. But looking into DeMatteo's eyes, Sean is able to see the truth in his words, and the fear and sadness his mate feels batters his mind. Sean is also not prepared for the crushing pain he feels at the thought of losing his children.

He realizes that while he never planned to have children so soon, the need to protect and love them is almost crippling now that he knows he is pregnant. Realizing his mate still needs him to say the words, Sean walks over to the stressed-out Alpha, grabbing his hands and entwining their fingers.

"I'm sorry, DeMatteo," he starts, "for not trusting you and for overreacting. I just was shocked by not only learning that I could get pregnant, but that I was in fact already carrying a child. I am still confused and have so many questions, and I am not sure where to start." Sean pushes closer to DeMatteo for comfort and support.

He has no idea what this is going to mean for them as a couple or him as a person, but he knows he doesn't want this to be the thing that comes between them. It's just been one thing after another; the minute he seems to come to grips with an impossible thing, something else pops up.

If anything, he deserves a fucking medal for only freaking out a little.

DeMatteo is still at first, but soon Sean can feel the tension melt away as he returns the embrace. The new place in his mind is filled with warmth and affection, and he relaxes more, that new primitive part of his brain basking in the attentions of their Alpha.

DeMatteo ~

It takes almost a full minute for DeMatteo to comprehend what Sean is telling him. His lion understands immediately and calms with the knowledge his cubs are safe.

Sean is sorry and has questions? Does that mean...?

DeMatteo pulls his mate into a tight embrace. He still needs confirmation. "So we are keeping the cubs?" he asks hesitantly.

"Yes, DeMatteo, although I'm scared and still confused. I already love this baby or babies and could never hurt it. Or you."

That last part is added so softly DeMatteo almost misses it. The relief and joy he feels fills his heart to bursting.

"I love you, Sean," DeMatteo confesses, covering Sean's face with kisses and sweeping him off his feet. "First I must feed you, and then we will talk, I promise," DeMatteo announces as he carries Sean towards the dining room.

Sean ~

"Can we eat in private? There are a few things I have to know, and I'm not ready to face everyone," Sean asks once he realizes they are heading to the main dining room.

Even though he enjoys eating with the others, there are things he needs to discuss now. Yesterday, after breakfast and between sex, he had spoken to his father and staff; they had been surprised by his long absence and shocked by the news of his marriage plans.

In order to make their story true, Sean and DeMatteo are planning to fly to New York to get married in two weeks. Sean's parents are flying in on Thursday to meet his fiancé. It seems strange that his father so easily accepted everything he said, but Sean does not have time to figure out why.

"Of course, mate, we can do whatever you like," DeMatteo answers as he places him on his feet. "Just let me gather our lunch, and I will meet you upstairs."

Sean grabs a tray with coffee and pastries and heads back to the master suite leaving DeMatteo to do the heavy lifting. Placing his contributions on the dresser, Sean considers all the planning he would need to do.

Not only does he need to explain that he is marrying a man, now he needs to explain this child. He can't explain it to himself, let alone anyone else. Things in his life are changing so fast he is struggling to keep it straight in his head.

DeMatteo enters the bedroom with three of his sisters in tow. After setting up the table and chairs and spreading out their meal, the women quickly leave, shutting the door behind them. Sean is amazed by the amount of food in front of him; it smells delightful and reminds him that he is starving. Shoveling in a few mouthfuls, Sean delights in the tender meat.

"This is delicious. Is this the elk you caught this morning?" Sean asks between mouthfuls.

"Yes it is. I'm glad you like it. I'm also pleased to see you're such a carnivore since you will now require extra protein and iron," DeMatteo boasts, looking smug and very cat-like.

Sean is suddenly reminded of his questions and puts down his fork. "DeMatteo, how long will I be pregnant? What will we tell people about the child's mother? And please tell me how this baby will be born, seeing as I am lacking the necessary birth canal and vagina."

DeMatteo ~

The questions are fired so rapidly that DeMatteo doubts his mate takes a breath in between them.

"Pregnancy usually lasts between eight and nine months with human mates. It also depends on the number of the cubs."

"So exactly how many cubs are we having?"

DeMatteo chooses his words carefully. "Normally cubs are born as triplets, unless it is an Alpha or Omega. They are only born one at a time," he explains, and DeMatteo doesn't think Sean's eyes could get any bigger as his brows nearly reach up into his hairline.

Sean gapes a few times before he finally gasps out, "So it is most likely that I'll be having more than one baby?"

Stroking his fingers through Sean's hair, DeMatteo tries for a tone that he hopes will be reassuring. "Yes, although we will not know until you are around three months. As for telling humans about the children: we will say I used a surrogate. Luckily you will not look pregnant until the end. You will gain weight but will be able to hide it in loose-fitting clothes."

DeMatteo sips his coffee, trying to give himself time to figure out how to explain this in a way that will be less terrifying.

"Around your sixth month, you will need to stay on the pride lands. You will feel the need to *den*. By that I mean you will tend to want to stay near and prepare the birth site. This is completely normal instinct for your lioness," DeMatteo adds quickly. "Not to mention you will start growing at a rapid rate and delivery can occur at any time after eight months. We can't risk you being near humans at that time."

Sean ~

Sean sits quietly, food temporarily forgotten, as DeMatteo explains what's to come as calmly as if he hadn't just rocked Sean's world.

Utterly shocked by what he is hearing, Sean decides to bench the conversation in favor of eating. He is ravenous and needs the distraction to truly put together everything that has happened.

I'm going to be a father, Sean ponders. *Actually I'll be the father and mother.*

This is crazy. In just over two weeks, he's become a husband, not quite human, and now pregnant with what will likely be multiple babies. A fool might wonder what could possibly happen next, but there was no way Sean will be tempting the fates.

Looking at his mate, Sean can't help the smile that tugs at his lips as he sees how proud the man looks. After clearing his plate and having seconds and thirds—fuck, his mate is a good cook—Sean sits back, pleasantly full.

"DeMatteo, you never told me how the babies would be born."

DeMatteo chokes on his coffee. "Luckily, after the birth, you will not be able to get pregnant for three years," DeMatteo hesitates, taking a deep breath. "Since you don't have a vagina, the babies will be born via the anus."

Sean's head jerks up. "The fuck you said?"

DeMatteo repeats, "The birth will be through the anus or, worst case, a C-section if necessary. Timothy is trained to perform the birth either way."

Sean can't breathe. "No! No way. I want a C-section. No way is a baby coming out of my ass. Are you crazy?"

That is not happening. Of all the insane things that have happened, this takes the fucking cake.

"C-sections are very dangerous for the cubs because of the sedation, but you and Timothy can come up with a birth plan when the time comes closer. I will support any choice you make, mate." DeMatteo strokes his arm, and Sean can feel his presence through their bond trying to calm his rising pulse.

"DeMatteo, I am not sure what part of *I have no plans of shitting out any babies* you don't understand. But, fuck no! If Timothy is trained to do C-sections, then that is what I plan on getting!" Sean knows he sounds hysterical but that is, in his opinion, the only rational response to his mate saying *ass babies*.

DeMatteo ~

"Sean, I know all of this is coming as a huge surprise, but you have to believe that I would never do anything to put you or our cubs at risk. I can imagine the thought of the birth is foreign and scary."

DeMatteo pauses at Sean's snort, waiting for the man to calm before going on.

"But as Timothy no doubt explained, your lioness will allow you to partially shift, creating the necessary birth canal and allow you to give birth with no damage. Your lioness will also work to keep the pain manageable, and as an Alpha, I can take the leftover pain."

DeMatteo watches as Sean mulls over the information. While overwhelmed, his mate is a logical man and when presented with all the information was likely to agree to the safer option.

"I know this is a lot of information, but Timothy can walk you through the entire pregnancy. I just ask you to believe that I will always have your best interest in mind."

"This is all just so crazy, DeMatteo. Until I met you, I never knew there were anything other than humans, and now I have to rearrange the way I look at the world. You are going to have to be patient with me," Sean pleads.

Chapter 12

July 18, Saturday, 4 p.m.

DeMatteo jumps from his seat and pulls his mate into his arms. "Let's not worry about going over every detail right now. I promise, I will be with you every step of the way," DeMatteo reassures him.

Sean opens his mouth to reply, but DeMatteo silences his words by taking his mouth in a tender kiss. Sean moans low in his throat as DeMatteo pulls him closer by the back of the neck and immediately deepens the kiss.

DeMatteo fucks into his mouth with bold swipes of tongue that make all thoughts of their earlier disagreement vanish from Sean's mind. Sean puts up a token protest, shoving his tongue into DeMatteo's mouth, fighting to get the upper hand.

DeMatteo responds quickly by capturing Sean's tongue and nipping on it sharply, earning a high-pitched moan, and Sean falling pliant against him.

When air becomes vital, DeMatteo finally pulls away.

"We will be okay," he soothes the frazzled man in his arms.

"Okay," Sean whispers, rearing to attack those lips again; DeMatteo quirks a brow, sensing his mate's arousal.

"Okay, but first we have a wedding to plan, so no fucking around," Sean quips. Two can play this game.

"No problem, Sean," DeMatteo teases, but doesn't back up an inch. "We will plan the wedding; I already made some arrangements that I think will blow your mind. And I want you to spend some time in our libraries. The books Timothy gave you are a good start, but there is still so much for you to learn," DeMatteo answers, his voice husky, as he reaches down and palms Sean's growing erection. Guiding him back, DeMatteo presses into his mate until his butt balances on the edge of the dresser.

DeMatteo mutters into Sean's ear, "But first, I'm gonna suck your dick. I need to taste you. That is… if you think we have enough time?" He drops to his knees before Sean can catch his breath.

DeMatteo wastes no time divesting Sean of his pants. He only takes a few moments to nuzzle Sean's balls where his musky scent is thick with want and fertility. DeMatteo pulls his pants further down so he can fondle his mate's heavy balls. He expertly rolls them in his palm before gently pulling them away from his body.

Slowly dragging his lips back up Sean's shaft, DeMatteo swirls his tongue around the crown. He dips his tongue in the slit, swallowing the pool of pre-cum that has formed there.

Gripping Sean's thick cock, DeMatteo bends lower to suck one of Sean's balls into his mouth. Sean squirms in his arms as DeMatteo looks up, eyes flashing Alpha red; it makes his dick twitch with want, witnessing Sean's lioness pushing forward to mate with him.

Sean's legs begin to shake as DeMatteo hums and tongues the sensitive flesh. Pulling away when Sean starts humping his face, DeMatteo makes sure to give its twin the same attention. Once Sean is reduced to begging, DeMatteo takes pity on him, swallowing him to the root in one quick motion.

"Fuck, so good, baby," Sean praises as he is forced to grip DeMatteo's mane to keep from falling over.

Sean ~

Sean feels the need to orgasm tighten up his balls; he tenses his entire body to hold it off, but the way DeMatteo is sucking him ensures he won't last long.

DeMatteo flicks his tongue over the sensitive tip and slides his finger in his mouth bathing the digit in saliva. Pulling out his finger, DeMatteo drops his head, taking Sean back to the root, swallowing when Sean's cock bumps the back of his throat.

"Yeah just like that, swallow me, take it all. Damn, baby, you are doing that so fucking well. Fuck! Too good, you're gonna make me come." Sean moans louder as he feels a lone finger probing at his hole.

It is taking all his control to hold back the orgasm that is curling his toes as he balances on the dresser. DeMatteo has the nerve to laugh at his mumblings around the dick in his mouth.

He bucks his hips tentatively and DeMatteo moans his approval. When that digit pushes in his ass, Sean growls and slams his cock down his mate's throat. Knowing the end is near, Sean picks up the pace, fucking harder and looking down at the man whose finger is keeping pressure on that hungry spot deep in his ass.

DeMatteo ~

DeMatteo glances up through his lashes and locks eyes with the man brutally fucking his throat. Moaning at the lust in his mate's eyes, DeMatteo has to finally free his neglected hard on. He is leaking so much he doesn't even need lube as he begins to furiously stroke his own cock.

Sean lets out a roar then tenses. Suddenly the cock in DeMatteo's mouth twitches, hardening further and pulsing, coating his throat with Sean's release. Swallowing quickly to consume every drop, DeMatteo finally loses his load when he hears his mate whisper, "God, I love you, DeMatteo."

Sean collapses back on the dresser, his legs unable to hold him up. DeMatteo doesn't bother to get up, only lying his head on top of Sean's thighs, trying to catch his breath.

"Say it again," DeMatteo rasps. *A cock down your throat will do that to you.* He wants to hear Sean say the words.

"I love you," Sean repeats as he combs his hand through DeMatteo's sweaty hair.

"I didn't want to say those words for the first time during sex, but when you looked at me I just had to tell you."

"Don't hide from me," DeMatteo admonishes. "I love you too. We'll get through this together."

Climbing to his feet, DeMatteo holds out his hand to help Sean up.

Sean ~

Once on his feet, Sean runs his hands under DeMatteo's shirt, feeling each sweaty muscle. "So, do I get to get my Alpha Mate tattoo now?" Sean asks as he traces DeMatteo's tattoo that covers his entire side, ribs to hip.

"Yes, after we announce the pregnancy next week at the pride meeting, Samantha will tattoo you." DeMatteo then asks, "How did you know what my tattoo meant? Do you read Greek?"

Sean laughs. Tempted to tease his mate, he remains silent as DeMatteo straightens his clothes in an attempt to make him look less just-fucked. After a few seconds Sean folds, deciding to not let his mate believe he is some linguistic genius. Sean admits, "Your brother told me."

"And just when I started to believe you were a scholar of dead languages."

Sean laughs. "Ah, so you have some kind of nerd kink. Should I start reciting the periodic table?"

In a blur of movement, DeMatteo has him pressed into the wall. "I'd love to show you all my kinks." DeMatteo's mouth grazes his lips with every word.

Sean moans against his lips, grinding his slowly filling cock against his leg. He feels like he is still in heat; he didn't even have this many erections when he was a teenager. If there is one definite plus side to mating with a shifter, it is his new, supernatural refractory period.

Pushing away, DeMatteo smirks. "Later. For now, we have a pride meeting and a wedding to plan."

With that, DeMatteo adjusts his cock and walks into the bathroom. Sean has to lean against the wall as he watches his mate through the clear shower door, the sight of DeMatteo's perfect body wet and soapy doing nothing to curb his growing erection. Sean decides to take the time to send out a few more emails before heading to the library; hopefully the mundane task will help him will his cock to behave.

After sending a carefully worded message to his secretary, Sean is back in control of his libido. Or he is until DeMatteo walks over in a scrap of cloth too small to begin to cover him—damn that man. Sean is curious: is it possible to fuck someone to death?

Hugh ~ Saturday, 6 p.m.

"Hugh, what is the status of the new houses? They need to be ready in time for the pride meeting next week." Samantha always seems to eye him suspiciously. Hugh is beginning to believe that she is also under a spell, even though she has always been a bitch.

"They've all been inspected; I'm just waiting for the Alpha to give his final approval. Are we having guests for the pride meeting?"

"That's good. I'm going to need all the keys; I'll be taking the Alpha on the final walkthrough. I'm not at liberty to discuss it; the Alpha will be explaining all the new goings on at the meeting."

"What?" Hugh seethes. "I always escort the Alpha through the new builds! Since when have the pride meetings been a matter of secrecy?"

"Since the Alpha and the Alpha Mate will be touring the houses. I'm sure even you can see how that would be disrespectful to the Alpha Mate."

"Disrespectful?"

"Yes, Hugh, you are his ex-lover. Your lack of respect for the Alpha Mate is disrespectful. Oh, I see how you look at him when you think nobody's watching. But you failed to realize I am always watching. I told you years ago not to get attached. I warned my brother not to use you to warm his bed. But neither of you listened, so here we are. This is not a debate. Just hand over the fucking keys," Samantha growls while flashing her eyes and fangs.

Hugh has no choice but to tip his head in submission, but his lion is furious at the other shifter's dismissal. One day Hugh is going to settle this feud with his mate's siblings, but not today; he needs to bide his time. Once they are able to get Sean away from DeMatteo and break the spell, they are all going to spend a bit of time on their knees.

"Is there anything else I can help you with?" Hugh presses out between clenched fangs. He swallows the growl that threatens to erupt as he buries his claws into the palm of his hand; the tinge of copper assaults his nose as blood oozes out between his fingers.

Samantha looks at Hugh's hand and scents the blood in the air and narrows her eyes at the other shifter. "Watch yourself, Hugh. I would like nothing better than a reason to put you down. You may have had DeMatteo fooled, but I see you," Samantha warns.

Satisfied that she has settled the issue, keys in hand, Samantha slams the door on her way out of the office. She is going to have to keep an even closer eye on that man. He is not to be trusted; both her and her lioness are sure of it. The problem is convincing her kind-hearted Alpha that Hugh is not the poor helpless lion cub he pretends to be.

DeMatteo ~ Saturday, 5:30 p.m.

"You know if you keep looking at me like that, we are never going to actually get out of the bed," DeMatteo teases playfully as his mate tracks his every movement.

Sean licks his lips when the towel falls to the floor. "That's untrue. The last time was against the dresser. Besides, if you expect my mind to be anywhere other than the gutter, then you are going to need to wear more clothes."

"Mmhmm… but maybe I like you like this, reeking of lust for me, even though I can still smell my seed seeping out of you," DeMatteo confesses as he blatantly scents the air, enjoying the smell of them joined together, along with the fresh combination of pre-cum and pheromones Sean is producing.

DeMatteo prowls over to Sean and nuzzles into his neck, pressing the proof of how much he enjoys that scent into Sean's equally interested dick.

"No. No way. You have completely wrung me out. If I come again, it'll be just blood. Besides, I asked your sisters to go with me to the library." Sean moans as he attempts to put some space between him and the insatiable Alpha.

DeMatteo smiles and pulls their hips together. "Are you sure? I think I can get you to come again. Look at you. You're already so hard for me."

Despite his earlier protest, Sean whimpers and presses in closer. "Yes, I'm sure you could, but I don't want you to."

DeMatteo takes advantage of his mate's receptiveness by sliding his hands down to his muscular ass, groping each cheek and pulling them slightly apart. Sean's heart races with anticipation as he momentarily gives in, before twisting away.

"Maybe later. Your sisters will be here any minute, and I refuse to have them catch me with my dick out, getting mounted." Sean pants as he tries to heed his own warnings, but he knows if DeMatteo touches him again, he will be naked and spread out like a whore this time.

DeMatteo sobers with that thought, kissing his mate softly. "Don't ever wanna let anyone see you like that."

Sean smiles. He is secretly pleased his mate is so jealously possessive he would die rather than share any part of his mate. Sean is taking that secret to the grave. Hearing Samantha and Carla climbing the stairs, Sean gives his mate a cheeky look.

"See, here they come now."

DeMatteo ~

DeMatteo sighs as he moves to pull on some boxers; nudity in the pride is common, but with Sean's lioness so dominant, he isn't willing to provoke an attack. Sean is gaining better control by the day, but so soon after mating, his lioness could snap without much warning.

"Are you two love birds decent?" Carla calls from the other side of the door.

DeMatteo winces as he stuffs his aching cock into his too tight jeans before he answers. "Yeah, come in."

"So there is my favorite brother-in-law," Samantha jokes as they enter the den.

"Well, since I'm your only brother-in-law, I'm not so sure that is a compliment," Sean jokes back as he grabs a notebook and pen.

DeMatteo pins Carla with a serious look, "Okay, I expect my mate back in one piece, and I'd appreciate if you didn't fill his head with nonsense stories. Let's stick to the history and skip the fairy tales and bedtime stories."

"Yes, brother dearest," Carla snarks.

Samantha adds, "You take the fun out of everything."

Sean ~

As Sean leaves with DeMatteo's sisters, he silently basks in the easy acceptance he has found with his mate's siblings. Being an only child, he had often wondered how it would have been to have brothers or sisters, but now, in this pride, Sean feels as if he fits in. His lioness purrs as she acknowledges her pride mates.

The hairs on the back of Sean's neck rise as he senses someone watching him. He tries to keep his pace even as he scans around him for what his lioness feels is a threat. He almost writes it off as paranoia, until he notices Hugh watching them from the doorway of his office. Sean silently bares his distended fangs at the shifter when their eyes finally meet, and Hugh quickly lowers his gaze before closing the door.

Chapter 13

Sean ~ July 21, Tuesday, 2 p.m.

After riding for an hour through the trees, Sean can see why DeMatteo lives here; it is so beautiful: no neighbors and no smog. Sean isn't sure he has ever seen so much open space. Arriving at a clearing, Sean notices what appears to be a large stage with about twenty chairs.

"We will sit on the stage with the pride enforcers and our Omega," DeMatteo answers his unasked question. "After the meeting, Samantha will tattoo you and the pride will go for a hunt. You will remain here with two enforcers until we return with the kills and then eat together to celebrate the Alpha mating and cubs," DeMatteo reminds him as they walk up to the stage.

After they had dressed, DeMatteo had informed him of the ritual for an Alpha mating ceremony. Although he is excited and curious, Sean can't help being nervous about getting his first tattoo in such a large gathering.

He doesn't want to scream and appear weak in front of the pride, but fuck, this is going to be a huge tattoo. Sean relaxes as DeMatteo pulls his back into his chest, reading his thoughts again.

DeMatteo whispers, "Relax, mate, you will do fine; it will take about two hours. While you are getting it done, the pride will hunt for you and feed you. Then I will take you home and lick every inch of you before fucking you through the mattress." Sean shivers as DeMatteo purrs and nips at his ear.

Three hundred and fifty shifters slowly fill the area; a buzz of excitement grows as word spreads of the Alpha's recent mating. Sean looks into the sea of faces, of the strangers who have become his new family, and he instantly recognizes Hugh—the man that confronted him that first night.

The shifter stays out of his direct line of sight, but there are times when Sean catches him watching with nothing less than hate. Not wanting to alarm his mate, Sean simply keeps his eyes on the man; there is something about him that keeps Sean's lioness on edge.

His hackles rise as he eyes his mate's former lover. The man has been mostly absent since that unpleasant encounter, but Sean feels a distinct threat in his eyes. Sean relaxes slightly as his mate wraps his arms protectively around him.

"What's wrong? I can feel your tension, sweetheart." DeMatteo's husky voice fans across his nape.

"It's nothing," he lies, not wanting to needlessly worry his mate. Sean has made it a point not to flood the mate bond with his suspicion of the other shifter. DeMatteo tries hard to be a fair Alpha, and as the Alpha Mate, Sean will also be looked at to care for all pride members.

Before DeMatteo can question him further, Sean turns in his arms and thoroughly kisses him, completely derailing his train of thought. His mate is not the only one who can use his body as a distraction, although Sean gets equally distracted.

After pulling away, Sean gazes up through his lashes and whispers, "Let's get this over with so you can take me back to bed."

Needing no further encouragement, DeMatteo takes center stage, grabbing everyone's attention. "Welcome home, pride mates. As all of you have no doubt heard, tonight's gathering has turned into a celebration."

DeMatteo waits for the excited purring and chuffing of the lions to settle before continuing.

"I am excited to introduce you to my true mate, and my new co-Alpha, Sean Herr." DeMatteo announces.

Sean watches in total shock as every member of the pride falls to their knees and bares their throats as he steps up beside DeMatteo.

"Your acknowledgment is noted." DeMatteo continues, "Your Alpha Mate and I would also like to announce that we are expecting our first litter!" The roars of celebration are deafening but Sean's eyes are glued to Hugh, who lets out a strangled gasp.

They lock eyes and Sean can feel the hatred rolling over his adversary as the man bares his fangs in a clear threat. Not backing down, Sean can feel his lioness rising up in the face of her challenger. Feeling a strange tingling sensation working through his body, Sean realizes that he is beginning to shift.

DeMatteo ~

DeMatteo senses his mate's agitation seconds before he hears the warning Sean growls. His own hackles rising with the need to protect his family, DeMatteo scans the crowd, searching out the possible threat.

Immediately, his eyes fix on Hugh, whose own eyes are lowering, but DeMatteo doesn't miss the contempt in them. DeMatteo is moving before he fully forms the thought to attack, grabbing Hugh by the throat and pinning him to the ground. The crowd gives a wide berth as DeMatteo growls, his fangs bared.

"You dare to threaten and disrespect my mate again!" DeMatteo snarls, his voice barely human and his face shifting.

Hugh stills, tilting his head offering his submission. Hugh can't suppress his whimpering at his mate's act of aggression.

"Take him to the security rooms and lock him in a cell until further notice. Hugh, you are being formally charged with challenging the true Alpha Mate. For this, your life is forfeit; however, I will not let your disrespect sour my mating, so you will be imprisoned until I render final judgement," DeMatteo orders.

Four pride enforcers hurry to surround the rogue male and unceremoniously drag him to a vehicle. Two more enforcers follow in a separate vehicle to ensure their prisoner makes no further outbursts or attempts to escape.

DeMatteo desperately tries to calm his lion, who is demanding that he hunt down and kill the man that has threatened their mate for the second time. Heading back to his mate, who is surrounded by the remaining enforcers, DeMatteo considers his options. The choice is clear: he decides to cancel tonight's hunt; he wants to deal with Hugh now.

As soon as DeMatteo is within reach, Sean wraps him in a bruising embrace. Stroking his hands through Sean's short hair, DeMatteo slants their mouths together as a way to reassure both his lion and mate that all is well.

After just a few swipes of tongue Sean looks up at his mate and says through their mind link, *DeMatteo, you need to continue the hunt. The pride needs to be calmed after that.*

Startled by Sean's calm thoughts, DeMatteo looks down at him, already shaking his head, but Sean stalls whatever he is about to say.

"I'm fine; I will be here with your sister and two enforcers. Plus, we leave tomorrow for a week. They need this. Let our mating be a positive thing."

DeMatteo has to admit that Sean is right; he needs to take his pride for a run. There have been so many changes, and with more to come, he needs to make sure the pride stays stable. The incident with Hugh shows that he needs to touch base with each member of his pride.

Sean leans into DeMatteo, trying to soothe the irritated lion—he even gets angry like a cat—that still vibrates with barely-controlled rage. Reaching up on his toes to brush their lips together, Sean sighs when he feels his mate start to uncoil.

Pulling back, Sean urges DeMatteo through their mind link to continue on. He does not want to let that jealous shifter ruin his mating ceremony any more than he already has. As DeMatteo once again takes center stage to have the pride priest perform the bonding ritual, Sean notices a line of SUVs approaching the clearing.

You have got to be fucking kidding me. Now what? Sean grits his teeth. God knows what's about to happen. When DeMatteo jerks his head towards him, Sean realizes he projected.

DeMatteo's gaze drifts towards the sight that has caught his attention. After a beat, Sean begins to relax as he sees the huge smile spreading across his mate's beautiful face.

"It seems my Uncle has come to celebrate our mating," DeMatteo says as he reaches for Sean's hand and pulls him into his side.

As the vehicles get closer, every shifter falls to their knees and bows their heads. As the cars come to a stop, Sean feels the power pour out before the doors even open. An impossibly huge man and woman finally exit the middle vehicle and stride towards them.

Sean is instantly floored by the devastatingly handsome man, who looks like an older version of DeMatteo. The woman that is with him is of East Asian descent and so beautiful Sean is mesmerized. Sean follows his mate's lead bowing his head in greeting, DeMatteo seems unprepared for his Uncle to pull him into his arms.

"Nephew, I have come here tonight not solely as the Alpha Apex, but as a proud uncle. This must be your mate, Sean," Richard says, releasing DeMatteo and facing Sean.

"Alpha Apex and Alpha Apex Mate, may I present my mate Sean Herr. Sean, meet my Uncle and Aunt: The Alpha

Apex of all American lions, Richard Santiago, and Alpha Mate and Guardian, Tien Santiago."

DeMatteo ~

DeMatteo can't help the burst of pride he feels as he introduces the most important person in his life to the people who have become his second parents. Sean extends his hand to Richard and he too is quickly pulled into a tight embrace.

After Richard embraces the man who will become his son-in-law—DeMatteo and his siblings have grown to see Richard and his mate as their surrogate parents—he addresses the crowd. "Everyone rise. I have come here today to celebrate with you in my nephew's mating."

After the cheering ceases, the priest takes center stage to perform the ancient bonding ceremony. Sean had been shocked to learn that Alphas were required to claim their mate sexually in front of the pride. He'd almost sagged in relief when DeMatteo had broken and told him that part had become optional decades earlier.

"Don't worry, mate, my lion is a jealous, possessive bastard," DeMatteo had chuckled when Sean shivered.

"What if the pride demands it?"

"They would have to take that up with my lion."

After the ceremony is complete, everyone starts to strip. From lowest ranking up they shift, each one coming up to be stroked by DeMatteo and then Richard. After every member has finished shifting, DeMatteo strips off his clothes and shifts into his lion.

Sean ~

After being stroked by Richard, DeMatteo stands by Sean, rubbing his body against him, marking him with his scent. Sean is taken off guard when Tien strips off her clothing and proceeds to shift into the largest polar bear Sean has ever seen.

"As you can see, there are many types of shifters, my mate is rare. There are only a handful of her kind on the planet," Richard explains as he removes his own clothing.

After his shift Sean notices that Richard is just a hair smaller than DeMatteo. As the lions begin their run, Sean has the chance to appreciate how graceful and powerful his mate is. Turning around, Sean runs directly into Tien.

"Oh gosh, I'm sorry. I thought you went on the run with the others," Sean apologizes before realizing that she is unable to speak to him in this form.

"No, she stayed behind to supervise your tattooing and offer you her magic as a blessing," Samantha answers as she walks up behind him.

"Offer me her magic?" Sean asks, struggling to make sense of what she is telling him while he is busy staring at a giant, magical polar bear. Sue him, Tien is fucking impressive.

"Tien is an ancient, not only a shifter spirit, but a guardian spirit created by the gods to protect us. She is also the first Alpha Mate shifter who was partially human," Samantha offers as she motions for him to come with her.

Walking to the platform on the rear of the stage, Samantha motions for Sean to remove his clothing and lie down. "She told me that she has had a vision of you and your unborn cubs. This is the real reason she and Uncle Richard flew here."

"What... What kind of vision?" Sean stammers as the priest starts chanting. Tien towers over Sean and gently places her large paws on his head and stomach. Heat spreads through his body as a melodious voice drifts into his head.

Be calm, Alpha Mate, for you have truly been blessed. The gods have deemed both you and your lioness worthy of great power. You will become a Guardian just as I am, and you and your mate will replace me and mine when we leave this earth. Just like you, I was born human and the gods chose me to guard over and carry the magic of the shifter race. Tien explains in his mind.

"But you are able to shift. I thought humans were unable to take complete animal form," Sean stammers, trying to understand all the conflicting information being shoved at him.

Normal human mates cannot fully shift. But you, Sean, were infused with powerful magic before your birth that was released during the claiming. You will be able to fully shift, just like your mate. Take care, for there will be many who will threaten both you and your family, but you will have the power to both heal and protect, as well as the power to destroy those who attack you.

This litter will be unique amongst shifters, and you must protect them at all costs. The world is changing, and we must change along with it. Your sons will be the first in a new breed of shifters. They will be the immortals of myth. You and your offspring will gather the scattered shifters and bring them back from extinction. I will be here to help and guide you on this path, but it is you who will have to walk it, Tien explains.

Sean has so many questions as he listens to Tien, but his words are lodged in his throat. Suddenly his lioness floats in his mind surrounded by light, roaring. Darkness claims Sean as his lioness rejoins his soul. Sean hears his bones breaking as his lioness takes form, but he feels no pain. It is almost as if he is a spectator watching the events taking place.

Tien rubs her paws through his fur as warmth spreads through his body—more intense than the burning of his mating, but a soul-deep wave that seems to reach every molecule of his being. Through his mind's eye Sean can see his lioness. Although Timothy had explained that the spirits have no gender, just two entities that are bound to one another, Sean is still surprised to see his lioness takes on the shape of a male lion. Timothy had explained his spirit was that of a lioness, but the form before him looks distinctly male.

We have always been one, gender is a concept only humans fixate on, but now you see me as I truly am. The Alpha Mate. Sean immediately recognizes his lioness's voice. It is the same voice he always hears in his mind. Slowly he returns to his body as be begins shifting back into a man.

DeMatteo ~

DeMatteo races back to the clearing—his uncle told him that Tien had a vision of his mate when they had shifted after several kills—his mind churns with the possibilities. Reaching the stage, his vision blurs when he comes upon his unconscious mate.

"Easy, DeMatteo. Your mate is fine, just resting after his tattoo," Tien soothes as she stands beside Sean.

Reaching Sean's side, DeMatteo is instantly comforted by his mate's relaxed and peaceful sleep. "Uncle told me of your vision. What was it?" DeMatteo demands, annoyed that he was the last to know of this.

"This is not the time," Tien states flatly as she looks around at the gathering shifters. "Your mate will have much to tell you when you are alone," she finishes as Timothy stops to check on Sean.

DeMatteo has to push back his hypervigilant need to protect his mate. He knows his aunt would never do anything to put the human or their cubs at risk. Still, the need to protect his growing family is strong enough to force his fangs to slide down.

Tien doesn't react other than to palm his face, "Relax, Alpha. Your family is safe," she says.

Either the words or her familiar touch is enough to get the lion pacing under his skin to listen to reason.

Sean ~

Sean's eyes flutter when he hears DeMatteo's voice.
As he starts to rise into awareness, Sean feels as if he had a
full night's sleep, feeling refreshed and energized. DeMatteo
rushes to help his mate to his feet, securing the robe that had
been placed to hide his nudity. Sean leans into the touch,
humming his approval as DeMatteo dips in for a quick kiss.

Probing their link for a clue to what has happened,
Sean quickly assures him all is well and they will speak in
depth later. As the shifters gather again, DeMatteo shifts
quickly back to his lion and tears into the largest elk, dragging
most of the carcass to his mate. Shifting back, DeMatteo tears
a piece of meat and offers it to Sean.

"You can't expect me to eat that. It's um, it's raw,"
Sean whines, his nose curling up in disgust.

"Just try some for me, mate. You will need the protein
for the cubs," DeMatteo encourages, beaming a smile at the
unconvinced man.

Taking the proffered meal, Sean cautiously puts the
raw meat in his mouth. Flavor bursts across his tongue and
Sean moans in response. DeMatteo's smile grows impossibly
larger as Sean starts devouring the meal. Finishing his portion,

Sean smiles when DeMatteo pushes the remaining cuts of meat his way.

"It's the cubs," DeMatteo chuckles as Sean practically licks his hands clean. "You will need a lot of protein to sustain them. Rare is good, and raw is best; it will help keep your blood strong. You will also need to start taking this supplement." DeMatteo grabs a bottle of pills that Timothy suddenly appears with.

"Ah, ok. Anything else, Daddy?" Sean jokes, popping a pill and swallowing it dry.

Chapter 14

Sean ~ July 22, Wednesday, 7 a.m.

After they return to their bedroom, Sean reels off everything that happened from the moment DeMatteo had left. The Alpha sits silent as Sean recounts what Tien had said.

"That is unbelievable. My mate will be a shifter Guardian," DeMatteo says. "That's a lot to take in. You should get more sleep," he adds.

"I don't need sleep. I slept through the entire tattooing!"

Ignoring his complaints, DeMatteo drags him into the shower and insists on helping Sean apply the cream Timothy had given him for his new tattoo. By the time they make it to bed, DeMatteo seems to have forgotten his proclamation of needing sleep and proceeds to make love to him for most of the night.

Sean wakes the next morning deliciously sore, and smiles at the smell of bacon as his mate enters the room pushing a cart rounded over with food.

"Good morning, baby, I figured we'd start the day with a good breakfast before getting on the plane." DeMatteo beams as he starts piling copious amounts of food on a plate.

"This is wonderful, baby. Thank you for breakfast in bed." As he grabs a glass of orange juice to wash down his vitamin, pain courses through his new tattoo.

"Wow, that really hurts." Sean winces as he rubs his hand down his side. A tingling sensation follows his fingers and when he reaches the bottom the pain has completely disappeared.

"That's strange," Sean mutters as he tries to get a better look at the tattoo. "Holy shit, it's healed." Retracing the tattoo, Sean cannot tell he has just gotten it.

"Let me see it." DeMatteo turns him to get a better look. "That's amazing, baby. We heal fast, but that should have taken at least another day. Let's just keep this to ourselves for now. We need to shower and leave within the next few hours to make our flight window, and I still need to deal with the Hugh situation."

"Damn, what is that man's problem? I don't want to tell you how to deal with the pride, but my lioness does not trust that man. Should I come with you while you question him?"

"You are my co-Alpha and have just as much say as I, but my lion is uncomfortable with him near you. If he was to try anything again, I wouldn't hesitate to kill him on the spot, so I believe it would be best for Samantha to accompany me."

"That's fine, I really don't have anything to say to him so I'll just grab breakfast then."

"Thank you." DeMatteo kisses his mate soundly before heading down to levy judgement on Hugh.

Samantha ~ 7:35 a.m.

Samantha paces outside her Alpha's office. She wants to debrief him before he sets out to talk to the crazy shifter. The night guards reported that Hugh had spent most of the night talking to himself. After they repeated what they had heard, and she listened to the recordings, she had contacted Timothy earlier in the morning.

She motions to the guards to check Hugh's restraints as soon as she sees her brother enter the hall. "I hate to say I told you so, DeMatteo, but I never trusted that man to step aside if you found your mate. He seems hell bent on destroying your bond. The guards reported that all night he mumbled about getting rid of the mate-stealer and reclaiming his rightful place. I think he is mentally unstable and should be either destroyed or sentenced to lifetime prison with the Alpha Apex," Samantha whispers once the guards are outside of hearing range.

DeMatteo's face hardens and Samantha winces at her choice of words. "You may hate it, but you never miss the opportunity to say it. Don't you think you're being a bit hard, Samantha? I will not kill a pride member because he is jealous of my mating," he accuses.

"No, Alpha, I really don't, and that is why I asked Timothy to join us to try to get a read on his mental state."

"Okay, Samantha. We will talk with Hugh and have Timothy observe, and I will make my decision after we have all the facts."

"Yes, Alpha," she agrees, leading her Alpha to meet with his deranged ex-lover.

DeMatteo ~

Timothy is standing outside of the holding room with his hands pressed to the door when they arrive. DeMatteo can tell he is already trying to calm Hugh through the door. He hopes a night of confinement has cooled his ex-lover's temper, but by the way DeMatteo feels his temper flare as Hugh senses his Alpha, it seems that is not the case.

"Timothy, I just want you to observe the hearing. Do not try to calm him, we need to know what's going on in his head," DeMatteo orders. If he has to, he can easily kill the other shifter, but DeMatteo still hopes that he can talk some sense into Hugh before the choice is taken out of his hands.

"Yes, Alpha," Timothy replies before following his Alpha and lead enforcer into the holding cell. Timothy stands off to the corner while DeMatteo and Samantha go closer to the loosely shackled shifter.

Hugh moves without warning; his arms swing open, but before he can react, Samantha is there, "DeMatteo!" she warns, fangs erupting around her growl when Hugh tries to embrace him. She grabs him by the throat before he can make contact. "Show some respect when addressing the Alpha," Samantha hisses.

Hugh's only response is to bare his fangs and claws. Timothy slides further into the corner behind his Alpha.

"Come on, Hugh, shift; I want you to give me an excuse to gut you," Samantha taunts, and DeMatteo can see that she is moments away from making good on that threat.

"Enough!" DeMatteo roars, his lion pouring authority and barely contained anger into the room. He needs to get this calmed quickly before he is forced to kill the smaller shifter.

Hugh ~

"Alpha?" Hugh whimpers at his mate's aggression directed towards him, his lion receding from his mind in submission.

Samantha slowly releases her grip on his throat. Hugh tries to reach his mate with his emotions through the pride bond, but he feels their connection weakening.

"Hugh, I am here to give you my final judgement. Although I was reluctant to admit it, your outburst and disrespect today have shown me that there is no place here for you. For your challenge to the Alpha Mate, it is my right to take your life, or to sentence you to life imprisonment, as in accordance with pride law."

Apparently that witch is powerful enough to sever his ties to his pride, Hugh realizes as he listens to his mate's rejection. This is the final straw. There is no more time to wait for the other human to kill the witch. Hugh has to find a way to break Sean's control over DeMatteo. Hugh has only one way to convince DeMatteo that he is his true mate: it's now or never.

Sean ~ 10 a.m.

After a quick shower, Sean and DeMatteo are getting dressed to go to the airport. Sean had been surprised when he learned DeMatteo had a private plane; his firm had a plane to shuttle attorneys out to their clients in other states and for the occasional wooing of a client, but this kind of extravagance is on a whole other level.

"Exactly how rich are you?" Sean asks when DeMatteo informs him they are leaving from his private airfield.

"We will be comfortable; I can't give you an exact figure, but our finances are stable," DeMatteo replies as he selects a dark navy suit.

Sean prides himself on making a decent living, but he is quickly discovering that his earnings amount to his mate's spare change.

"Well, I am glad Samantha grabbed some decent clothes from my place. What am I going to do with my condo? I doubt you want to leave here," Sean asks as he wrestles with his tie.

"We can keep it, Sean. That way, when you want to stay in the city, we can stay at our home there," DeMatteo answers as he steps up behind him, wrapping his arms around Sean's waist.

"Don't worry, mate. Everything will be fine. Let's go." DeMatteo swats his ass as he steps back to grab his jacket.

The ride is quick; Sean watches the scenery pass by and he is struck by the thought that he is going to be a father of three. That was the one detail that he had not shared with DeMatteo, that on the day he received his tattoo, he had seen that they were having three sons.

It's not as though he wants to hide anything; he just doesn't want to get his hopes up if his vision is not accurate. He figures he will tell DeMatteo after the wedding, maybe at a romantic dinner, once the number has been confirmed.

"Ready to go, love?" DeMatteo squeezes his hand, pulling Sean out of his daydream. Thankfully Tien had taught him how to avoid projecting his thoughts, allowing Sean the ability to keep some things to himself.

As they take their seats, Sean can't seem to wipe the ridiculous smile off his face. "This is nice, DeMatteo. I've never taken a private plane for personal reasons."

DeMatteo ~

"And now you own one," DeMatteo jokes as he takes his seat beside his mate. Reaching over to rub Sean's belly, a feeling of peace and happiness sweeps through him. He can't believe he gets to have this; he only wishes his parents could have lived to meet their grandchildren.

"As soon as Dr. Santiago gets here we will be ready for takeoff, Alpha." The stewardess addresses DeMatteo and he can tell that she will soon be going into heat. Before he can warn her off, Sean growls a low and dangerous warning. Without removing his hand from Sean's belly, DeMatteo bares his fangs. The stewardess immediately bares her throat.

"Forgive me, Alpha. I meant no disrespect."

DeMatteo continues to soothe his mate even as he grumbles to the shifter, "I realize you are from the Texas pride, but surely you can scent our mate bond."

"Forgive me; I assumed he was a comfort mate. I apologize," the stewardess says, trembling; the acrid scent of fear fills the cabin as the young female realizes the depth of her mistake. Heat or no heat the female shifter can surely scent that they are together, even if Sean was only a human companion mate it would have been wildly inappropriate for her to flirt with the Alpha in his mate's presence.

"It would be wise if you remain in the back for the duration of this flight," DeMatteo warns. After watching the hapless woman tripping over herself to get away, DeMatteo senses his brother's arrival.

Timothy pushes his bags into the overhead compartment. "Sorry I'm late," he mumbles as he flops in his seat.

"Funny how the women managed to get here on time, but you—as always—came late." DeMatteo teases.

Timothy's cheeks grow red as he splutters, "Well, I am the only one that could deliver the cubs. There are three new Beta females in the pride, I might add."

Sean ~

Once airborne, conversations go smoothly. Sean is able to relax since he no longer has to deal with some female drooling all over his mate.

The six-hour flight goes so smoothly that it isn't until they were stepping off the plane at JFK that Sean remembers he is about to face his father and stepmother to try to explain the sudden changes his life has taken. Pure panic races through Sean as he wonders if his family will accept his mate and his new sexual orientation. Before his fear completely spirals out of control, Sean feels both DeMatteo and Timothy trying to calm him.

DeMatteo places his hand on his lower back. *Easy, mate. You are starting to shift.* DeMatteo's voice drifts into his mind as he stands in front of Sean, blocking him from any human's view.

Taking several deep breaths, Sean concentrates on DeMatteo's scent and heartbeat to help him relax. Once he feels confident he has his lioness under control, Sean tells his mate, "Let's go straight to the hotel and let the others get the bags."

Without a word, DeMatteo wraps his arm around his mate's shoulders and steers him towards the limo that is waiting, leaving his siblings to handle everything else. Sean does not speak again until they are inside the vehicle and pulling into traffic.

"I'm sorry, DeMatteo, but I couldn't help it. I started worrying about my parents and it just happened." Sean can't remember a time in his life where he felt less in control of his own body.

DeMatteo ~

DeMatteo doesn't want to frighten his mate, but he has never felt the kind of power that is radiating off the man. It is pouring off of him in such powerful waves that even he has trouble being close to his mate. "We will contact Tien when we reach the hotel. Hopefully she will know a way to help you control your magic," DeMatteo whispers, pulling Sean further in his arms.

It is early evening when they finally arrive at the Four Seasons, and as they make their way to the desk, Sean can't help but gape at the beautiful architecture. "I have a reservation. Matthew Santiago." His mate's voice snaps Sean out of his trance.

"Yes, sir, I see you have the Ty Warner penthouse for two weeks. Oh, and I see you also have a wedding this weekend. Will you or the bride need any special services at the spa? We can schedule you at any time."

The bubbly receptionist is almost drooling as she bats her eyelashes. Sean can feel his annoyance at yet another woman blatantly pursuing DeMatteo. Consciously, he knows that the man is beautiful, so he shouldn't be surprised that people pursue him, but this is seriously starting to piss him off.

"There is no bride, but I am sure my fiancé will call down to schedule his appointments," DeMatteo replies coolly as he slides his arm around Sean.

"Yes, sir. Of course, sir. Your concierge, Mark, will take you to your quarters. Congratulations, gentlemen, and welcome to The Four Seasons."

He has never seen someone's eyes get as round as this woman's does. He can't even get upset, seeing as the woman is so red it seems her head might explode. He offers her what he knows is a shit-eating smile as they follow the concierge towards the private penthouse elevators.

"The penthouse? Really, DeMatteo, this is too much. You didn't have to do all of this," Sean says as he leans into his broad chest, but DeMatteo can sense that his mate is pleased that he is so well provided for.

"Nothing is too good for my family," DeMatteo purrs into his ear, while snaking a hand around to touch his still flat stomach.

"Besides, this will be our honeymoon suite, and I want you to have the best of everything," he finishes just as they step into the room.

Walking inside, Sean knows his mouth is on the floor as Mark gives them a tour. The penthouse is over four thousand square feet with floor-to-ceiling windows. There is a three-hundred-and-sixty-degree view of the city and four glass balconies.

"Your stay includes a twenty-four-hour personal butler; I will be at your service for twelve hours, and Chris will replace me tomorrow. You also have access to a Rolls-Royce chauffeur, an art concierge, personal trainers, all-inclusive access to the spa and dining venues, and unlimited international telephone calls. What time would you like your turndown service?" Mark walks from room to room, all without missing a beat.

"Nine will be good. Are our reservations for dinner confirmed?" DeMatteo asks.

"Yes, sir. Dinner at eight thirty for four at the TY bar. Will that be all, gentlemen?"

"Yes, that is all. Goodnight," DeMatteo answers as he hands him a roll of bills.

"Thank you, sir, and please call me if you need anything."

"Wow. Just wow!" Sean exclaims as he takes in the fabulous view of the New York skyline.

DeMatteo wraps his arms around his mate, pulling Sean's back tight to his chest. "I'll take this to mean you are pleased with our honeymoon suite," he says as he places love bites on the strong column of Sean's neck.

"Yes, this is perfect," Sean says as he turns to face DeMatteo. "Thank you, baby. You've made everything so amazing. I can't believe I am about to be Mr. Santiago." Sean gives his mate a mischievous look before whispering against his lips, "But first you have to meet the parents."

Sean chuckles at DeMatteo's pained groan. They have just enough time to clean up and relax a little before going downstairs to meet Sean's father and stepmother for dinner.

Chapter 15

Sean ~ July 22, Wednesday, 7:50 p.m.

"Good evening, gentlemen. My name is Kevin, and welcome to the Ty Bar, do you have a reservation?" the maître d' greets them as soon as they stop at the podium.

"Santiago," DeMatteo replies as Sean scans the dining room, searching for his father.

"Yes, sir, I see you've requested the private dining area. Your reservation is for four, and your guests are already seated. I see you have security; will they be dining as well?" Kevin asks as he peers at the hulking shifters that accompany the Alpha Pair.

"No, that is not necessary," DeMatteo replies. As they make their way towards the private dining area, Sean struggles not to fidget. How is he going to explain the sudden and dramatic twist his life has taken?

As soon as they reach the table, Sean's stepmother pulls him into a tight embrace, which helps calms Sean's nerves as they take their seats. Introductions are easy, and Sean is happy to see that his parents don't even blink when another man is at the table. It seems that he has completely underestimated his dad.

After their food arrives, Sean notices his father watching him out of the corner of his eye. "Is everything okay, Dad?" Sean asks, hoping that his parents are indeed taking the news as well as it seems.

"Well, Sean, I was hoping that you would have told me the truth, but I guess it isn't just your truth to tell. Isn't that right, DeMatteo?" Frank says, looking directly at DeMatteo.

Sean's mind blanks as he fails to comprehend his father's words. *What the fuck?* Sean asks his mate through their link.

I have no idea, DeMatteo answers cautiously as he calmly eyes Frank. Frank's dramatic sigh causes Sean to refocus on his stern expression.

"Well, I guess I am going to have to force the truth out of you two. Sean, do you remember your Aunt Ruby? I was down to see her a few months ago."

Unable to follow his father's logic, Sean answers, "Yes, I remember crazy Aunt Ruby. What does she have to do with you thinking I'm lying about something?"

Frank looks at his wife before answering. "Well, she told me about this, you getting married to a man. Or should I say mated with a shifter?"

Sean's heart nearly stops, and he feels both his mate and his enforcers bristle.

"Calm down, everyone. Before anyone gets upset I think I need to tell the rest of this story," Sean's stepmother, Rebecca, jumps in. "Sean, your Aunt Ruby and mother come from a long line of seers. Both your mother and aunt saw your fate before you were born. Your mother also knew that she would die trying to protect you, but she loved you so much and knew you would be okay."

Sean couldn't breathe; how could this be true? "Dad, what is going on? Is this true? How do you know all this, Rebecca?"

DeMatteo's presence in his mind is the only thing keeping Sean from shifting, his lioness needing to protect him and the cubs. His pulse races, and sweat breaks out on his skin. He feels his lioness restlessly pacing in his mind, wanting him to flee the stressful conversation.

Rebecca grabs his hand. "Son, calm down. This is the truth. You and your mate can scent that I am telling the truth."

And he does; he scents her honesty and love as easily as he hears his own heart rate escalate and his breath stutter.

"Before your mother died, she told your father all of this. She also told him how to meet me. There was a little girl around twelve years old that died at the exact moment your mom died. They were able to bring her back, or they thought they did. Her spirit was too weak to continue, but I was strong. Sean, baby, I am your mother."

DeMatteo ~

DeMatteo can't decide if he is furious that they have hid this from his mate or grateful that Sean's parents know about the supernatural—until his mate tries to stand, only to collapse. Fury quickly wins out as he cradles his unconscious mate.

"Call Timothy!" DeMatteo barks at Kyle, one of his enforcers, who is already on his phone.

"He is on his way; he should be here in five minutes," someone answers.

But Sean is already starting to stir as his parents gather around him, concern and fear rolling from them as they call for Sean to wake up. DeMatteo can't suppress his growl as they reach for Sean.

"He is *my* son," Rebecca rebuts stubbornly, as she grabs onto Sean's hand.

"Yes, your son, but he is *mine*, *my mate*, and I will not allow you to cause him any more harm," DeMatteo growls back.

Sean's eyes open. "I'm okay, love. Rebecca… Mom, I'm alright," he whispers weakly. Sean clutches her hand as he pulls himself out of DeMatteo's arms.

It's a struggle not to pick up his mate and rush him back to their makeshift den, but DeMatteo knows that Sean needs time to confront the parents that have hidden so much from him.

DeMatteo was born a shifter, so he has always known of his kind and the magic users. He can't imagine what it must be like to be thrown into this world with no warning. Watching the human female closely, DeMatteo can now sense the strong magic that is radiating out of her; she must have somehow been hiding the telltale stench of magic with some sort of spell. This explains why Sean seemed so in tune with their connection from the beginning.

Our mate is more than just human, and we will be even greater together. His lion rumbles boastfully and DeMatteo has to agree, although he has no idea what being half-magic will do to their bond. He vows to speak to Tien at length and find out exactly what she has envisioned.

Sean ~

"Mom, is this true? Why didn't you tell me?" he asks, not trying to disguise the pain he feels at being left to believe his mother was dead.

"When I died, the Goddess told me that you were destined to fight in a great battle. She said you were going to need the support of all those who love you to succeed. I was given the opportunity to return to prepare you, but I was not allowed to tell you until after your mating. You had to get here on your own," Rebecca answers as tears roll down her face.

Sean can't be angry with the woman who has always loved him. As he pulls her into his embrace, they both weep, crying tears of regret and sadness and of love and forgiveness.

Timothy eases into the room. "Excuse me. I was told Sean needed me," he hedges, obviously unsure of how to proceed with the humans in the room.

"Yes, the Alpha Mate passed out while talking with his parents. I want you to make sure both he and the cubs are okay," DeMatteo answers gruffly. Sean wants to chastise his mate on his behavior, but right now all he can focus on is that somehow his mother is alive.

"Cubs? What do you mean, cubs?" Rebecca stammers as she holds Sean tight to her bosom.

"Uh… Mom, Dad, I'm pregnant!" The room becomes deadly silent as Sean glances at his stunned parents.

Timothy breaks the stillness by walking toward the Alpha Mate while pushing out his calming influence. "I just need to check your vitals," Timothy states once he reaches them.

"Yes. Yes. I'll wait over here," Rebecca stammers as she backs away toward her abandoned seat.

Sean pleads with his mate through their bond to smooth things over with his parents. There are a lot of secrets between them, but he is desperate to keep them in his and his cubs' lives.

"Mr. and Mrs. Davis, after Timothy is done, we should retire to our suite. There is a lot we need to discuss," DeMatteo says.

"Yes, that is a great idea. And call us Mom and Dad," Frank answers, looking DeMatteo straight in the eyes. Sean releases a breath he hadn't even realized he was holding. Maybe things are going to be alright.

"So, Sean, you're pregnant?" Rebecca asks as she moves closer to her only child.

Sean smiles softly as he watches his step… no, his mother reach for his nonexistent baby bump as if she wants to touch but isn't sure she is allowed. While there are so many questions he wants to ask, he figures his surprise is the only thing on his parents' mind.

"There's not much there yet, but you can touch me," Sean offers as he closes the distance until her hand is pressing gently against his stomach.

DeMatteo ~

DeMatteo figures it is a good idea to let Sean and his mother have a few moments alone, and he needs to speak with Frank to find out the entire story. He needs to know how this will affect his children. "Mr. Davis, you look like you could use a drink."

"Yes. Do you have any bourbon?" It is clear that, although outwardly poised, Frank is still reeling from the pregnancy shocker. "So explain to me how my son is pregnant. I mean, I thought I hit the limit when I learned that my dead wife's soul had ended up in a young girl's body, but this has taken strange to a whole new level."

DeMatteo slowly sips his drink as he tries to find the words to explain magic and mating, things that even he doesn't understand. It's just something he has always known to be true, but then, Sean is something else altogether.

"I understand he is part magic, but even my wife was stunned. I mean, where is it even gonna come out of?" Frank continues, grimacing.

"Yes, it is magic. True mated male shifters have always given birth. But this is one secret that we have kept from everyone. There has never been any written record because our descendants always feared what humans would do with this knowledge. As for the birth, it will not be so different from how females birth their cubs."

Even as he fears the human's reaction and possible rejection, he refuses to be anything but honest. His mate would expect no less.

DeMatteo watches with slight amusement as the blood drains from his father-in-law's face as he comes to the right conclusion of how his grandchildren will be born.

Quickly draining his glass, Frank stands up. "I think I'm going to need another drink."

"Yes. This is indeed a cause for celebration," DeMatteo quips before grabbing his glass.

It takes several hours, but in the end, Sean's parents go back to their suite excited at the prospect of being grandparents.

Sean ~

"So while we are already dealing with one crisis, tell me what happened with Hugh earlier today," Sean says after his parents leave.

DeMatteo rubs his hands across his face and makes a pained sound as he takes a seat across from Sean.

"Well, that doesn't inspire much confidence." Sean grimaces just thinking of that man. He's sure there is some jealousy, but mostly Sean felt unease around the other shifter.

His lioness sees Hugh as a threat to them and their cubs' safety, and she is constantly demanding that Sean eliminate the enemy. While Sean does not completely understand his lioness, he understands that thought because even his human senses are on constant alert around Hugh.

"The hearing went a little worse than I anticipated. It appears Hugh is more unstable and dangerous than I first believed."

Sean pulls up his legs and wraps his arms around himself, as if he needs to hold himself together to hear any more. DeMatteo can tell that his mate is fighting his lioness for control; the fact that he is winning impresses him.

Sean has adapted to and gained control over his lioness quickly. DeMatteo had been warned that it could be years before his mate would be stable in high stress situations, but like with everything else, Sean proves to be the exception.

"He is convinced that he is my mate and that you somehow have me and my lion under some kind of spell. He is completely irrational, going as far as to lunge after me in an attempt to mate bite me."

DeMatteo reaches out to squeeze his mate's hand when Sean sucks in a surprised breath and starts shaking in both fear and anger at the attempt to break their mate bond.

"I was obviously able to subdue him," DeMatteo states when he notices Sean glancing at his shoulder. "But there is no chance that he will be able to stay with the pride. Samantha and Timothy are both in favor of putting him down as a feral shifter, but I am having him shipped to my uncle to pass final judgement. My lion is too tempted to kill the asshole for me to be able to render an impartial judgement."

"Why?" Sean demands, his lioness hissing her disapproval of the rival's life being spared. Sean wants to rip that fucker's throat out. To actually try to mate bite his mate? Fuck no! Now that shit is taking things way too far. Hugh has announced, beyond a reasonable doubt, that he is a rival set on stealing Sean's mate.

"Hugh has made some friends in the shifter community. Any hints of a wrongful kill could lead others to believe you coerced me to be rid of your rival. I will not have this cause any more damage to the pride than it already has."

Sean takes a deep breath, and then another, before he trusts his voice. "Okay. But until then, where will he be?" His eyes flash Alpha Mate orange with his annoyance, but his mate is right. Being the Alpha Pair means they have to act with due process and not let their emotions rule them.

"He will stay in his cell with a guard twenty-four seven. I would rip his throat out with my bare hands before he ever got close to you or the cubs."

Sean all but crawls into the larger man's lap; hearing his worst fears all but confirmed leaves both him and his lioness unsettled. They both need the comfort and safety of their Alpha; the stress of the day has Sean wanting to hurt someone.

Before the mating, Sean never cuddled just for the sake of contact with his lovers. But between his lioness and his cubs, Sean needs the comfort of his mate and his pride.

Learning that he would also have his parents to lean on has taken an extra weight off his shoulders.

DeMatteo ~

"Come on, little one, let's get you to bed," DeMatteo says, gathering the smaller man in his arms.

Gently setting him on the edge of the mattress, DeMatteo carefully undresses his mate before stripping off his own clothes. Even his fastidious lion seems unconcerned as he tosses their clothing across the room and shuffles Sean under the covers. Pulling Sean in close, DeMatteo wraps himself around his mate's smaller frame.

"Just sleep, Sean. I will take care of it. Just trust me and sleep."

Sean entwines their fingers, pulling them up to kiss DeMatteo's knuckles. "I trust you with my life."

DeMatteo just kisses the back of his head, smiling that he is able to comfort his mate.

Chapter 16

Sean ~ July 23, Thursday, 6 a.m.

It isn't often that Sean is awake before DeMatteo, but his increasing appetite is starting to dictate more of his life, so he takes a few seconds to watch his mate sleeping. So much has changed since that day DeMatteo walked into that conference room, but he wouldn't change one second if it meant losing his mate.

"It's creepy when you stare at me like that," DeMatteo says, voice rough with sleep.

Sean brushes the hair off DeMatteo's forehead. "You're creepy," Sean jokes.

DeMatteo's eyes sleepily blink open. Looking at his mate, Sean feels that familiar fluttering in his chest as he sees DeMatteo's breathtaking smile.

"So, Mr. Herr, are you ready for me to make an honest man out of you?"

"I was an honest man until you left me in a motherly way." Sean's easy smile shows how he truly feels about his current situation.

"Yeah, I did." DeMatteo leers as he smooths his hands over his barely-there baby bump.

Sean stills those wandering appendages. "Hey now, we have too much to do today. We don't have time for any shenanigans."

DeMatteo wrinkles his nose. "Shenanigans? Really?" He shakes his head fondly.

"That's right, so keep your hands above the waist, Alpha."

DeMatteo ~

DeMatteo's gaze darkens as he reaches up to gently pinch one of Sean's nipples, causing his mate to suck in a sharp breath.

"Now, now. You said to stay above the waist."

Ignoring his mate completely, Sean immediately pushes his chest further into DeMatteo's hand as the little nub pebbles with the attention.

"You know that you are not playing fair, right?"

"Yes," DeMatteo concedes easily.

DeMatteo just watches, mesmerized as his mate purrs and coos as he teases one nipple then the other until each one is swollen and red. With a stuttered moan, Sean grabs his free hand and shoves it onto his erection.

"If you are going to touch me, then do it right..." Sean rubs up against DeMatteo's hand.

"I am touching you. I thought you wanted me to stay above the waist?" DeMatteo chuckles at his mate's obvious frustration.

"God, DeMatteo would you just stop playing around and fuck me?"

DeMatteo leans over to capture one of those abused nipples. "So now you want me to do this?"

DeMatteo grins up at his mate without detaching from the task at hand, and reaches down to stroke Sean's cock properly. Sean's hips jerk up, seeking more and earning him a sharp nip before DeMatteo finally releases him to trail kisses down his chest.

DeMatteo sucks at Sean's cock through his boxers until his jaw aches and Sean is begging. Satisfied with the incoherent babble streaming from his mate, DeMatteo finally relents, ripping the offending fabric and flipping the sobbing man onto his belly.

"Shit, DeMatteo," Sean moans.

DeMatteo pulls away long enough to slide a second finger into his mate. Sean is sloppily wet; the squelching sounds are obscene as DeMatteo shoves both fingers in as far as they can reach. Just when DeMatteo thinks it can't get better, a distinctive scent permeates the air.

A thick, slick liquid starts to slide out of Sean and around DeMatteo's fingers. DeMatteo had hoped this would happen before the birth, but there had been no guarantee. His mate is self-lubricating outside of birth or his heat.

"DeMatteo. DeMatteo!" Sean screams.

The edge of fear in his mate's voices pulls DeMatteo out of the stupor he has been in as he watches more and more of the lubricant squeeze out of his mate's hole.

"What the hell is that, DeMatteo?" Sean squeaks out as another dollop of fluid drips out of him and soaks his thighs. DeMatteo dips in for a taste, and the honey sweet liquid has him licking and sucking at the spasming muscle.

Sean ~

Sean groans and licks his lips; it's pointless to pretend he isn't into this. His painfully hard dick alerts his mate to exactly how much Sean aches for his touch. Sean pushes his head further into the pillows, trying desperately to muffle the screams that are crawling up the back of his throat. He gasps and writhes as DeMatteo eats him out; one finger joins his tongue, bent on pushing an orgasm out of him.

"You are perfect. That is your body craving me, Sean," DeMatteo growls around a mouthful of fangs. Sean is eternally grateful that his mate's fingernails have remained mercifully blunt, especially considering their current location.

"You're getting all wet for me like a bitch in heat."

The words should have embarrassed him. Hell, being called an animal should have pissed him off. But instead of righteous indignation, Sean feels even more turned on by his mate's crude language.

"Oh my god, yes!" Sean shouts as he pushes back on those devious digits, needing his mate on him, and in him, immediately. Spreading his legs as far as they will go, Sean proceeds to clench and grind, silently begging his mate to give them both what they need.

"Yes, baby, just like that. You are so greedy for it. Your hungry little hole just begging for my cock. Say it, baby. Tell me how much you need it."

DeMatteo ~

DeMatteo tries desperately to think of anything to hold himself back from slamming his painfully hard dick into his mate. His good intentions are swept aside when Sean slams back on his fingers, whining high in his throat. It's that sound that finally breaks DeMatteo's control. It's urgent and desperate, and DeMatteo's lion instantly breaks free from deep inside. Their mate is begging… their mate needs.

"Jesus, DeMatteo, please."

DeMatteo kneels back and slowly teases Sean's rim, trying to give himself a second to calm down. He can feel that his fangs have already dropped and his fingertips tingle with the threat of claws.

"I'm gonna have to knot you."

"Yes, please, I want that. I want you to knot me," Sean gasps out as he tilts his hips higher in offering.

DeMatteo's hands shake with how desperately he wants to slam into the slighter man, but this is his mate—his mate who is with cubs—and he deserves to be treated with care.

DeMatteo winces slightly and sucks in a breath as he eases the head of his cock in. Sean shifts his hips, stuttering out a moan as DeMatteo circles his hips and buries himself inside of his lover.

"Fuck! Shit, shit, baby, you are still so tight. You're going to squeeze my dick off," DeMatteo groans as he bottoms out.

Sean is too far gone for words; he can only manage to tighten around the length, and gasp out various attempts of his mate's name.

DeMatteo squeezes his mate's hip right before he slowly pulls out, letting Sean feel every inch before shoving back in. Sean rewards him with a quick intake of breath, followed by a barely spoken, "Oh god." Satisfied with his mate's comfort, DeMatteo sets a quicker pace, drilling into his mate's sweet spot over and over again.

"Oh god… DeMatteo. Shit!"

"You like that, baby?" DeMatteo asks pushing in deeper.

"Fuck yes! Harder, baby, fuck me harder. I won't break."

DeMatteo's claws finally break free as he grasps his mate tighter, given the green light to fuck the man just like his lion wants. Little beads of blood well up at the points of his claws as he begins to pound in, growling in appreciation as he feels Sean clench down.

"Son of a bitch!" Sean bellows out after a particularly hard thrust.

DeMatteo leans over his mate as he feels the familiar tingle of his knot forming. He is reduced to smaller thrusts to keep from injuring his mate. Careful of his claws, DeMatteo reaches around Sean to quickly jack his cock.

It only takes three pulls and Sean's cock jerks in his hand, spraying his ejaculate all over the sheets. DeMatteo bites deep into his mate's shoulder, holding him still as his knot quickly swells, tying them together. Sean moans and his cock feebly attempts to fill again as DeMatteo's barbs latch onto his prostate.

DeMatteo guides them both to their sides for the remainder of the knot. Sean pushes closer to him, and DeMatteo pulls his arms around his mate's barely there belly. Content to bask in the afterglow, he will take great care to lick Sean clean as soon as they separate.

It takes about a half an hour before he can pull away without injuring his mate, but as soon as he pulls free, DeMatteo crawls down to lap at that abused rim. He loves the musky taste of Sean's seed where it's rolled down to his perineum. All too soon Sean is pushing at his head, and DeMatteo gives up his treat, not wanting to hurt the sleepy human.

DeMatteo has just rolled off the bed to get towels to clean the rest of their mess when he hears the fluttering of a tiny heartbeat. Holding his breath, he returns to the bed and presses his ear closer to his mate's belly. What had once been one has now blossomed into three distinct, rapid heartbeats.

His cubs.

Sean ~

Sean grumbles and attempts to roll onto his stomach to avoid being woken by his suddenly over-affectionate mate, but the constant purring rumble that his mate always provides ratchets up a level.

"What's the matter?" Sean mutters, refusing to open his eyes.

"I can hear them. I can hear the cubs' heartbeats," DeMatteo says, his voice warbling over the word.

Sean shoots up, instantly awake. "You can? How many? How many hearts can you hear?"

"Three."

"Oh my god! Three! Are you sure? Be sure DeMatteo."

DeMatteo presses his ear to his mate's belly and concentrates on separating the various sounds until he can focus on the three strong heartbeats.

"I'm sure, baby. We're having three cubs."

Sean tries to blink away the stinging in his eyes, but between the shock and joy of learning they would be having three babies and the sound of awe in his mate's voice, it's impossible to hold the tears back.

"Holy shit! We're going to be dads. We are going to be dads for three babies. Holy fuck! How are we going to care for three babies? I'm gonna get huge!" Sean laughs hysterically.

Sean's babbling reaches levels of panic when three small, barely noticeable family bonds open. He instantly quiets when three tiny pulses of affection come towards him with a whispered call.

Mother.

"What the—? DeMatteo, I heard them. They called me mother. How is this possible?" Sean breathes out as he feels the familiar fluttering that indicates that the babies are moving.

Though this was happening more and more and the intensity is growing, it is still strangely comforting each time. Sean has struggled with the idea of how much faster cubs develop. Since they are in lion form, they grow much faster than human children.

Luckily they won't gain the most weight until the very end, but mentally they will be as smart as the average one-year-old. Even though they won't be able to open their eyes for the first few days, they will immediately walk on all four paws.

They won't be able to maintain their human form until they are at least three months old, but Sean has been warned that most shifter babies prefer to stay in their more mobile lion form. He had worried about not being able to communicate with them always being lions, but that seems to be a moot point now, since they can already communicate in the womb.

DeMatteo ~

"It's just like our bond. It's not words; it's more like feelings. Being their mother allows you to sense their well-being," DeMatteo offers, though he still can't take his eyes off his mate's belly.

DeMatteo has known his mate was pregnant, has watched his stomach slowly swell, and has noticed the subtle change of his scent. But hearing the heartbeat and feeling the bond form is amazing and something DeMatteo hadn't been sure he would ever have.

"I wish I could hear them." Sean doesn't mean to pout, but he can't help it. It seems so unfair that DeMatteo gets to hear their children's heartbeats before he can.

DeMatteo snorts. "You can. Concentrate on your lioness's hearing; listen through her senses."

Sean ~

With no small amount of coaching, Sean is able to shift just his hearing into that of his lioness. Slowly everything fades away until he is left with just the sounds of his children's hearts beating. Tears spill unchecked as he reaches for that tiny bond to which he whispers, *I love you.*

Pulling his senses back, Sean is surprised to see that his mate is also crying silently as he watches him.

"Thank you, baby." DeMatteo presses into his lips with barely there kisses.

"For what?"

"For accepting me and the bond, for loving me and giving me our children. I had always hoped, but I don't think I ever really believed that I'd find you. You have made me the happiest man on the planet, and I plan on spending the next few thousands of years of my supernaturally long life showing you how much I love you."

Sean blinks. That has to be the single most romantic thing anyone has ever said to him. He doesn't know how to express that DeMatteo means just as much to him, had given him that and so much more. What he ends up with is: "God, I love you, DeMatteo. Thank you for that, and more."

Luckily, that is enough. As he pulls his mate into his embrace, Sean feels love and adoration, both from his mate and their cubs. DeMatteo pulls Sean close, laying his hands protectively around his belly and kissing and nuzzling his neck until Sean drifts back to sleep, feeling cherished and safe.

Chapter 17

Sean ~ July 24, Friday, 10 a.m.

Sean attempts to hide his nerves as they wait for the ceremony to begin. He never imagined that all his friends and family, and a good portion of the pride, would fly out to be at his wedding. It's a heartwarming gesture that makes him both ecstatic and nervous.

"Are you ready, son?" Frank asks as the first notes of the wedding march begin.

"Yes," Sean answers honestly; he's nervous, but he is more than ready to start his life with DeMatteo.

Frank claps him on the back, all smiles as he says, "Well, let's get you married then." Sean tries to hide his grin as he steps out into the wedding hall.

But it's useless, his grin spreads wider as he looks to his left and sees DeMatteo being escorted by his uncle. They had decided that since there is no woman in the marriage, they will simply stand together in front of the priest.

Frank and Richard each stand two paces behind the grooms as a sign of support and to bear witness to the handfasting ritual.

The priest is already waiting as they arrive. It isn't until Sean sees him tilt his head in submission that he realizes the priest is also a shifter.

The priest clears his throat, getting the room's attention before starting the ceremony.

"We have come together here in celebration of the joining of DeMatteo Santiago and Sean Herr. There are many things to say about marriage, much wisdom concerning the joining together of two souls has come our way through all paths of belief, and from many cultures. With each union, more knowledge is gained and more wisdom gathered."

DeMatteo ~

DeMatteo can hear his mate's heat rate ratchet up as the priest begins the ceremony that will not only bind them as mates, but also make their relationship legally binding in the human world.

"Though we are unable to give all this knowledge to these two who stand before us, we can hope to leave with them the knowledge of love and its strengths and the anticipation of the wisdom that comes with time. The law of life is love unto all beings. Without love, life is nothing; without love, death has no redemption. Love is anterior to Life, posterior to Death, initial of Creation and the exponent of Earth. If we learn no more in life, let it be this: to love.

"Marriage is a bond to be entered into only after considerable thought and reflection. As with any aspect of life, it has its cycles, its ups and its downs, its trials and its triumphs. With full understanding of this, these grooms have come here today to be joined as one in marriage. Others would ask at this time, who gives one of the grooms in marriage? But as no person is property to be bought and sold, given and taken, I ask simply if they come of their own will and if they have their family's blessing?"

The priest raises his arms over the couple.

"Grooms, is it true that you each come of your own free will and accord?"

Both men reply, "Yes, it is true."

"With whom do you come and whose blessings accompany you?"

Frank steps up near the couple and announces, "Sean comes with me, his father, and is accompanied by all of his family's blessings," before stepping back to his place.

Richard steps forward and announces, "DeMatteo comes with me, his uncle, and is accompanied by all of his family's blessings."

After both men retake their places, the priest continues. "Please join hands with your intended and listen to that which I am about to say." The priest clasps their hands in his before saying. "Above you are the stars; below you are the stones. As time doth pass, remember... Like a stone should your love be firm; like a star should your love be constant. Let the powers of the mind and of the intellect guide you in your marriage, let the strength of your wills bind you together, let the power of love and desire make you happy, and the strength of your dedication make you inseparable. Be close, but not too close. Possess one another, yet be understanding. Have patience with one another, for storms will come, but they will pass quickly."

Letting go of their hands, the priest then blesses their rings before continuing.

"Be free in giving affection and warmth. Have no fear and let not the ways of the unenlightened give you unease, for God is with you always. DeMatteo, I have not the right to bind thee to your mate. Only you have this right. If it be your wish, say so at this time and place your ring in his hand."

DeMatteo can only smile at his mate, speaking the words he has felt since the moment he laid eyes on the man. "It is my wish."

"Sean, if it be your wish for your mate to be bound to you, place the ring on your finger." Sean's hands tremble as he slips the ring onto his finger. He can hear both his lioness and their children purring in excitement through the bond.

"Sean, I have not the right to bind thee to your mate. Only you have this right. If it be your wish, say so at this time and place your ring in his hand."

Sean's eyes flash Alpha Mate orange as he presents his token to DeMatteo. "It is my wish."

"DeMatteo, if it be your wish for your mate to be bound to you, place the ring on your finger." DeMatteo's eyes flash Alpha red in response as he slips on his ring, feeling grateful their backs are to the audience so none of the humans can see their eyes shifting.

Smiling broadly, the priest's voice rings out, "DeMatteo, repeat after me: I, DeMatteo Santiago, in the name of the spirit of God that resides within us all, by the life that courses within my blood and the love that resides within my heart, take thee Sean Herr to my hand, my heart, and my spirit, to be my chosen one. To desire thee and be desired by thee, to possess thee, and be possessed by thee, without sin or shame, for naught can exist in the purity of my love for thee. I promise to love thee wholly and completely without restraint, in sickness and in health, in plenty and in poverty, in life and beyond, where we shall meet, remember, and love again. I shall not seek to change thee in any way. I shall respect thee, thy beliefs, thy people, and thy ways as I respect myself."

DeMatteo repeats the words loudly, with a hint of Alpha in his voice, proud to be claiming his mate in front of so many witnesses.

"Sean, repeat after me: I, Sean Herr, in the name of the spirit of God that resides within us all, by the life that courses within my blood, and the love that resides within my heart, take thee, DeMatteo Santiago to my hand, my heart, and my spirit to be my chosen one. To desire and be desired by thee, to possess thee and be possessed by thee, without sin or shame, for naught can exist in the purity of my love for thee. I promise to love thee wholly and completely without restraint, in sickness and in health, in plenty and in poverty, in life and beyond, where we shall meet, remember, and love again. I shall not seek to change thee in any way. I shall respect thee, thy beliefs, thy people, and thy ways as I respect myself."

As Sean speaks, he is surprised that his voice stays clear and strong, although he feels choked with how much he loves his mate.

The priest then hands an old decorative chalice to DeMatteo. "May you both drink your fill from the cup of love."

DeMatteo holds the chalice to Sean while he sips from it before taking the chalice himself and holding it while DeMatteo sips. The chalice is then handed back to the priest, who sets it back onto the ceremonial alter. They repeat the process with a ceremonial bread, feeding one another.

"By the power vested in me by God and the State of New York, I now pronounce you husband and husband. May your love so endure, that its flame remains a guiding light unto you. Let us all bear witness of your consummation of this bonding with a kiss!"

Sean ~

"I can't believe we're married!" Sean whispers into his mate's ear as they sit at the reception table.

The reception is turning out to be just as beautiful as the ceremony, with Sean's parents and DeMatteo's uncle all giving speeches that don't leave a dry eye. The shifters have incorporated some of their traditions by providing the fresh game that is served to the guests.

Sean should have known something would throw a wrench into his evening, and it comes in the form of a fiery redhead calling his name. Seeing his secretary making her way to the table, Sean quickly excuses himself so they can speak properly. He has been dreading trying to explain how he had a *secret* relationship. Mary is more than just his secretary; he counts her as a dear and trusted friend. The thought of lying to her does not sit right, but he has an obligation to his mate to ensure their secret remains secret.

"Congratulations, boss. Although I can't believe you never told me about your relationship," Mary accuses as she embraces him.

"Yeah, I meant to tell you earlier but…" Sean blushes, trying to come up with a reasonable answer.

"I know coming out can be difficult. Better to make sure it's real before changing your life," Mary offers.

"Yeah, exactly... I'm really glad you understand, Mary. I always thought of you as one of my closest friends. And the woman who keeps me in a steady supply of coffee."

Mary snorts out a laugh. Yes, Sean has a lot to explain, and things will get muddier before the end, but it seems as though their friendship will survive his initiation into the supernatural.

"Well, at least now I understand why you snapped when he came into the office."

Sean almost chokes as he remembers how he had nearly ripped the poor woman's head off. "Uh... yeah about that..."

Mary halts whatever lame apology Sean is about to offer by giving his shoulder a squeeze. "Don't sweat it. I would've clawed your eyes out if the situation was reversed."

Sean laughs long and loud; she has absolutely no idea how true that statement is. Before she can question him further, DeMatteo appears beside him, wrapping his arms protectively around his new husband. It is obvious that something has the shifter on alert, so Sean smiles at his friend before making an excuse to leave.

"Sure thing, boss. You two have *fun* on your honeymoon." Mary grabs Sean back for a quick hug that he pulls away from quickly, feeling his mate's body stiffen with the contact.

DeMatteo wastes little time guiding Sean through the crowds and out towards the gardens, and each step plummets Sean's heart further into his stomach. Once Sean is sure no humans are in earshot, he rushes out, "What's wrong, DeMatteo?"

DeMatteo barely slows his steps as they pass another small group of what Sean suspects are humans. As soon as they are once again out of sight, DeMatteo tersely replies, "I don't know, but something is happening with the pride. People are hurt and scared. I need to get somewhere private to call in."

They are well on their way to the parking garage before the pace slows enough for Sean to ask, "How do you know?"

DeMatteo answers as he calls their security detail to inform them that they will be returning to the rooms. It is then that Sean realizes that DeMatteo has brought them out into public without their ever-present security. That alone convinces Sean that the situation is dire.

"I can feel it through the pride bonds. If you focus on it, you will feel it too," DeMatteo replies as he pulls out onto the city streets. Sean tries to get a feel for what is going on in his pride, but he can only sense jumbled emotions. While his perception isn't as clear, he too can sense all is not well back at home.

Reaching their room, Sean begins to pack. Now that he is focusing on the pride, his lioness is insisting that they need him. It's pointless to fight her directions, but Sean can't think of one thing he can do for the pride.

There is much we can do, insists the lioness.

Sean's knees almost give out as the lioness inside him lets loose a mournful howl, just as DeMatteo lets out one of his own. Ignoring his own, sudden pain, Sean races towards his mate; what he finds is enough to snap him into action.

DeMatteo stands in the middle of the living room, partially shifting, his suit ripping to shreds around his still growing muscles.

"We have to go home now, Sean. Hugh is missing, and his guard Nathaniel is dead. And my sister Carla has been shot," DeMatteo lisps angrily around a mouthful of fangs.

"Oh my god!"

Chapter 18

DeMatteo ~ July 24, Friday, 11 p.m.

DeMatteo can't believe the sight that greets him as he walks into the pride lands shifter hospital. Every shifter hospital is set up the same, with enormous beds on the floor large enough for the biggest of lions. Carla is lying in the middle of the bed, still in her human form, hooked up to various IV lines that all seem to be infusing her with blood. She looks almost lifeless and so small lying in that large shifter bed.

Timothy walks into the room after spending time with the other doctor who's treating Carla. Wordlessly, he begins adjusting the covers while letting out calming and healing Omega pheromones. The covers move and reveal that her lower body is turning an awful shade of black, with pus seeping from a multitude of wounds.

DeMatteo freezes as he instantly recognizes the telltale signs of hemlock poisoning. Carefully scenting the air, DeMatteo is hit with the same sickly sweet smell that had clung to his parents' bodies; it had taken months for the lingering scent to dissipate from the pride house.

Taking in the extent of her wounds, he realizes that it might be what kills her as well. Yes, the doctor had done well, but Timothy's abilities as an Omega might have saved the guard's life and improved his sister's condition.

DeMatteo whirls around a finger pointed accusingly at Timothy. "Why isn't she shifted? We heal faster while we are inside our lions," he snarls.

"It's pretty bad, Alpha. I'm going to do everything I can, but the bullets were coated in hemlock. This poison is geared specifically towards large cats and causes our advanced healing to work against us. So every shifter in the pride has been donating blood to keep her transfused and alive," Dr. Hammond answers as he enters the room.

He growls at the shifter as he makes his way to Carla's bed. "How the hell is that possible?" DeMatteo asks.

"Hunters have been working for years to make poisons that would be deadly to shifters. It looks like someone has finally succeeded," Timothy says.

He can feel his fangs slide into place. "Will someone please explain to me why a hunter would risk so much to kidnap Hugh? Is it possible that someone from his old pride has set this up? And how the fuck did one person get in and off pride lands undetected?" DeMatteo demands. With this many shifters in one place, how could hunters breach their perimeter?

"Alpha, from what we can see, there was no sign of struggle. It appears as if Hugh left willingly with this person; it also seems that this person had extensive knowledge of the pride lands. They avoided all guards and cameras until they entered the holding rooms."

"So you are telling me that someone in the pride, most likely Hugh, gave information to a hunter that resulted in one of my guards being killed and my sister to be shot? This is what you're telling me?"

"That is the way it appears, Alpha. Of course I'll be able to tell you more once I'm able to study the poison. With Timothy's help, I am sure we will be able to reverse the poisoning. But our initial testing indicates that somehow the hunters have been able to engineer a poison that binds to our DNA, allowing it to replicate itself as the shifter attempted to heal."

Whatever DeMatteo is about to say is interrupted as Sean bursts into the room. He ignores the three shifters as he moves towards the injured woman. After sniffing her neck, Sean lets out a hissing sound before climbing into her hospital bed.

"Sean? Baby, what are you doing?"

DeMatteo tries to pull his mate off his sister and is surprised when Sean answers with a growl of his own. Mostly shifted into his partially shifted form, Sean presses in closer, purring and rubbing his hands over every available inch of her skin as if he is assessing her damage. Sean then switches to licking Carla's face and neck as he curls his body around the wounded lion, much to DeMatteo's displeasure.

DeMatteo's jealous, possessive growl is ruined when his lion begins to whimper. Stunned, he watches as their mate continues to purr and shift into a full lioness although physically he looks more male than female. A vibrant yellow glow flows out from Sean and begins to surround the entire bed in a pulsing wave of magic.

Carla's heart monitor goes haywire as Sean's lioness aggressively grooms her. All three older shifters can only watch in awe as the black begins to recede and the worst of her injuries start to close and heal before their eyes.

"Holy shit! I've never seen anything like this!" Dr. Hammond exclaims as he takes several steps back from the pair.

"I don't think anyone has seen something like this. His magic seems to be fighting the poison and healing her," Timothy adds as he too steps away from the magic he can feel swirling around the room.

DeMatteo is forced to back away as his lion whimpers and whines. Sean's power whips through him. Not even his Aunt Tien has ever exuded this much energy. All he can do is hope that Sean's lioness is able to use so much magic without endangering his mate or cubs.

Sean's lioness whimpers in pain as their magic seems to fold back into them; it's clear that whatever was in that bullet would have surely been enough to kill Carla. DeMatteo's not sure if even being a Guardian is enough to filter the sheer volume of poison Sean seems to be drawing from her.

By the time Sean crumples to his side, he appears to be barely able to open his eyes. DeMatteo offers his mate some semblance of a reassuring smile, and Sean's mouth twitches slightly before he completely passes out.

DeMatteo ~ July 26, Sunday, 2 p.m.

"You can't seriously be considering going back to work?" DeMatteo asks as he watches his mate pulling a suit from their closet.

"Yes, I've been out on vacation for almost a month. I have to go back while there is still a job to go back to," Sean answers distractedly, choosing and discarding several shirts that have no hope of hiding his baby bump.

"No, you don't," DeMatteo says adamantly. He makes more than enough to provide for his mate and cubs; there is no reason for his mate to go back to his firm.

That seems to grab his mate's attention as Sean whirls around in an unbuttoned shirt. "Excuse me?" he asks testily.

DeMatteo may not always be the sharpest knife in the drawer, but the danger is clear and present in Sean's face so he proceeds with all due caution, "What I mean is that you don't need to go back to work. I make more than enough to support us and the cubs. Besides, you just spent almost twenty-four hours unconscious. You don't need all the added stress of working."

"You're joking, right? Please tell me you're joking. First off, I love my job. I worked my ass off to get to where I am, and I hope you don't expect me to walk away. Second, I passed out from using magic, which isn't exactly a stressor that will come up at work. There is no reason for me to stay home until I absolutely need to."

"How about the fact that Hugh and whoever helped him are still out there? If they are trying to hurt me, you will be their first choice. If they are trying to hurt you, you will be an easy target at your office, without the pride there to protect you," DeMatteo argues. "Please, Sean, I am asking you to do this for me."

"DeMatteo, I know you are worried, and so am I, but I am not going to run and hide because I think Hugh is hiding in every corner. And I am anything but an easy target. Believe it or not, I was taking care of myself long before I had a pride."

Sean ~

"That's not what I meant—" DeMatteo tries.

Sean cuts in, "No! That is exactly what you meant. You might do well to remember that I am more than capable of dealing with any threat." Sean has to pause to take a breath as the triplets start to squirm inside him.

They seem to be especially sensitive to Sean's emotions, so while he is justifiably pissed, his first instinct is to protect the lives growing inside of him. Once he is calm, he walks to where DeMatteo is leaning against the wall with his arms crossed defensively.

"But I am nothing if not a reasonable man. If it will make you feel better, I will take someone with me. That way, I am free to do my job, and you can have peace of mind knowing I have some protection."

DeMatteo fixes his jaw stubbornly, and Sean scrubs his hands down his face, preparing to appeal to DeMatteo's more rational human side.

"DeMatteo, I need you to work with me on this. I am not going to be held hostage in my own home. I need to go back to work, visit my parents, and spend time with my friends. And so do you. We have been secluded for a month; eventually we have to go back into the real world."

DeMatteo's lion reaches out through their mind link, and Sean seizes the chance to show his mate how important his sense of independence is to his happiness. He knows his mate has accepted his choice when DeMatteo deflates, huffing out a breath.

"You realize that this is our first fight since we've been married?" DeMatteo says as he gently massages Sean's shoulders.

"Yes, but it won't be our last. We are going to bump heads, even more so when these guys get here, but as long as we work as a team... Things will work out," Sean reasons as he holds his mate's gaze. "Don't think I haven't realized you didn't answer the question."

"Yes. Yes, you are right, and I agree to your stipulations. You do realize this goes against all my instincts, right? My lion just wants to bury you in the back of our den and not let anyone near you," DeMatteo confesses.

Sean smiles wide, "Yes, I know, but you will work on it because you are such a good mate and Alpha," he says, kissing DeMatteo's chin.

Not happy with that, DeMatteo pulls him closer, kissing his lips as he says, "No. I will do anything to make you happy, because I love you."

Sean returns the kiss with one of his own. "I love you too," he tells the other man as he heads back to the closet.

Sean ~ July 27, Monday, 7 a.m.

It takes nearly two hours, but Sean finally relents and pulls on one of the new suits he bought at the big and tall men's store while in New York. The drive into the city is quiet, and it doesn't take long to make it into his office.

"Oh my, looks like the prodigal son has returned," Mary proclaims as Sean walks up to her desk. Even after his recent absence, Mary is still a constant, someone he knows will always be there for him.

"But yet you have no coffee prepared for me?" he jokes.

"Yeah, because I've brought in a cup every day in hopes of your return? Not hardly. In fact, I'm out twenty bucks in the pool that you wouldn't even return to clean out your office," Mary says as she walks over to pull him into a hug.

It's awkward to keep his belly from making contact, but somehow it seems to go unnoticed. "Oh, how I've missed your special brand of sarcasm," he drones out smarmily.

"What's with the two linebackers over there?" Mary asks as she points to the shifters DeMatteo had assigned as his personal babysitters.

Sean dismisses the men with a flick of his wrist. "Oh that is David and Frederic. They are personal security specialists for me and the office."

Sean hopes that his blasé attitude would keep his friend from wondering too hard why he suddenly needs protection. It's not as if he deals with hardened criminals, and before his mating, Sean had hardly seen a fist fight—let alone a real threat.

Mary's body stiffens. "Personal security specialists? Sean, what is going on?" she asks, and this is not the conversation he wants to have. He should have known that there was no way Mary was just going to go with it with no questions.

"It's a long story, but nothing is wrong. Let's just say my husband is a security Nazi, and it is easier to go along with his OCD than it is to try to talk him out of it." He holds his breath, hoping for once his best friend just lets this go.

Mary takes her time gauging all three of them, as if she is trying to ascertain the truth without words. After a few tense seconds, her eyes soften as she offers Sean her go-to snark.

"OCD? Well, it had to be something, he seemed way too good to be real. But if overprotective is his only flaw, consider yourself blessed," she teases and Sean wants to sag in relief.

Mary pulls Sean in for a tight hug; despite what others would think from her banter, Sean can sense how happy she is to see him. After his sudden departure from the wedding, Sean hadn't had a chance to contact his oldest friend.

"So now that we've had our Lifetime TV moment, I'm going to grab you some coffee," Mary announces as she steps away from his door. She is halfway to the elevator before she seems to remember that they have guests.

"Would you gentlemen like some coffee, tea?" she asks the shifters.

"No, thank you, ma'am. We've brought our own refreshments," Frederic, the head guard, answers.

"Ma'am? Lord have mercy. Big, handsome, and well mannered? Looks like you hit the motherlode of sexy men at your beck and call." Mary sighs as she mock-swoons at the two shifters before strutting off into the elevator. Sean has to cover his mouth to keep from laughing at the shifters' scandalized looks.

"Is she always like that?" David asks, continuing to watch the now-closed elevator doors with a scandalized look.

"Yes, but that was Mary on her best behavior. She didn't want to scare the new guys," Sean answers easily as he walks into his office, leaving a stunned David and Frederic staring at his retreating form.

Sean ~ 3 p.m.

Amazingly, there is little to do in the office. His father had not been joking when he said he would keep Sean's cases up to date. So after catching up on the office gossip with Mary, Sean decides to spare his guards her unique brand of flirting by heading out to visit his parents.

Pulling up to his childhood home, Sean is still floored when he sees his mother, his birth mother reincarnated, in the front yard tending to her flowers.

"I was wondering when you would get around to visiting. After the scare you gave DeMatteo, we weren't sure he'd let you leave the house," Rebecca says, wiping the dirt off her hands.

She pulls him in for a hug as soon as he's within touching distance. "It was a close call, but really, Mom, I'm fine. It was the amount of magic I used that caused me to pass out. It's not like I even knew I could do something like that before it happened. Which leads me to part of the reason I am here," Sean says, hesitating slightly as he returns the hug. He is still trying to wrap his head around the fact that this is his birth mother's soul inside of someone else's body.

"Oh, so this isn't just a social call?"

"Mom, I'm—" Sean starts.

His mother cuts him off, "Sean, relax; I was just teasing you. What do you want to know?" she asks, taking his hand and leading him into the house.

The living room is exactly how he remembers it, and Sean has to stop and remember how long it's been since he last visited. He has spent so many years angry at his dad for just moving on so quickly after his mother's death. Now, knowing the truth, Sean hates himself just a little for being so selfish for so long.

His musings are cut short by his mother's voice. "Let's have some tea and talk," Rebecca says as she heads to the kitchen.

Sean takes a seat on the antique floral couch that his mother had purchased in Italy on her honeymoon. He remembered how his mother had adored it, and how much he hated whenever his stepmother had dared rearrange anything. Now that he knows that his stepmother is his mother, in some strange reincarnation thing he still can't understand, all his memories take on a new shape. He is just getting comfortable when she returns with drinks in hand.

She hands him a cup. "So what do you want to know?" she asks, sitting across from him in her chair.

"After I woke up, I raided DeMatteo's library looking for anything I could find about magic users, but their information was limited."

Rebecca hums, sipping her tea. "I'm not surprised. We are both children of the Goddess, shifters and humans. Shifters use a form of magic, magic that allows two souls to dwell in the same vessel and allows them to shift. The Goddess gifted both of her children with unique skills, but your type of magic is rare even among the most special of humans. They work better when we aid each other, but that is another story," she says.

"Okay, but why do I now have so much power? Tien is also a Guardian, but she has never seen anything like what happened."

"You are vastly more powerful than Tien. There has never been anyone like you or my grandchildren. And there never will be again, which is why so many have been sent in preparation to aid you," Rebecca answers with a smile.

"Aid me in what?"

"That is a path that you will need to find on your own, but I do have many things I can share with you," his mother says, holding out a set of keys.

"What are these?"

"These are the keys to the safety deposit box that holds all the information I have, and to the property you now own. You will find the deed to some land that is right outside of the pride lands. It is protected, hallowed ground. You will only be able to enter the main temple with the triplets after they are born."

His hands go to his belly. "What do my babies have to do with this?" he asks nervously.

"These things were already in process before we were born, and everything has a purpose. The Goddess has been making your path since the beginning of time, and just like the Goddess, you will have enemies that will try to stand in your way."

Sean is stunned. How is it that he has some predestined magical fate that no one has seen fit to tell him about until now? "How am I supposed to just believe in all this? Just a year ago, I was nobody, and now suddenly there are going to be people after me?" he finally gets out.

"You, my son, were never nobody. I hid your existence from the mages who were waiting for your birth. But the spells I used to hide you and suppress your magic were old, powerful spells. They weren't made for someone like me so they left me weakened, which is why I was unable to heal after the accident."

"You did all that trying to protect me? Did you know that casting that spell would kill you?" he asks and he has to know. Did his mother knowingly commit suicide trying to protect him?

Rebecca takes his hand. "Yes and no. I knew that I would die while you were young, but I did not know when or how. I used that spell to protect you. I died because I was hit by a car. But the Goddess allowed me to take this body to continue to watch over you until you mated and came into your powers," she answers, tears gathering in her eyes.

Sean wipes the tears welling up in his own eyes, "Okay. So are you going to die now that you don't have to protect me anymore?" he questions urgently.

Rebecca slides onto the couch beside him. "No. There is still a little magic left in me, and there is still much to be done for you to fulfill the prophecy. Trust yourself and trust your mate; you will find all the faith you need in time. This is all I can tell you. I don't know everything, except that you are on the path you are meant to be on," she says, kissing his forehead.

Sean laughs. "I think I liked you better before you started talking in cryptic riddles," he jokes, sitting his cup on the coffee table.

"I know I liked it better when you couldn't talk; that was the only time you didn't talk back," Rebecca rebuts.

"Ah, ten points to mother dearest."

"Now if we are done with the supernatural talk, come here and let me love on my grandbabies," Rebecca says, reaching out to touch his ever-growing stomach.

"You do realize that you're talking to your pregnant son? I don't think we'll ever be done with the supernatural."

Hugh ~ October 12, Thursday, 11 a.m.

"It has been weeks since my escape. I think it would be safe for me to get into the pride house and poison him," Hugh grinds out between clenched teeth, as he paces the shack he has been left rotting in.

He is spending all his time on the phone with his contact within the pride, keeping tabs on the witch who stole his mate. His only source of protection is the human who had rescued him from execution. They too had lost a mate to Sean and his coven.

Now Hugh just has to wait for the perfect moment to kill the witch.

"That is why I'm the one that does the thinking, Hugh. You only needed to bide your time until the poison was ready and slip it into the food of that witch that stole your mate, but no..."

Hugh stops pacing long enough to glare at the smaller woman; up until now, she has been one of the few people who has been on his side. "But you had no idea what that bastard did! He—" Hugh protests.

"I don't care what he did! I care what you did! You had to draw attention to yourself, had to get yourself captured. Do you know how much trouble it was to free you?"

Hugh grimaces as the human continues to mock him, her voice taunting him. Hugh leans against the wall, staring in shock as they pack an assortment of vials and weapons. He knew that he should have waited, but when DeMatteo had announced the witch's pregnancy, Hugh had just lost it.

Those should have been his babies; they would have been his if Sean hadn't placed a spell on DeMatteo after killing his parents. Hugh knew that if DeMatteo would just give him a chance to explain how evil Sean is, he could make him understand, but no. Sean's dark magic has tricked him into believing that Sean is his true mate.

"Do you know that now I am exposed, and that witch is probably trying to destroy me? I could have just left you to die in the cell. You know that witch would have made your mate kill you, don't you?"

Unknown female ~

"I know! I'm sorry but…" Hugh sobs as he slides to the floor.

"I don't want you to be sorry. I just want you to do as you're told! I know what it's like to lose a mate, Hugh. That is why I didn't leave you there. That is why I'm going to help you rescue your mate, the same way I wish someone had been there to save mine," his protector croons as she kneels beside the broken man.

"You're right, and I'm sorry. I just want to go with you. I want to be able to see my Alpha."

"I know, sweetheart, and if you get me close to the witch, I'll make sure you get to spend the rest of your life with DeMatteo." Placing a kiss on the shifter's head, the hunter smiles with the knowledge of just how short that life will be.

"Of course. I will get my contact to meet us. He will be able to get it into the food and call us when it's ready."

"Perfect, and after I dismember the witch's body, the spell will be broken, and DeMatteo will recognize you as his mate." It takes every ounce of strength the hunter has not to laugh at the man as he cuddles closer to his executioner.

Chapter 19

Sean ~ December 17, Thursday, 10 a.m.

Sean collapses on his side after his soft cock slides out of his mate. He has been the one taking DeMatteo as sex had become increasingly uncomfortable as the triplets started to put on weight.

Last Monday marked to start of his first week of maternity leave. Officially he is out with an injured back. He had grown to the point that there was no more hiding the fact that he is a heavily pregnant man. So from this point on, he avoids all contact with any humans other than his parents.

"So, we need to talk," Sean blurts out.

"Oh god," DeMatteo groans as he starts to roll over.

"Hey! It's not bad. Stop reacting before I even say it."

"No pleasant conversation in the history of the spoken word has ever begun with the *we need to talk*."

"You don't need to take time off work to stay home with me, DeMatteo. It's been months since Hugh's escape. He has probably left the country, and I have at least two months before the babies come."

"Maybe I just want to be home with you, or are you sick of seeing my face already?"

"Ha Ha Ha. Nice deflection. But I don't need super hearing to know you are lying. You need to have more faith in me and the pride that we can survive a few hours without our big bad Alpha to protect us."

"I trust you, Sean. I trust you with my life. More importantly, I trust you with the lives of our children. I just don't like the thought of you being unprotected. No, before you cut in, I know you can protect yourself. Even more so since you have better control of your magic and your lioness, but with you being so pregnant, I just feel like I need to be near you."

Sean cannot ignore the pleading in his mate's eyes, and with all the things that have gone wrong, it's understandable that both the man and his lion are on edge. Sean stretches out so his belly is tucked up as close as the obviously swollen bulge will allow.

"How about we make a deal? Starting tomorrow you go to work every other day for just a few hours. I will stay in the pride house with my babysitters while you're away."

"You'll stay in the house? With your guards?"

"Yes. I understand that you have used all your restraint to not be the possessive asshole your lion wants you to be, but you have responsibilities and I don't want you to lose clients," Sean sasses, just because he understands his mate's motives doesn't mean he has to pretend to like being placed under lock and key and assigned babysitters.

Either DeMatteo is choosing to ignore his comments or Sean needs to work on his sass delivery because DeMatteo just smiles and nods. "Okay," he agrees easily.

"Okay? Really? No argument?" Sean splutters.

DeMatteo shrugs. "No arguments. You are right. I do trust you," he says giving Sean a peck on the lips.

Sean can sense how hard the Alpha is struggling with his lion's instincts to allow him to have some semblance of normal. Always a fan of positive reinforcement Sean rewards DeMatteo with a decidedly less chaste kiss. "Perfect. I love you," he says once they separate.

"I don't deserve you. But I'm going to keep you, because I love you."

"Well now that you got me all dirty again, I'm going to take another shower," Sean quips. "Alone. And you can shower in your office and send out all those emails that need your attention."

"Trying to get rid of me already?"

"Yup, now that I've had my wicked way with you, I'm sending you off to make me some money," Sean says, giving DeMatteo a wink. "I am going out to work on the gardens, maybe Skype with my parents."

"Sounds perfect. I'll have Nick bring you lunch," DeMatteo says.

Nick ~ 11 a.m.

"Nick! I'm headed to my office to handle some pride business. Do me a favor and pack Sean a lunch and take it out to the gardens in about three hours."

"Of course, Alpha. Does he want anything in particular?"

"No, he isn't that picky. Just make sure the meat is rare, and take the fruit basket."

"You got it, Alpha."

"Thanks, Nick," DeMatteo says before he jogs upstairs to his office.

Nick watches DeMatteo until the door closes. Looking around to make sure he is alone, Nick quickly walks to the kitchen to place his call.

"Hey, if you are going to do it, we need to do it now. Yes, you have two hours to get it to me. Okay. I'll have everything ready on my end. You just need to be in position. There will be two guards to take care of."

DeMatteo ~ 1:40 p.m.

DeMatteo walks into the garden to speak to Sean, but he stops in his tracks when he notices both of his guards lying darted on the ground. Rushing past them, he races to the picnic tables and almost vomits when he notices Sean's lunch scattered on the ground.

"Sean!" DeMatteo roars to his pride.

His mate is missing, his cubs are gone, and even their link seems to have disappeared.

He fights to keep from shifting as he waits for his pride to answer his call; the lion under his skin is demanding to be let free. The need to find his mate is almost enough to overwhelm his ability to think rationally. He wants to hunt down whoever is responsible and kill them in the most painful way he's able to imagine.

His claws and fangs are already out, and fur is starting to cover his skin when his head enforcer crashes into the field.

Samantha ~

Samantha was headed back to her room when she hears her brother's call, his roar of unimaginable pain and anger. Samantha lets out her own call as she races to her Alpha, hearing the pride call out in response. "DeMatteo! What happened?"

"Sean. The hunters have taken Sean; they have my cubs!"

Samantha has never seen her brother so devastated. Not even the murder of their parents had left him looking so vulnerable. She swears then and there that she will make sure everyone, shifter and human alike, involved in this will be put to death.

"We have to set up a hunting party. Whoever has him has somehow blocked our connection. I can't feel him or the cubs, but I know they are alive since I'm not yet feral. But we have to find them now."

DeMatteo roars before shifting into his lion. Everyone quickly strips and shifts to try to find their Alpha Mate and kill whoever dared to take him. The fact that someone had considered entering pride lands and kidnaped the pregnant Alpha Mate is a call to war. If they fail to find Sean and the cubs, or they are killed, their Alpha will go feral and need to be put down.

Chapter 20

Sean ~ December 17, Thursday, 3:47 p.m.

"When you get this message, fucking call me," a distorted female voice shouts somewhere in the distance.

Sean hears a voice talking, but he can't understand why he feels like his body has been filled with lead balloons. He tries and fails to open his eyes. He just knows that he needs to wake up.

Sean tries to piece together what happened. The last thing he remembers is making love to his husband, taking a shower, and heading out to the gardens. The more Sean struggles to remember, the fuzzier everything becomes, before he is pulled back under.

Sean's memories swirl in and out of focus until he can see himself clearly in the garden on his phone with his parents. He had called to Skype with them after working in the garden with his guards standing a few feet away.

"How are my grandbabies doing?"

"Nice, Mom. Don't even ask about your only child, just the grandbabies. I'm hurt." Sean pouts as he looked into the camera.

"Well, if my grandbabies are good, that means you're good." his mom beams.

"Well, in that case, they are doing great, although they are a bit confused about day and night. You won't believe how big they have gotten since last week, I'm huge!" Sean complains as he attempts to get comfortable on the picnic table.

"Are you still coming to visit next week?"

"Well that's why I'm Skyping. We don't think I should leave the pride lands anymore. I am so big that there is no way to explain why I look so pregnant. And since I have no desire to be studied as the world's first pregnant man, we think you guys should visit me here," Sean answers.

"So what you really mean is that your paranoid, possessive mate doesn't want you leaving, so we need to come to you?" his mother asks knowingly.

"Yeah that pretty much covers it." Sean chuckles.

The memory grows fuzzy as they continue to catch up. The next thing that comes in clear is Nick bringing him lunch.

"Hey, Sean. DeMatteo wanted me to bring you lunch. I also brought your favorite tea." Nick winks as he hands Sean

the glass. He then spreads out a variety of foods and desserts, the babies beginning to kick non-stop as the scent makes his mouth water.

"You are a godsend. These three are starved!" Sean exclaims as he takes a long drink of raspberry iced tea. "Perfect, sweet just the way I like it. DeMatteo always skimps on the sugar," he says as he finishes the glass; the babies have him constantly thirsty.

"I know, so I added a lil mor to th be syr..."

Sean blinks as Nick's words started to jumble together, everything starts to shift and blur. The last thing he really remembers is Nick's smile growing wider as his vision blurs out of focus.

Sean ~ 4:30 p.m.

Someone shakes his shoulder roughly. "Wake up," a cheerful woman's voice encourages.

Sean fidgets as he struggles to wake; that voice sounds so familiar, but something is definitely wrong. He can't move his arms, he can't move his legs, and that voice shouldn't be here.

He's shaken again. "Come on, Sean. It's time to wake up," the voice says again but this time it seems more angry and demanding.

Sean blinks as the room twirls in his vision, waves of nausea hitting him as he tries to focus on just one spot.

"There you go. Welcome back, Sean. I thought I was going to have to start this party without you," the cheerful voice says. There is something familiar about the sound that helps Sean anchor himself to the here and now.

Sean peels open his eyes and at first the light is blinding. He blinks into focus and sees the smiling face of his ex-girlfriend. "Sara? What are you doing here?" he croaks, his throat is dry and his head still fuzzy.

Sara's face twists into a smile that can only be described as cruel as he tries to move his heavy limbs. It takes a few seconds for Sean's drug-impaired brain to realize that he is in serious trouble: woozy, tied to a chair in the middle of a dirty room, with someone from his past that he never expected to see again.

"Hello, Sean, aren't you happy to see me? It was so hard to get a word alone with you, so I must apologize for tasering you, but I've missed you." Sara smiles as she picks at some nonexistent lint from her clothing.

"You just disappeared off the radar, not so much as a goodbye, it's been, what, seven months? I didn't even get invited to your wedding. At first I felt slighted, hurt, but now I can see that you've just been busy."

"Um… Sara, I don't know what you think is going on, but if you let me go now, we can just forget about this whole thing."

Sara's laugh is high, lacking any kind of humor. "Let you go? Oh, sweetie, we are well past the point where you can just walk away. I tried to give you that, a chance to walk away, but you chose to put yourself here."

Sean reaches for his lioness, knowing that if he can shift he can get away, but he feels no connection. He reaches further and still nothing, like his lioness is completely gone. Starting to panic, Sean reaches for DeMatteo and the pride; when he finds nothing, a new level of dread wraps tight around him.

"I'm not sure what was worse, pretending to care about you or letting you put your disgusting hands on me. I could never get clean afterwards; your stench lingered for hours. You know that witches and shifters are abominations, don't you?" Sara asks as she strokes Sean's belly. Fear shifts into terror as Sara pulls out the biggest knife he's ever seen and uses it to cut away the buttons of his shirt.

Focusing on his babies, Sean knows he has to remain calm, whatever Sara had given him somehow blocked him from his lioness, his magic, and the pride. Every time he reaches for that thread binding him to his pride, he pulls up nothing. But he can still feel his cubs, and they are starting to feel his panic.

"Sara, please don't hurt my babies. I'm sorry for what happened, but please don't hurt my babies."

Sara begins to pace in front of him. "You know that I was trying to save you. Once we realized what you were, I was sent to you to keep you human."

"Who sent you? Just tell me what you want. I have money. I could help you get away; just let me go and I'll do it." Sean recoils as she sits on his lap, hands back on his belly.

"I was willing to spend my whole life keeping you from their evil plans, but then you went and threw it away for an even filthier shifter. Do you have any idea how much I sacrificed for you? I gave up my chance at happiness. I was sterilized to prevent you from ever infecting me with your children. But look at you now."

Ice cold fear snakes down Sean's spine from the look of insanity in Sara's eyes. There isn't a hint of the woman he thought he knew; the kind and loving Sara who had spent months in his bed has been replaced with this heartless madwoman.

"I never pegged you as a faggot, but you are just full of surprises. But faggots and shifters are both abominations so I guess it's no wonder they lie together. So tell me, Sean, how is it to be fucked by an animal? I've never understood bestiality. Is his dick as freaky as the rest of him?" Sara taunts.

Sean continues to fight the drugs and ropes that subdue him, blocking out the hateful rants being hurled at him. He just needs more time to get free, then he'll show that bitch how freaky he is.

"I know what you are thinking, but no one is going to save you or those little abominations inside of you. Do you know what happens to an Alpha that loses its mate?"

Sean yelps as Sara grabs his pinky, twisting it violently when he fails to answer quickly enough. "No!" he wails.

"No? Well, let me tell you. It's nothing pretty; they go completely insane. You see, they are not human, not really, and when push comes to shove, the animal always wins. They will kill any and everyone they come across until someone finally puts it down like a rabid dog. Because that is what they are, rabid animals that need to be culled. Some people think we can train them, domesticate them if you will, like pets. But just like any wild animal, I don't think you can ever really trust them not to turn on their masters," she warns, but Sean can't focus on her words, he's too focused on the knife that swings closer and closer as she rants.

A blinding light blasts from Sean before the blade can pierce his belly, flinging the deranged woman across the room. Sean only has a few seconds to realize that his babies have protected him and are now desperately calling to DeMatteo before the darkness of unconsciousness pulls him under again.

Sara ~ 5:57 p.m.

Sara pulls herself towards the door. Her shoulder is badly dislocated, but it is the angry roar off in the distance that decides her path. Sean seems to be out cold and she could finish the job, but she wouldn't live to finish her mission.

"Shit, fuck…" Sara hisses as she tries to stand. Realizing her leg is also damaged, Sara decides to leave her tools behind. She has to crawl, no doubt getting her wounds infected and leaving a trail. Finally, she makes it to her vehicle, pulls herself inside and drives off.

"Fuck!" Sara screams as she slams her hands on the wheel.

She needs a new plan. Hopefully Hugh and Nick are still in play. Running isn't an option. Her entire life has been for this moment, and somehow that abomination has snatched it away.

Checking the rearview mirror, Sara can't help but wonder what those filthy animals will think of their Alpha Mate once they find out he brought hunters in. There is little doubt that they will find out who she is. The Council will sell her out just like they did her grandparents. No matter what she has to do, she will bring both of them to their knees.

"Where the fuck are you, Hugh?" Sara growls into her phone as soon as it's answered.

"Sara! I just got back to the safe house. Is it done?" Hugh answers, obviously winded.

"Is it done? Is it done? No, it's not fucking done, Hugh. Do you wanna know why it's not done? Because you fucked up, again! Because you seem incapable of doing as you are told. You had a simple task, Hugh. You were supposed to meet me at that cabin! Did you know that he could do magic?"

The nerve of this guy! Sara wants to cut his fucking heart out and feed it to him.

Hugh ~

"I was… I was taking care of Carla. Of course he can do magic; he is a fucking witch! How do you think he stole my mate?" Hugh replies as he plays with the knife he had used to open Carla up.

Gone was the timid, almost fearful way he had of talking to the hunter. It had taken everything in his power to deal with her, but now that she has failed to deliver his mate, Hugh has no need to even pretend to care about what she says.

"Carla? Are you kidding me? You went to the house when you were supposed to be backing me up?"

Hugh ignores her as he drags the blade across his thigh and watches as the flesh splays open obscenely. His lion seems to bask in the scent of blood, even his own, as his nostrils flare.

"Did you kill her?" Sara asks.

"No. I wounded her, but I was interrupted." Hugh smiles as he remembers how it felt to slowly pull out her intestines, watching her eyes widen in horror as she got to visually see the carnage he wreaked.

"Just fucking great! So now they know you're still here. You are a fucking idiot; I should just kill you myself!"

Hugh's voice is quiet when he answers. "I would be careful if I was you."

"What?"

"I said, I would be careful if I was you. Threatening the wrong person can have catastrophic results," Hugh repeats as he watches his wound slowly close.

"Are you threatening me?"

"Threatening? No. I am simply informing you of the dangers you face. I know you may think I'm weak, but trust me, you have no idea what I am capable of. Are you almost here?"

"No. I'm headed to a new safe house; I've been hurt, and I need medical attention. Which is why I called, to tell you to lay low and keep the phone with you until we can meet up. We need to come up with a new plan, so I have to meet with some contacts."

Hugh sighs. "Okay. Well, I'll keep the phone, but I think I'm going to take supplies and head out. Find a new spot, just in case there is enough of a scent to track."

"Yes. That's good. I'll be in touch," she says and Hugh laughs as the call is disconnected.

Time to pack.

Maybe it's for the best that Sara is injured and escaping to a different place. If she had walked in the door, Hugh would have undoubtedly killed her on sight. His lion is on edge, anxiously pacing; this house is no longer safe. He needs to move far away from the scent trail he undoubtedly left on his way back to the hideout.

Collecting the food, money, and assortment of weapons, Hugh heads out in one of the many vehicles Sara had left at the house. He would come up with his own backup plan to rescue his mate. His lion reminds him that he has never trusted the woman to get the job done, and they will do better on their own.

Henry ~ 9 p.m.

"Honey, I need you to take the children downstairs as I handle some business."

Henry watches until he hears the basement door lock before opening the door for the person he had once seen as a daughter. "What are you doing here, Sara? You know the Council has voted your clan out," he whispers.

"Yes, Henry, I am more than aware of the betrayal of my family after generations of faithful service. But I am here for a favor—" Sara begins.

Henry cuts her off, "Sara, you know I can't..." he hisses, careful to keep his voice low. He doesn't want his wife to see Sara here.

Sara's face twists in anger as she sneers, "Can't what? Be a man and do something without checking with the Council for permission? Jesus fuck, Henry, you know me! Are you really going to turn your back on someone who you once loved as one of your own? You know what? Fuck it. It was a mistake coming here." Sara turns to leave, making sure to exaggerate her limp and expose her bloodied clothing.

"Sara, wait. Jesus, what happened to you?" Henry relents. It goes against the code to aid a hunter after they've been voted out, but this is Sara, and he raised her as if she was his own.

"I was attacked by a shifter. I think they recognized me as a hunter, I just need some medical attention. There is no way I can explain these injuries at a human hospital. I just need to get patched up so I can leave town," she says, limping towards him.

Henry opens the door and steps out, placing an arm around her waist. "You're leaving?" he asks, taking her weight.

Sara grimaces but leans heavily against him. "Yeah, I can't risk staying here now that I'm exposed. The Council will never believe that I was attacked unprovoked, and without their protection, those animals will kill me."

"Jesus, Sara, come inside. I'll do all I can. My wife can patch you up," the old man says as he helps her inside.

"Thank you, Henry. I owe you," Sara says as he closes the door.

Sara ~ Thursday, 9:45 p.m.

"We're almost done. It's so good to see you. I couldn't believe it when Henry told me you left town after that horrible accident," Jessica says as she finishes the last row of stitches.

Sara smiles, not the least bit surprised that the Council had covered up everything. Jessica had been like a second mother to her after her own mother had died. No wonder Henry had hidden the truth from her.

"Yeah, I just had to get away from the constant reminders."

"I can't imagine. But you were just a child. No one would have blamed you; it's amazing you were able to control the car at all. I'm just so glad to see you again, although I wish it could have been under better circumstances. Even though I am not surprised you took up the family trade, you were always a natural."

Sara holds still as Jessica places the last of the bandages, happy to see that her old friends seemed to have made such a beautiful life for themselves.

"Do you have any pain killers?"

"Sure thing. I bet you do need something for the pain," Jessica answers as she leaves to retrieve the medicine.

"Here you go. That script is good for two refills, and there are thirty pills in the bottle."

Sara embraces her old friend in a tight embrace.

"Thank you, Jessy," she whispers into her ear right before slamming the blade into her throat, stifling any screams before they raise the alarm. She continues to hold the woman that was like a mother to her, as the light fades from her eyes.

Sarah is careful to make sure the body is completely hidden in the tub before closing the curtain. She doesn't want one of the children to find her if they come down to use the bathroom. After cleaning her bloodied hands and returning the blade, Sara looks at her reflection in the mirror. Satisfied her face is clean, she heads upstairs to speak to the man she had once loved more than her own father.

"Where are the children?" Sara asks when she enters the kitchen. Henry is alone, standing in front of the sink, cleaning what looks to be dishes from dinner.

"I put them to bed. I figured you would like to talk, in private."

"Do you want me to tell Jessica that we need to talk?" Sara offers. If he goes to get her, Sara will be forced to kill him sooner than she planned.

"That won't be necessary. I told her as much before she cleaned you up."

"So what do you want to talk about?" Sara asks with feigned innocence.

"What do I want to talk about? How about where you've been for the last decade?" Henry seethes as he turns to face her. He looked so much older than Sara remembers, older and tired, not at all the man her father had sent her to befriend.

"I left to train. You couldn't expect us to stay after you and the others abandoned us. You excommunicated my entire clan because of the death of some filthy animals and an accident!"

"Animals? What kind of nonsense have they been filling your head with? Your family was censored after what happened to those two Alphas. Your grandparents were tried and found guilty of their crimes. After what you did, we had no choice to but excommunicate you, even though most of us understood it was your father who was pushing you."

"What I did was an accident! Ask Jessica. She believes me," Sara hisses quietly as she begins to pace in front of the table.

She eases the knife out of its sheath. There is no point in continuing this charade. Henry doesn't want to acknowledge the wrongs he and the Council instigated against her family. They are just as bad as the animals she hunts.

"She believes you, Sara, because I never told her exactly what you did. How you drove over twenty miles to your victim, how you avoided everything as you swerved to hit her head on. And how you fled the scene and tried to destroy the evidence. Yes, we protected you from the police, but you had to be punished for your crime. Surely you understand what you did was wrong?"

Henry ~

Henry feels uneasy as the girl he once knew starts laughing uncontrollably. There is something off about her, something dangerous. Before he can react, Sara clears the space between them and presses a knife to his throat.

"My crimes? How is it a crime to rid the world of those evil abominations? If you want Jessica and the kids to live through this, you won't do anything stupid. Now I want to know everything the Council is up to."

"You can get everything you want off my laptop," Henry offers.

"Oh yeah? And where would I find said laptop?"

"It's in my office," he says while pointing towards the stairs.

"Well then, let's take a walk." Sara keeps the knife pressed tight to his throat as she walks behind him.

"If memory serves, we have to pass the children's bedroom. Better be quiet; don't want to wake them," Sara whispers in his ear as they reach the top of the stairs. As they enter the office, Sara shuts the door behind him and leads him to his desk.

"Very nice. Now I will require the passwords for the laptop and the desktop," Sara orders, as she stands behind him, knife still tight to his throat.

"There are no passwords," Henry growls as she presses the knife just shy of drawing blood.

"No passwords? Henry, you are getting sloppy in your old age," Sara teases.

"Don't need them. No one is stupid enough to steal from the Council. Sara, if you stop now I can still help you. I know you don't want to hurt me; I know your father has brainwashed you into all of this. Just put down the knife, and we can go back downstairs, get Jessica, and figure out how to get you out of this mess."

Sara ~

Sara watches the sweat beading down the back of his neck as he speaks. She can hear his heart thundering away as he pleads for his life. She eases up on the pressure on his throat as he reaches out for that young girl that had once curled on his lap and wept for her dead mother.

"You would do that for me? Even now?"

"Always. Sara, you are like a daughter to me. I would never abandon you."

"I'd like that, but I'm afraid Jessica is already dead," Sara says right before she slits his throat. Too bad for them that the girl they loved had never really ever existed.

She watches as his eyes bulge with the realization that his wife had been killed first, that he was begging for a life that was already gone. Sara follows his body as it sags to the ground, she graces him with a final smile as she mops the sweat from his brow before standing.

"Now if you'll excuse me, I've got to go tuck in your kids." She can still hear his gurgled screams as she heads down to the bedroom where the children sleep. Under normal situations, Sara would have let the children live, but this isn't a normal situation, and she can't afford to leave anything behind.

The sun is rising as Sara loads her vehicle with all of her belongings, along with the hard drives of the laptop and desktop computers. She had taken her time to find all the recording devices she knew Henry kept in the house.

Luckily Jessica was her size, so she changed into a smart business suit she had found in the closet. She sits in her vehicle about a mile away, watching the flames burn high in the sky, burning away any trace of her late night visit.

She just needs a safe place to heal and regather her troops. She has been given some obstacles to overcome, but she is determined to exterminate every single abomination in the Santiago pride; after all, she is a very patient woman.

Chapter 21

DeMatteo ~ December 17, Thursday, 5:30 p.m.

They have traveled several miles searching for the pregnant Alpha Mate, but whoever has him had not only been able to sneak onto pride lands undetected, but had also taken down two shifters before disappearing without a trace.

DeMatteo shifts into his human skin to search the storage shacks, wondering how far they could have possibly gotten on foot, when he is suddenly hit with a desperate call. Looking around, DeMatteo feels a blast of magic reverberate through the air with such intensity that his lion perks up.

"Sean!"

At first, he can't identify the voices calling to him; in his desperate bid to find his mate and cubs, he almost misses the family bonds blazing back to life. DeMatteo's lion, however, has no trouble identifying the new call and rips through his mind to get to its cubs.

DeMatteo wastes no time shifting back into his lion, racing towards his family. He will kill anything that tries to get in between them. He just prays to the gods that he is not too late.

Timothy ~

"Where is he going, Samantha?" Timothy asks.

"I have no idea, but we need to follow him," Samantha orders, not waiting for his response before she shifts to follow their brother.

He turns to find Kim running up to meet him. "I need you to go back to the pride house and look after Carla," Timothy tells his mate.

Kim grabs at him, "Timothy! You can't go out there! What if the hunters are there? What if…"

Timothy pulls away. "Kim, I have to go. That is the Alpha Mate and his cubs out there!" he says and shifts, racing to catch up with the hunting party that had all followed after their distraught Alpha.

Carla ~ 3 p.m.

Carla barely registers the prick on the back of her neck before she hears her attacker whisper, "Surprise!" into her ear.

"Bet you never thought you'd see me again, did you? I was hoping to one day get my hands on that bitch of a sister of yours, but I guess I'm just gonna have to settle on making you suffer," Hugh says. Carla blinks rapidly, trying and failing to get any part of her body to move.

Hugh watches her carefully, laughing, and she realizes that he is completely insane and she is about to die.

"No. No. Don't exhaust yourself; we have so much to do together. Shhh... It's okay. I know your *mate* will be sad when he realizes I've taken his chance to slit your throat, but I have to have some of the fun, right?" he continues, and Carla is forced to watch in silent horror as he pulls out a knife and gloves.

Carla screams in her head as she realizes that she and her lioness are both paralyzed. She has no way to call for her pride, to let them know who is about to kill her.

Then the horror truly begins.

Each slice feels like she's being burnt alive. Whatever Hugh gave her makes it impossible to move, but she can feel everything. At some point, she had heard DeMatteo's roar. For a brief moment, she believes she's about to be rescued.

As more and more calls sound, Carla realizes that the pride is running further into the pride lands, sentencing her to a slow and painful death at the hands of someone she once counted as a friend.

Hugh ~

Hugh eases onto the mattress next to the paralyzed shifter. His smile broadens as he watches her eyes widen as she recognizes who he is.

"Bet you never thought you'd see me again, did you? I was hoping to one day get my hands on that bitch of a sister of yours, but I guess I'm just gonna have to settle on making you suffer," Hugh says, not expecting an answer.

The drug in that needle is fast acting and long lasting, more than he'll need to leave his message.

"No. No. Don't exhaust yourself; we have so much to do together. Shhh... It's okay. I know your *mate* will be sad when he realizes I've taken his chance to slit your throat, but I have to have some of the fun, right?"

Hugh pulls on his gloves before selecting the curved blade. This one isn't laced with hemlock. No, this one is just for taking his time. He has plans to slowly gut the woman, to leave her organs exposed—the same way they ripped out his heart when he was kept away from his mate and forced out of the pride.

"Now, Carla, don't take this as my personal feelings towards you. Consider this a favor. It would be shameful to let some pathetic human kill you. Right now, Nick is blissfully unaware that he is about to die. You will be my masterpiece, but he is my ticket back inside. Now we better hurry up and begin; timing in this case is crucial," Hugh offers conversationally.

Rolling her to her back, Hugh immediately sets to work, starting his first cut low in her abdomen. He has no intention of just cutting her open—oh no, he plans to disembowel her slowly, letting her heal, so he has to cut her over and over and over again. Maybe then someone will understand how painful his lover's rejection really was.

That first cut is surprisingly easy, the heavy paralytic doing more than its job. The only sign that his toy is alive are the tears welling up in her eyes as he drags the blade up to her belly button. His lion chuffs in excitement as the sweet metallic tang of blood floods the room, and Hugh finds himself momentarily dazed as he watches the wound bloom wider as Carla sucks in a breath.

He drags his glove-covered fingers into the hole, feeling the muscles bulge and quiver as her healing kicks in, trying to close the wound and slow the bleeding. After a few seconds, the unblemished skin is begging him to begin again, so he does, this time sliding the knife deeper through flesh and muscle.

The scent of her pain and panic fill the room and Hugh can almost hear the *oh god, oh please…* Carla is undoubtedly begging in her head.

Hugh hears DeMatteo and the others roar out in the distance. He can see the hope shine in Carla as she hears their calls. "Oh no, baby girl. Seems as if your Alpha is taking the pride on a hunt. Soon he will find that witch dead, only to come home to find you dead as well. And I will have gotten here just in time to kill that human you bedded and comfort my hurting mate. It's a shame this couldn't have been Samantha instead. You were always so sweet. I am going to miss you. Do you know how many times I wanted to warn you about Nick? He is obsessed with killing you. I never understood it," Hugh says as he plunges the knife in again.

"You always seemed too good for him in my opinion, which is why I couldn't let Nick kill you. As a matter of fact, I am going to enjoy killing him for you, because the things he planned to do to you..." Hugh shakes his head in disgust about the way Nick had planned to sexually violate her before killing her.

Hugh smiles when he is finally able to hook a finger around what has to be her lower intestines, and he starts to pull.

"No, you deserve better than what he planned to do to you. You deserve for it to be a friend, someone who wants to have your death mean something. I think that is something you would have wanted; the pride will grieve for years from the loss of you, my sweet," Hugh coos even as he slowly begins to pull out her intestines.

"What the fuck?" Kim screams, and Hugh spins around to face the woman he hadn't heard approaching. "Hugh! Get away from her!" she says as she begins to shift.

"Kim! You don't understand! I need to do this, DeMatteo needs me!" he tries to explain.

Hugh barely has time to react before a half-shifted lioness crashes into him, burying her fangs deep in his shoulder. The blinding pain pulls his lion to the forefront and he slashes wildly, catching her several times in the face.

One deep slash to her stomach forces his attacker to retreat, and Hugh is given a moment to shift into his lion and escape as she is distracted by her partially-eviscerated pride mate.

Kim ~

"What the fuck?" Kim screams as she takes in the carnage around her.

It had taken her a while to get back to the pride house. She had taken time to stop and check on the children that had been left by the others, not knowing that Hugh had somehow come back into the pride house and attacked the injured shifter.

"Hugh! Get away from her!" Kim snarls around her fangs before she attacks.

"Kim! You don't understand! I need to do this. DeMatteo needs me!"

Kim doesn't bother to answer the crazed shifter as she lunges for his throat. Hugh manages to dodge the vicious swipe, and he drags his claws across her side. She counters, burying her claws in his hip. Kicking out, he catches Kim in her sensitive belly, causing her to stagger back. Hugh capitalizes on her injury to escape and Kim nearly chases after him before she hears Carla's barely audible whimpers. When she takes a closer look at her injured pride mate, Kim is horrified by the sheer amount of damage Hugh had inflicted on the other shifter.

There is no way Carla's lioness will be able to heal the wounds where pieces of what must be Carla's intestines lay exposed. Kim has to suppress a gag as she cuts into Carla's stomach with her claws to push her intestines back inside. Carla can heal, but she needs to be whole to heal properly. Kim's lion whimpers at her pride mate's weak and pain-filled sobs as she pushes down harder.

Carla's lips are moving but even with her lioness's hearing Kim still has to concentrate to hear Carla whisper, "Find Nick. He's been sedated."

"I'll find him, I promise. Just rest. You need your strength." Kim smiles gently at the slowly healing pride mate before going to search for her human.

Carla ~

Carla thinks, *At least that treacherous bastard Nick will also meet his end today.* It is her only comfort as her vision bleeds out, her lioness laid out motionless in her mind.

Voices carry as Carla struggles to open her eyes; her lioness is dragging itself forward at the sounds of a battle raging around them. As the drugs dull, pain flares brightly, almost knocking her back out, before she recognizes the scent of the shifter pushing on her wound.

"Find Nick. He's been sedated," Carla manages to whisper as her stomach is cut open again, this time by claws, allowing her sister in-law to push her guts back inside. Her throat feels ripped and ragged, from the constant struggle to scream.

"Kim, I'm fine. Find Nick and bring him to me," Carla wheezes as her lioness roars back to life, pushing her healing into overdrive. Carla tries to remain still while Kim checks the wound to make sure it is indeed healing.

"Please, Kim I need you to find my mate," Carla begs as she remembers who had set her up. Kim flinches at the flare of aggression, Carla grimaces before smiling at her sister-in-law in apology.

Carla closes her eyes and waits; she will pay Nicholas back in kind for his betrayal.

Carla ~ 6 p.m.

Carla had drifted off, curled up in a chair, but she stirs when she hears footsteps headed towards her room. Her lioness, poised for another attack, has her partially shifting and crouching down beside the bed. Carla relaxes as Kim enters carrying a still-unconscious Nickolas.

"Hugh must have gotten to him first. I found him drugged in the downstairs bathroom. I sent Cassandra to find and tell DeMatteo of Hugh's attack, I didn't tell her the extent of your injuries. I don't want to distract him from searching for the Alpha Mate, but he needs to know about the attack," Kim explains as she carefully lays the human on the bed, still soaked with her blood. Carla will question him thoroughly before repaying her *mate* for his betrayal.

"Thank you, Kim. But I will need to speak to you in private as soon as possible. We have another traitor in our pride," Carla says as she makes her way over to Nick's play box.

Carla's heart twists as she grabs the ropes Nick had often used during their play sessions; she can't help but wonder how many times he had thought to kill her when she allowed him to have her in such a vulnerable position.

"Who?" Kim growls as her eyes flash.

"Not now. Just help me secure him to the bed. I want to make sure we are not overheard in case there are others in on this plan. Who all was left behind?" Carla answers as she hands Kim a length of rope to secure his legs. Carla doesn't want him getting any ideas of escape while she isn't there.

"Just me and Cassandra. I was left to watch over you, and she was taking care of the cubs."

"Kim, this wasn't your fault. In fact, you saved my life. If you hadn't gotten here when you did and fought him off..." Carla shudders as she remembers all of the things Hugh had said to her. "Who knows what he would have done to you and the cubs after he killed me? So thank you. You saved us all today."

Carla takes a moment to hug her pride mate, part in thanks and part in comfort. Kim has never been a fighter; being the runt of her litter, she has always been protected. Carla vows then and there that Kim will receive special status in the pride for her selflessness and bravery in the face of a truly insane larger shifter.

"Now help me tie him to the bed, then we will go to the office and I will explain everything."

Nick ~ 6:20 p.m.

Nick blinks slowly as he tries to remember what happened. His head aches and he is tied to his and Carla's bed. A million different scenarios play out in his head but none of them end with him walking away from these animals.

He can only hope that Sara and Hugh have finished the mission, killing Sean, DeMatteo, and Carla, and that Sara has gutted Hugh for all his troubles. Nick had known going in that there was a real chance of him dying when he entered the pride, but he had considered it an honor to die in order to save humans from these animals.

Nick braces himself for an attack as the bedroom door slowly opens, and he can't help but gasp as Carla enters the room. His heart races as he tries, and fails, to come up with a spin on things that will end with him living. He thinks his prayers are answered when she smiles, bright and open, at him.

"Thank the Goddess, you're awake," Carla says as she makes her way over to the human.

"Yeah... But, baby, why am I tied to the bed?" Nick hedges, trying to keep his heartbeat even as the shifter walks into the room. The fact that she is still alive is surprising; maybe Hugh had bugged off before he ever made it to her.

"Oh! Sorry, sorry. We thought it best to restrain you so you couldn't hurt yourself if you woke up alone. I didn't know if your head was injured and didn't want to take the chance," Carla explains as she unties his restraints. "What happened to you, Nick? You were unconscious for a long time. How are you feeling? And someone took the Alpha Mate! The pride is out looking for him," Carla asks worriedly as she rubs his sore wrist.

Nick tries not to smile at that. He has to make sure his alibi for everything that had happened is above the board. They must realize by now that Sean's food was spiked, and since he's the one that delivered it, he would be suspect number one. "The Alpha Mate! Oh god, where is DeMatteo? Have they found him yet?"

When she remains silent, Nick's fear starts to creep back, so he decides to give her something to throw off her suspicion. Nick grabs his head and sways, looking to cash in on the sympathy Carla first displayed when she walked in.

"I'm not sure what happened. I was in the kitchen eating lunch. Then the next thing I know I woke up in our bed.

Oh god, the food! I was eating the extra that couldn't fit in Sean's lunch!"

"No. They haven't found him yet, and I still can't feel him through the pride bond. I was asleep when the pride left on the search. I didn't even know he had been taken until after Kim found you," Carla says as she lays her head on his shoulder.

Nick pets her hair gently as she speaks; he needs to keep her calm until he hears from Sara. He hopes his phone is still in the kitchen. Luckily, he had taken the time to lock up the poison in his safe before poisoning the Alpha Mate.

"So you didn't see or hear anything? You have no idea who did this to you?" Carla asks, concerned.

Nick has never been a religious man but he is thanking every deity that he has come out of this situation clean. He looks her over, amazed she had somehow survived and that he will still have the chance to kill her himself. As she sits up in the bed, Nick reaches over to kiss her, and that is when he really notices her bloodied, torn clothing.

"Oh my god, Carla! Are you okay?" His surprise is honest, since Nick is sure that Hugh would have drugged her before trying to kill her.

"Yes. I was also attacked and sedated. I thought they were going to kill me!"

"Oh god! Thank Christ you are okay. What happened?"

"I'm not sure, I was asleep when someone drugged me, and they stabbed me a few times before they fled. I heard them talking to someone saying it was you who wanted me dead, and they were just beating you to it."

That fucking dirty, stupid fucking shifter! Nick has to fix this quickly; he has to convince everyone that he is madly in love with her and is also the victim of the crazy shifter.

"What!" Nick wails, jumping up from the bed. He stumbles with the quick movement but every fiber in his bones is screaming danger, and he wants to put as much space between himself and the shifter as possible. "I would never! Carla, you know I would never ever hurt you. I love you! Hugh has always been fucking crazy. You know this. You know that I would never betray you or our pride."

Nick's heart is about to beat out of his chest; this is do or die. The only thing standing between him and death is a scent blocker and their history together. This is a performance of a lifetime, and if the shifter smells any trace of deceit, he is a dead man.

"Of course I believe you, Nick. I know you. We have been together for years, and I have always trusted you." Carla smiles as she comforts the human, kissing him gently on the lips.

Nick takes a deep breath and smiles at the shifter; if it wasn't for the fact that Hugh was so obviously crazy, Carla may not have taken him at his word. Nick realizes he has to find a way to contact Sara and warn her that Hugh has gone completely renegade and had almost blown his cover.

"Hey, Nick?" Carla calls out as he heads to the closet.

"Yeah, babe?" Nick answers as he turns back towards the shifter.

"I never said it was Hugh," Carla growls as she shifts.

Nick slams back into the wall, his hand raised as if to fight off the attack. "Carla, please!"

His pleas are cut short as Carla grabs him by the throat, completely decapitating him. Carla sniffs around the lifeless human. Satisfied that he is dead, the lioness lifts her leg to urinate on what is left of the corpse.

Carla ~ 7:10 p.m.

"Did you get everything on tape?" Carla asks once she has shifted back into human form,

"Yes. Video and audio, although I would think our testimony would be enough," Kim answers as she steps over what is left of Nick.

They had left Michal, one of the older cubs, in charge of the younger ones and gave him explicit instructions to keep them in the pride house's basement. But Carla knows it will only be a matter of time before the smell of blood reaches them.

"No. I just hope that it is enough. Remember I just killed a longtime companion. The Council will investigate, and I will need proof of his betrayal of not only me but the entire pride. They will not just take my word for it."

The killing of a human is strictly prohibited; the only exception was self-defense. Carla has no intentions of lying about what had happened in this room. The execution of a human is only to be done by an Alpha, and even then there are guidelines they have to follow. Protection of the whole pride, or Alpha and Alpha Mate, is the only exception. She can only hope that the video shows that Nick was in on the kidnapping, and possible murder, of the Alpha Mate and cubs.

"What do we do now?"

"Now we grab a tarp and clean up. The bedding, my clothes, his body—they all need to be burned in case we need to bring in the human police to report Sean missing. We need to hurry before any of the cubs get curious and come up here to see what we are doing," Carla answers as she grabs the bedding.

"Dammit, it soaked through, the whole mattress will need to go. The carpet too," Carla says distantly as she looks around her bedroom.

Kim ~

Kim leaves to gather the tarp they need in a daze; things have spiraled so far from normal that she has no idea what the proper reaction is. She is on auto-pilot by the time she returns to the room. Carla has already stripped and begun tearing up the carpeting. Kim silently lays out the tarp, rolling Nick into the center before joining her pride mate in removing the evidence.

"Do you have any regrets? I mean, he was your companion mate for a long time. It couldn't have been easy to kill him," Kim says as they pile all the bloodied towels on top of his body.

Kim's hands shake as she grabs the cloths Carla had thrown under the body to soak up the blood that is still oozing from the mangled remains. The stench of urine burns her nostrils as she attempts to wrap Nick in some of the towels.

It is not unusual to deal with the bloodied corpse of a recent kill. Kim had gutted more than a few unfortunate deer, but the sight of someone that—up until minutes before his death—was considered family is making her stomach twist as her lioness batters at her senses.

"It was incredibly easy to kill him; I only wish I could bring him back just to kill him again. This man planned to kill me, Kim. He helped to kidnap the Alpha Mate and cubs. The only thing I regret is that his blood has ruined my carpet."

Kim stares at her pride mate in horror. Carla is the least violent person Kim knows. Now she is talking about killing a human with the same emotion she might discuss killing a deer. Any response Kim may have had was silenced as a single call cuts through the pride lands.

Both Kim and Carla freeze and stare off in the direction of their Alpha's pain-filled call.

Epilogue

January 10, 2016

"My contact in the Council informed me that your identity has been revealed and that Nickolas was killed by that abomination. It might be time for you to pull out and let them catch that monster that helped you. Maybe that will allow you a chance to get out of the country."

Sara grits her teeth, struggling to keep her temper in check as she responds to Chris. She'd wanted the fucking shifters dead even before they'd murdered Nick, and now she has yet another reason to kill every single one of them.

"No. This is my mission. We all knew the chances when we started this, Nick included. I have plans for my pet, but he is a bit unpredictable. Now that we know for sure that Sean is the key and those freaks he is carrying are those of the prophecy, it's of greater importance that we don't fail," Sara responds.

So much has been sacrificed to keep this from happening, but the treachery of others has constantly gotten in the way. Shifters might have managed to trick most hunters into thinking they wanted to coexist peacefully, but she knows they are just biding their time before they turn on the humans.

"We also need to deal with those on the Hunter Council who have gone against the code and sided with the shifters. They've issued a kill on sight order on you and that shifter, so we can only trust those who have remained loyal," Chris warns.

Sara almost snorts. She hadn't expected anything else from that spineless conference of old men. They had shown their lack of character when they had refused to move against a witch working magic that endangered the public. Even after the sacrifices her mother had made to protect the witch's innocent human victims, the Council had done nothing to honor her death.

"I already have a plan in place to strike at those who have put their greed above the code. I have found that many of the Council members have business and personal relationships with the shifters. Once we expose their treachery, I am sure we will get more hunters on our side. They'll see that the planet belongs to humans—not these animals."

Chris laughs before sobering. "Your mother and grandparents would be so proud of the hunter you have become."

"Does Sean know about his mother's death?" Sara asks.

"No. It doesn't seem like anyone has pieced that part of the puzzle together yet." Chris chuckles.

"Good. So we still have an element of surprise. If we can get to his parents, we might have leverage to pull them both off of pride lands. If not, we go after the children. One way or another, we will get our revenge and save the human race at the same time."

"Happy hunting, Sara, and good luck," Chris says, his voice an odd mixture of both proud and fond.

"Thank you. Good luck, and happy hunting to you," she says, smiling as he ends the call. She looks out of her window at the New York city skyline, knowing it is almost time to leave the city behind and head home.

Her wounds are mostly healed, and she would soon be ready to hunt her prey. They now know who she is, but they have no idea the level of destruction she was about to bring.

Losing Nick had taken her by surprise, but they had all known what was at stake. All of them are willing to risk it all, and she will make sure he didn't die in vain.

There is one more move she needs to make before declaring war on those animals. Grabbing a throw-away phone, Sara prepares to set loose her number one distraction.

"Wow, I was starting to think I'd never hear from you again."

Smiling into her glass of wine, Sara puts on her friendliest voice. "Well, hello to you too, Hugh."

To Be Continued…

About the Author

Sharon Johnson is the pen name for a natural born story teller. The youngest of five, Sharon found the art of creating tales that had her parents often wondering if her adventures were real. Born and raised in New York City, Sharon spent most of her after school hours curled up with a book.

An avid reader from childhood young Sharon took to expanding on her favorite stories, creating fan fictions. A former United States Marine she has a quick wit and a vocabulary that would make most sailors blush. Sharon spends most of her days as an ordinary electronics technician. If by ordinary you mean a heavily tattooed, pierced, and fiery redhead.

Sharon now resides in the beautiful Pocono Mountains with her husband, four children, two dogs, and two cats. She sets out every day to prove that you can never have too much on your plate if you love what you do.

Mostly Sharon is a believer in love no matter what form you find it in. She specializes in M/M with Alpha males who are complex and flawed but are willing to fight for their HEA.

Word of mouth is vital for any author. If you enjoyed this book please leave a review where you purchased it, on Goodreads, or post it on your social media site. Sharon spends most of her nights writing but would love to hear from you.

You can email her: mail.sharonjohnson@sharonjohnsonauthor.com

You can find her on Facebook: Facebook.com/SharonJohnson1979

You can Tweet her: Twitter.com/SJohnson_Author

Visit her website: www.SharonJohnsonAuthor.com

Check her blog: http://sharonjohnsonauthor.com/blog.html

Visit her on Instagram: www.instagram.com/sharondjohnson

Visit her website to sign up for Sharon's monthly newsletter. Get sneak peeks, deleted scenes, be the first to know future release dates, first glance at cover reveals, a chance to receive free ARC's, join her beta team, and so much more!

Also Available

Erasing All Doubt (Alphas Rule)

Book 0.5 in the Doubt Series

Eighty-six thousand, four hundred seconds. One thousand, four hundred and forty minutes. Twenty-four hours. One day. In his twenty-five years of life, DeMatteo Santiago had often taken for granted how much could change in a single day.

When DeMatteo crawled to bed at 10:30 pm on May 7, 1980, there was no way of knowing how the next twenty-four hours would forever alter his life. As a young Alpha lion shifter, DeMatteo has left his pride in search of his mate and a pride of his own. But the fates have been conspiring for centuries to lead him to this precise moment in time.

May 8, 1980, 10:30 pm: a moment in time that will forever change the life of Matthew "DeMatteo" Santiago. Facing the challenges of being the new Alpha of the largest pride in the United States, DeMatteo must find a way to lead in the face of his own personal tragedy.

Where Doubt Remains

Book 2 in the Doubt Series

The story continues for Alpha DeMatteo Santiago and his mate. After the nightmare of having his pregnant mate kidnapped and tortured, DeMatteo begins the seemingly impossible process of piecing together the truth. Forces against them take this time to regroup and launch an all-out attack. Lies and half-truths fall apart as the past is investigated, but it's a race against time and failure could prove to be fatal…

This release is an M/M paranormal shifter romance. This series will contain scenes of graphic violence, graphic sex, graphic language, Mpreg, and graphic birth. What it will not be is an instant mate fairy tale, as forces set out to destroy everything and everyone around him.

A League of Gentlemen

Book 1 in The Gentlemen's League series

Dominic has spent his entire life fighting and hiding. After leaving the Marine Corps, he is embarking on a new chapter in his life and cutting all ties to the man he was before.

He's in a new place with a new name. But some ugly truths from his past, truths he thought were long buried, will come back-- and these truths are refusing to be ignored.

Ladies and Gentlemen

Book 1.5 in The Gentlemen's League Series

Natasha Tsarsko is a CIA agent with a dubious past. She is second in command for a specialized unit of operatives that work in the shadows of organized crime.

She's built her career on capturing the worst kinds of criminals. In her world, getting close to the wrong person can get you killed. But what happens when someone she trusts wants her to risk it all?

Coming Soon

Only Truth Remains

Book 3 in Doubt Series

Philip Cooke is the Alpha of the Montana Wolf Pack; they have served as the head enforcers for the Joint Counsel for over a hundred years mostly because of their ability to remain neutral. But when a call from Richard Santiago, Alpha Apex of all shifters in North America, summons him to hunt down a rogue lion, his options of remaining neutral disappear.

Once in Seattle, Philip meets Alpha Mate Sean and Alpha DeMatteo Santiago, nephew of the Alpha Apex and target of the rogue lion's affections. The case takes a bizarre turn when the rogue lion is killed in a failed attack, but his death leaves more questions than answers. Talk of the true mated gay Alpha had reached the pack lands, but Philip had dismissed the talks as mere rumors. Now with the undeniable evidence all around him, Phillip has to reevaluate all he has ever known and sacrificed.

When all the players are identified, one of the hunters appear to be the lost offspring of one of his own. Soon Phillip will learn that his pack is more deeply involved in this plot than anyone had ever realized, and choices made long ago have explosive consequences today. The death toll rises, but the case is far from over. In fact, it seems to be headed even closer to home.

Coming Soon

No Man Left Behind

Book 2 in The Gentlemen's League Series

The trail heats up in the search for the mole hiding within the Hive, but in the game of espionage there is always another game being played just below the surface. New passions heat up and take center stage as we continue Dominic's journey to a new life.

Up and until a few months ago, Samuel Wright has never spent any significant time thinking about his love life. Although to be fair, few of his conquests spanned beyond a couple of sweaty encounters, and until very recently, he had never seen a need for more. Men, women, and everything in between, Samuel liked to think of his bed as a sexual United Nations. There was no reason to limit his options.

Well, that was true until a certain spook joined their team...

www.ingramcontent.com/pod-product-compliance
Lightning Source LLC
Chambersburg PA
CBHW070751280626
47162CB00016B/146